"I'm not ready, Toby."

Corinne couldn't meet his eyes.

He stared at her for a long moment. "I'm willing to give up everything, Corinne. I'll follow you, anywhere you want to go. I'm willing to do just about anything, except wait. Except listen to any more of your excuses. I'm offering you everything I have."

He lifted her chin with his thumb and forced her to meet his gaze. "But I won't take one bit less from you."

Dear Reader,

We've got a special lineup of books for you this month, starting with two from favorite authors Sharon Sala and Laurey Bright. Sharon's *Royal's Child* finishes up her trilogy, THE JUSTICE WAY, about the three Justice brothers. This is a wonderful, suspenseful, *romantic* finale, and you won't want to miss it. *The Mother of His Child,* Laurey's newest, bears our CONVENIENTLY WED flash. There are layers of secrets and emotion in this one, so get ready to lose yourself in these compelling pages.

And then...MARCH MADNESS is back! Once again, we're presenting four fabulous new authors for your reading pleasure. Rachel Lee, Justine Davis and many more of your favorite writers first appeared as MARCH MADNESS authors, and I think the four new writers this month are destined to become favorites, too. Fiona Brand is a New Zealand sensation, and *Cullen's Bride* combines suspense with a marriage-of-convenience plot that had me turning pages at a frantic pace. In *A True-Blue Texas Twosome,* Kim McKade brings an extra dollop of emotion to a reunion story to stay in your heart—and that Western setting doesn't hurt! *The Man Behind the Badge* is the hero of Vickie Taylor's debut novel, which gives new meaning to the phrase "fast-paced." These two are on the run and heading straight for love. Finally, check out *Dangerous Curves,* by Kristina Wright, about a cop who finds himself breaking all the rules for one very special woman. Could he be guilty of love in the first degree?

Enjoy them all! And then come back next month, when the romantic excitement will continue right here in Silhouette Intimate Moments.

Yours,

Leslie Wainger
Executive Senior Editor

Please address questions and book requests to:
Silhouette Reader Service
U.S.: 3010 Walden Ave., P.O. Box 1325, Buffalo, NY 14269
Canadian: P.O. Box 609, Fort Erie, Ont. L2A 5X3

A TRUE-BLUE TEXAS TWOSOME

KIM McKADE

Silhouette®
INTIMATE™MOMENTS®

Published by Silhouette Books

America's Publisher of Contemporary Romance

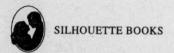

SILHOUETTE BOOKS

ISBN 0-373-07915-X

A TRUE-BLUE TEXAS TWOSOME

Copyright © 1999 by Kimberly Harris

This edition published by arrangement with Harlequin Books S.A.

® and TM are trademarks of Harlequin Books S.A., used under license. Trademarks indicated with ® are registered in the United States Patent and Trademark Office, the Canadian Trade Marks Office and in other countries.

Printed in U.S.A.

Dear Reader,

I'm thrilled beyond belief to have my first book published by Silhouette Intimate Moments, as part of MARCH MADNESS. Toby and Corinne's story is set in a small Texas town because I grew up in a town much like it, and that was where I fell in love. Though I don't live there anymore (there's no mall, you know), I miss the warmth, simplicity and sense of community that come from living in a small town. I tried to capture those emotions in *A True-Blue Texas Twosome*.

From my earliest memory, I knew I was a writer. It wasn't until I fell in love myself, though, that I decided to write romance. I thought there couldn't be anything more interesting, rewarding and just plain *fun* than writing about that moment when two people take that leap into love. And you know what? I was right!

Enjoy!

Kim McKade

This book is for Darryl—
for showing me what a hero should be.

Chapter 1

Aloma, Texas, hadn't had this much gossip—not legitimate gossip anyway—since Barbara Massey got on "The Price Is Right" and won that trip to Hong Kong. Of course, Corinne Maxwell was a bigger celebrity than Barbara would ever be. While Barbara *had* gotten to hug Bob Barker, Corinne Maxwell was actually shot on national television. An event like that was destined to be fuel for conversation over more than a few pots of coffee down at the Dairy Queen.

Who would have ever thought she'd come back, even temporarily? She'd been itching to get out of this one-traffic-light town since the day she was born at the county hospital. A cotton-farming town like Aloma didn't have much to offer a girl who wanted to hobnob with politicians and break the lead stories on the evening news. Certainly being the substitute English teacher at Aloma High School was a step down for the woman who'd been on the verge of national stardom.

Traffic bogged down the aisles of Aloma's one grocery store, with people speculating how Corinne's adventure in the big city had changed her. Was she still as pretty as she'd been? Did she still have that spark that kept her the center of attention, no matter who else was in the room? Phone lines were practically melting off the poles.

The few who had seen her said she'd changed, that she'd mellowed out. Like a colt finally filled into a mare. They said she looked kind of sad now.

Of course, they figured, getting shot would probably do that to a person.

Toby Haskell had heard it all, and then some. Several times. In fact, it was becoming downright irritating. So she had come back. Big deal. Did it necessarily mean that people needed to line up on his doorstep to tell him about it?

He watched her jog down the high school track now, all long legs and flowing hair. Even from forty yards away he could tell. That quality, the one that got her noticed no matter where she was, was still there. In abundance.

His lazy stance, leaning against his Jeep with one booted foot crossed over the other, did a good job of masking the queasiness in his stomach. He wasn't wearing the trademark Haskell crooked grin, the one that had set the hearts of every girl within three states to fluttering at one time or another. In fact, his mouth was set in an uncharacteristically flat line. Damn, but she looked good.

She finished her lap and those long legs crossed the patchy grass toward him.

"Hello, Toby," she said casually, as if she'd just seen him last week. Her voice was as throaty and rich as he remembered, and it still made his heart lurch. Hearing it every night on the news—along with a couple million other viewers—hadn't made him immune. Dammit.

"Hello, Corinne." He took off his Stetson, then wondered why he'd done it. But he didn't put it back on.

He would not tell her how good she looked. He would not. She stuck her foot up on the bumper of the Jeep and stretched her hamstrings. God, her legs were a mile long.

She did look good, even though she was hot and sweaty from her run. Her face was flushed, a golden glow to her apricot complexion. A light sheen of perspiration showed on her arms and legs. She'd had him drooling since the sixth grade, and damned if she didn't have him drooling still. After a decade of not seeing her, he figured he'd be over it.

He figured wrong. He remembered a skinny, long-legged girl with bony knees and big feet, her heart full of fire and passion, leaving this hick farming town and ready to take on the "real world." Leaving him.

Now those limbs were shapelier, a woman's body in place of the girl's he remembered. She was still long and slim, but there were more curves than the last time he'd seen her, face-to-face.

"You'll be back," he said, with what he hoped sounded like determination.

"Of course. I'll come visit every chance I get."

"Not to visit. You'll be back to stay."

"Toby," she sighed, exasperated. *"I'm not moving back to Aloma. Ever. I'm off to Dallas. Then maybe New York. Washington, D.C. I want to go everywhere. Aloma is nowhere. I don't belong here, I never have. There's nothing for me here."*

The hurt must have been plain in his eyes then, because she ducked her head. "I mean, I can't have a career here, Toby. I'm no one here. What would I do? Broadcast the farm report on AM radio?"

He gripped her arms, bitterness dripping through him that what they had wasn't enough for her. "Go ahead, then! Go off, go to school. Be a big-shot reporter, if it means so much to you. See the world. But you remember one thing."

Her eyes grew wide when he advanced on her; he knew he was frightening her. He couldn't stop himself. "You remember one thing," he said again, forcing his voice back down. *"You belong with me. You're mine, Corinne Maxwell. God put you on this earth to be with me. And when you get done, get all this out of your system, I'll be here. Waiting. And we can get on with our lives. Together."*

He groaned inwardly as he remembered all too clearly the rash confidence of an eighteen-year-old boy, sure that everything in his life would work out just as he thought it should.

He ducked his head and chewed his lip. If he thought his life hadn't turned out like it should, he wondered how Corinne must feel. She was back, all right. But it wasn't for any of the reasons he would have liked.

She straightened and brushed a strand of honey blond hair away from her face, meeting him eye to eye. Those who had seen her were right—her amber eyes were sad. No, not sad. Just kind of lifeless.

He stared at the scar that ran along her jawline, then he glanced away self-consciously when she tucked her chin down. She'd been through a lot since they last met, more than he could ever know. There was a wariness about her now, too, and that bugged him. Before she left Aloma, she hadn't worried about anything more than winning her mother's approval. If she'd stayed here as he asked her—well, it was too late for that.

She smiled finally, wide moist lips, even white teeth, still breathing deep from her jog. She put long-fingered hands on her hips, as she squinted the sun out of her eyes. "It's good to see you."

"Yeah." Great. Impress her with your eloquence, Haskell.

"I didn't know if you knew I was back."

"Are you kidding? People were lining up at my door to tell me you were back. I probably knew before you did."

Corinne laughed, bent her knee and reached behind, pulling on her foot to stretch her thigh. "Some things never change."

"Yeah," he said again. Brilliant.

Actually, that was the reason he'd finally stopped. People had been telling him for a week that she was back. As if the first thing he was going to do was run right over to her house and start tagging around after her like a puppy. Just like the old days.

Except it wasn't like the old days. He'd spent enough of his life being led around by the nose by Corinne Maxwell. He wasn't getting his heart tangled up with her again. She was only here for a few weeks, a few months at most.

Hell, he didn't have to see her. He'd lived the last ten years without seeing her. He figured he could go the rest of his life doing the same.

Aloma, Texas, was a small town, though. And at least fifteen people made sure he knew she was staying at her mom's house. It was getting a little awkward and pretty stupid besides, *not* seeing her. He felt as if he were avoiding her.

And that was dumb. This was his town, the town she'd been too good for. She was the one who went off and married someone else. He wasn't going to drive blocks out of his way to avoid her.

Rounding the corner in the sheriff's Jeep just a few minutes ago, he'd recognized Corinne in an instant, jogging down the deserted high school track.

And just to prove to himself that he was okay with this, that he was completely over her and there was no reason why she should mean any more or less to him than any other female on the planet, he'd pulled the Jeep over.

He was ten kinds of a fool, too.

"You look good," he said, then looked around for something to bash himself in the head with.

"You, too," she said. "Protecting your town from the criminal elements, I see." She reached out a manicured nail and lightly flipped the star on his chest.

He looked down at it, experiencing the flash of embarrassed pride he felt when anyone pointed it out. Her smile was a little teasing. He remembered her reaction when they were sixteen, when he first told her he wanted to follow in his father's footsteps and someday run for sheriff.

"In Aloma? What a cushy job. The only crime here is when someone gets drunk and runs over someone else's mailbox."

"I do my best," he said, setting his lips in a firm line. He would not let her make him feel like a bumpkin, the modern-day version of Sheriff Andy Taylor from Mayberry. He had followed in the footsteps of one of the greatest men he'd ever known. She could think he was small-town and quaint if she wanted; he was proud.

"I'm sure you do. And I'm sure it's a challenging and rewarding position."

He grinned. He remembered Corinne enough to know that the more uncomfortable she got, the more piercing her comments became. It was her defense mechanism. Make them feel stupid. He'd seen her use the tactic many times when she was interviewing a particularly slippery subject for the news. It usually worked, too. She'd cock that eyebrow and have them babbling defensively before the first commercial break.

But not this time.

He winked and deliberately exaggerated his drawl. "That it is. It's a twenty-four-hour-a-day job, running this town. And I rule it with an iron fist. Just ask anyone."

"Of course you do. And of course, you're an upstanding pillar of the community, too, aren't you?"

He hadn't realized how much he missed their verbal sparring. A simple conversation with Corinne had never been simple. "You can bet on it."

"Like you bet on it, Sheriff? In that friendly, albeit illegal poker game, held weekly in the back of the feed store?" She grinned saucily at him and did that little eyebrow lift she used to do, the one that had him torn between shaking her senseless and kissing her into submission.

He nodded his admiration. "Just a few days back in town, Corinne, and already you've nosed out corruption in high-ranking local officials. Good work. I guess we'll be seeing a late-breaking public defender segment in the *Aloma Sentinel* this week. Don't be starting any riots out here, now."

She lowered her gaze, and her face grew shuttered. Again he felt like looking for something to hit himself with. Way to go, Haskell.

"Touché," she murmured. She turned her face away and ran a hand through her shoulder-length swing of hair.

"I'm—ah, hell." Toby took a deep breath and blew it out in a gust. "That was uncalled-for. I'm sorry."

"It's okay," she murmured. He knew it wasn't.

They stood awkwardly in silence. He tried to think of something to say to steer the conversation back to safe ground.

"We're off to a great start, aren't we?" Her lips pressed together tightly.

He attempted to tease her. "I don't know. We probably went a full five minutes before we got each other mad. That might be a record for us."

Her mouth tipped up crookedly, but the gesture was devoid of humor.

"It might be. I guess we haven't changed that much. Maybe we shouldn't be talking to each other. The last conversation we had wasn't exactly pleasant."

He rubbed his chin and looked at the ground. "No. No, it wasn't."

He hadn't been sure if he should bring up their last conversation. He'd hoped, actually, that it wouldn't be necessary. But the intervening years only seemed to magnify the hurt feelings. It was between them now, as big and solid as the Jeep against his back.

"I'm only here for a few months, anyway. We could probably avoid each other for that long, even in Aloma," she said, idly toeing a line in the dirt.

"Maybe," he said, though that was the last thing he wanted. Why was it that with any other female in the world, he knew just the right words to say, and around Corinne he couldn't open his mouth without tripping over his tongue?

"Or maybe—" her voice was a little shaky, and he cut his eyes and saw her lick her lips, biting the bottom one softly "—maybe we should start over."

He raised his chin and looked at her, and just for a second— less than a second—he thought he saw a little fear in her eyes. Fear mixed with hope.

And it was all he needed. "That's a better idea."

They stood looking at each other, the tension shimmering between them like a fine thread. How to go about starting over, with all that lay between them, both good and bad? Suddenly the self-assured glamour girl was gone, and she looked a little like she did when she was a bony thirteen-year-old, getting all worked up over an algebra test or something.

He did what he'd done then. He reached out, took her hand in his, and smiled.

She smiled back, though hers was a little wobbly. She took a deep steadying breath, and he did the same.

"So," he said.

"So," she echoed.

"You really do look good."

"And you've still got the most wicked smile of any man within a hundred miles," she said. Warmth crept into her eyes, making his heart squeeze painfully in his chest.

"I like this conversation better than the other one." He flashed his dimples at her, casually leaning one elbow on the hood of the Jeep. "Let's talk some more about how good you look."

"Toby Haskell, you could charm the skirt off a Sunday school teacher."

"Yeah?" He arched his brow cockily. "How about an English teacher?"

She just rolled her eyes and leaned back against the Jeep, her hands lightly rubbing her arms. She looked out over the cotton fields on the other side of the track. "I remember looking out at these fields and thinking it was the ugliest sight in the world. I couldn't wait to get away from all this cotton."

"It can get pretty ugly, looking at it from the business end of a hoe."

She shook her head. "I was such a snob," she said softly, almost to herself. "I still think hoeing cotton was the hardest work I've ever done."

They both knew that wasn't true, but he wasn't going to talk about it unless she insisted. "I'll bet teaching will be harder."

She shrugged. "Maybe. At least I won't get blisters. I hope."

"You glad to be back?" The question blurted out of his mouth before he knew he was even thinking about asking it.

She looked at him, then back at the cotton. She didn't answer for a long time.

"Glad?" She shook her head and furrowed her brow, as if this were the first time she'd thought about it. "I don't know, Toby. I'm here, at any rate."

"Nothing better to do, huh?" Even to his own ears, his laugh sounded fake.

She shrugged. "I had no good reason not to come. The school needed help. Aunt Muriel said Mr. Sammons was desperate to find a substitute. And Aunt Muriel was getting tired of watching me mope around and feel sorry for myself. I figured I could coast along here as easily as in Dallas.''

Toby had a hard time believing she felt sorry for herself. Corinne wasn't the type for self-pity, no matter what had happened to her.

But her attitude irked him. ''Coast along, huh?''

''I know it sounds terrible. I've got a job to do, and I'm going to do it. I think I'll be a good teacher, for as long as it lasts. But as far as being glad or happy or hopeful or anything else...I just don't know.''

''Times have changed. You used to know everything.''

He more than half expected her to get mad again, but she didn't. She returned his smile ruefully and nodded. ''Life was a simpler thing then.''

''I guess it was.''

''Maybe that's what I needed. Coming back to a simpler way of life.''

''But things aren't the same as they were back when we were in school.'' He wanted to say that he'd changed, but instead he said, ''The town's changed.''

''How?''

''Well...'' He racked his brain. It always burned him up how little respect she had for Aloma. Not part of the real world, she'd always said. As if Aloma didn't matter as much as the rest of the world. As if the people who lived there didn't measure up.

''Well,'' he said finally. ''We put in a new traffic light.''

''Oh, well then...'' She laughed. He realized how silly it sounded, and laughed himself. Maybe Aloma was a little like Mayberry, after all. What the hell.

''And we got a new video store. Did you notice?''

''So, there is something to do here after all.''

''There are still the old standbys. Dominoes every afternoon at four, at the Senior Citizens Center—not necessarily restricted to senior citizens. And, of course, the hotbed of activity that can always be found at the Dairy Queen.''

She laughed again, and he found that the sound did pretty much the same thing to his stomach that it did in the sixth grade.

He stuffed his hands in his pockets and leaned back against the Jeep. "You want to go to The Corral for dinner? Sort of a welcome home thing?" Again, the words took on a life of their own and leapt out of his mouth. He was going to have to find a rock or something and put himself out of his misery.

"Toby." Her expression grew distant again and she looked out at the track field. The sun was setting, red and amber shafts of light cutting through the trees and reflecting highlights in her hair.

"Never mind." He bit the words out, pulled his Stetson back on his head and moved to get back into the Jeep. How many times did a guy have to get his head chopped off before he quit putting it on the block?

"Wait." She laid a hand on his arm and stepped into his path. "Could you just—I mean—just wait. I need—" She stopped, sighing deeply. "Don't be mad."

"I'm not mad." He clenched his hands.

"Don't be. I'm just not ready for...for anything."

"Maybe you didn't hear me right. I said The Corral, Corinne. For dinner. Not the wedding chapel." He managed to mix a little mockery with the bitterness in his voice.

"Toby, could you just have a little patience? I'm not ready—"

"For dinner? What, did you give up food?"

"Toby." She sighed.

He moved around her and drew closer to the Jeep.

"I could use a friend." She clenched her teeth, and he realized how hard it was for her to admit even that much.

"You've got lots of friends here," he said, refusing to be swayed by her big brown eyes.

"I mean...look, Toby, you're right. When I left here, I knew everything. I knew who I was and what I wanted. I was so *sure* of everything. I knew what the world was like and what was wrong with it and what I was going to do to fix it. Now..." She shook her head. "Like I said, now I don't know anything. I don't even know what's real and what's not anymore."

He cleared his throat and took his hat back off. He was torn between getting out of there while he still had a little pride left, and taking her in his arms. Which would be the second stupidest thing he'd ever done.

"I really am sorry, Corinne. For what happened. I called you then." He didn't say that he'd actually flown to Dallas and hung around outside the hospital, along with a crowd of reporters and cameramen and thrill-seekers. He didn't say that he'd called from a pay phone in a coffee shop across the street from the hospital. "I don't know if your aunt told you. I called to see how you were. If I could do anything. She said you didn't want to talk to anyone."

"I *didn't* want to talk to anyone. Anyone, Toby, not just you. There were reporters and cameras and...everything." She waved a hand dramatically in the air.

"Pesky reporters," he said, trying to get her to smile again.

"Yes." She did smile, ruefully. "And I just needed some time to sort things out and...I don't know. Get my bearings."

"And somehow, you ended up back here."

She shrugged. "I needed a little quiet in my life."

"You'll get that here."

Since they'd been talking, not one car had driven by. Still, old Mrs. Thompson across the street had peeked through her curtain more than once since he'd pulled over. Before he got home tonight, half the people in town would know that Toby Haskell had finally talked to Corinne Maxwell.

"That's what I need. Quiet. And peace."

"And you think teaching high school English is going to give you peace?"

"It'll give me something to do besides sit around being afraid."

"You still get scared?"

She folded her arms across her chest and lifted her chin. "This is not the part where I break down and get all weepy, okay? I got shot. It happens. It's not the only reason I decided to come back." She looked off, and already he could feel her edging away. Not physically, but tangibly edging away nonetheless.

"Is that right? Are you going to tell me the other reasons, or let me dangle on that hook for a while?" He waggled his brows at her, teasing. He was suddenly afraid that if he didn't lighten things up a little, she was going to bolt on him.

"The reasons are my own, and have nothing to do with anyone except me, okay? You always did read too much into things."

"Can't blame a guy for trying. Okay, I'm out of your business."

"I didn't say I wanted you out of my business. I just said...I mean... God, Toby, you can be so difficult sometimes. I mean it. I really could use a friend."

"I wasn't suggesting anything else, Corinne."

"Maybe not, but you remember how it was between us."

He remembered. He remembered it too much, on hot summer nights when his memories of a long-legged girl with fire and passion made it even hotter.

"Okay," he conceded. "But friends do occasionally go out to dinner together."

"Charming and stubborn. Good qualities in a friend, you think?"

"The best."

"Toby?"

"Yeah?"

"I might be glad to be back."

"I might be glad you're back, too. A little."

"Say, friends are pretty good about doing favors, aren't they? Such as repairing things? Like hot-water heaters?"

"Only in dire emergencies. Why, is yours out?"

"Not out, exactly. Just not very hot."

"Sounds like an emergency to me. I'll be over tomorrow evening." He climbed into the Jeep. He could do it tonight. Hell, he could do it right now. But he had degraded himself enough for one day.

"No hurry," she said, backing away from the car.

"It's a bad idea to abuse the friendship. Emily Post would probably suggest a small but thoughtful gift of appreciation."

"I could fix dinner."

He shook his head. "At your house, unchaperoned? I don't know. Sounds a little intimate, for just-friends. How about a beer and maybe a cheese sandwich? I'll eat on the back porch."

She laughed. "Sounds safe enough."

He remembered to put his hat back on, and concentrated on getting out of there before he did anything really stupid—like try to kiss her.

She was smiling, though, and that made it a lot harder. Maybe he'd made her feel better. Which was really, he told himself, all he was interested in.

"Tomorrow," he said casually, determinedly putting the Jeep into reverse. He watched her from the rearview mirror all the way down the street, and he almost ran smack into Billy Myer's Dodge because he wasn't watching where he was going.

He drove the five blocks to the station. When he got there, he took a deep breath outside the door, then entered the outer office.

Luke Tanner, one of four deputies in Aloma County, sat at his desk, his head bent over paperwork, lines of concentration between his brows. Toby didn't say anything, just walked quickly and purposefully through the outer office as if he had a lot of important, official business on his mind.

He made it within three feet of his office door.

"So. You talked to Corinne, huh?" Luke asked, head still bent over his work. Toby could see the corner of his mouth tipped up.

"Shut up and get back to work, Barney Fife."

Corinne lurched upright in the dark of night and clutched the sheet to her chest, her hand to her throat. Her breath came in harsh gasps, and her heart jerked painfully in her chest. Sheets damp with perspiration tangled around Corinne's limbs like vines as she scooted back against the headboard and wrapped her arms around her upraised knees. She rocked back and forth.

After a few seconds she regained enough presence of mind to follow the instructions the doctor had given her. She clutched one wrist with the other shaking hand and felt for her pulse. It thumped fiercely away under her fingertip, and she began to count.

Still she rocked, unable to stop the movement if she wanted to, and counted. She heard her own gasps for air, loud and cruel in the silent house, and felt the brutal throb of her heart. But she kept counting. Everything in her screamed to reach for the phone, to get help. This time was really it. This time she really was dying.

But she didn't give in. She rocked and counted, and whispered to herself over and over, "This isn't real. This isn't real."

Finally, her calming techniques started to work. Almost imperceptibly, her pulse slowed, then slowed some more. Her breath came a little easier, deep gulps replacing the ragged gasps. A few minutes later, she knew the attack was over. This time.

Corinne swallowed against the raw pain in her throat, relief and humiliation flooding her in equal measure. Her weakness shamed her. But for tonight, it was over.

As her heartbeat slowly eased from its frantic thumping, she breathed deeply through her nose and listened to the whir and click of the ceiling fan, watched the rectangle of yellow streetlamp light that came through the opening of the Priscilla curtains over her bedroom window. She did everything except think about the shooting.

Knowing she was no longer in danger didn't help. Knowledge didn't stop the nightmares, and it didn't stop the panic attacks.

She closed her eyes again and took deep breaths, concentrated on letting the tension ebb from her body, but she knew it was no use. She was awake now, and would be for at least a few hours, possibly for the rest of the night. She swung her legs off the bed and padded silently through the dark house that she'd walked through thousands of times. And she felt just as alone in it as she always had.

At least her mother wasn't there to be awakened by her screams. She would never have agreed to take this job if her mother hadn't already moved to east Texas to be with her new boyfriend. It was bad enough waking herself up with her panic attacks. Having her mother witness them, having her mother look at her with mixed pity and contempt, was unthinkable.

Not that her mother would actually say that Corinne was a disappointment and a failure, that this scene was inevitable—not to her face. She at least tried to wait until she thought Corinne was out of earshot before she said things like that.

In the kitchen Corinne ran water into the old teakettle and set it on the stove. Hot chocolate wouldn't help her get back to sleep any faster, but it was something to hold in her hands until that time came.

Her doctor had warned her that the panic attacks could return, but Corinne had been sure she was past them. Being back in this house had added stress, though. And so had seeing Toby today.

Idly, she traced the line of the scar that ran from below her ear, along the side of her jaw. All things considered, it wasn't a bad scar. If the gunman had cocked his wrist an inch to the right, she wouldn't have been hit at all.

An inch to the left, and she would be dead.

Toby hadn't said anything about the scar, but he'd noticed. Just as he'd noticed the other changes in her.

She tried not to think too much about Toby. About him being here, in her mother's house, tomorrow. She looked at the clock on the stove as she poured the steaming water into her mug. Today.

She'd known, of course, that she would see Toby again. Aloma was too small to avoid anyone. But she hadn't given much thought to how seeing him would make her feel.

She sighed and sat back down at the table, stretching her legs out in front of her. She'd carried a sense of numbness around for months, thinking only of the next moment, the next task to get through. Refusing to let her mind probe any deeper than surface thoughts. The entire reason for coming back to Aloma was to get away from the world, to avoid stimulation of any kind. Not because the doctors wanted it that way. Because she wanted it that way.

She wanted to be invisible again. The feeling that she'd railed against while she was growing up—the sense that, at best, nothing she did or said mattered, or at worst was all wrong—was what she yearned for now. And what better place to find that blessed sense of nonexistence than here, in her mother's house, where she'd grown up with the certainty that she was just an unfortunate mistake? The fact that her mother wasn't here to reinforce that feeling, she was relieved to discover, did nothing to diminish her own sense of nothingness. That awareness was in the house, waiting for her to wrap it around herself like a familiar, comfortably shabby blanket.

Already, she was afraid, Toby was tugging at the edges of that protective blanket. It had been more of a shock than it should have been, seeing him. The pounding in her heart hadn't been simply because of the run. He'd looked so devilishly handsome, so soothingly familiar leaning against the Jeep in his tan sheriff's uniform, with that same casual cockiness that had always made her heart stammer. He was bigger now, though, his chest wide and his shoulders filling out the tan sleeves of his shirt. He looked so *solid* now. Sturdy and dependable.

His face was bronzed by the sun, his square jaw tense, even though she'd thought he was glad to see her. His lips were full; she'd had a hard time not staring at them as they talked. But his eyes were the biggest change. There had been a time when she was confident around Toby, could read his mind by looking into his eyes. But today, with those gray eyes studying her intently and not missing a thing, she'd almost shied away.

At once he was so comfortably familiar, but frighteningly foreign. She'd felt the urge to touch him as she'd once done, as easy with his body as she was with her own. And yet there was a wall between them that couldn't be removed. Shouldn't be removed.

Emotions she didn't want to feel again floated through her, and she smiled to herself, the small movement feeling foreign on her face. The thrill she'd had when she was twelve, and she knew Toby had gone out of his way to pass by her. How her heart had stopped when they were fourteen and he flashed those dimples at her. How important he'd made her feel, how smart and beautiful and worthy to be around.

How she'd panicked, the day after high school graduation when she fled Aloma in the gray hour before dawn, afraid to tell him goodbye.

How heavy with guilt she'd been when he called, four days before her wedding to Don Reinert, not believing she would actually marry someone else when they both knew they belonged together.

Why should she feel guilty, then or now? She was never less

than honest with him. From the time she was nine years old, she couldn't wait to get out of Aloma. And he wasn't willing to disappoint his father by leaving. There was no way for them, really.

She drained the last of the lukewarm chocolate, then stood and flipped off the kitchen light, moving back through the quiet house.

It was in this very house, in fact, she'd first discovered the way to make her mother forgive her, to earn her love and respect. To show her mother that Corinne's life was worth all the things her mother had been forced to give up.

Corinne remembered that moment still, as if it were permanently tattooed on her mind. She'd been nine when she watched her mother sit on this very couch, smoking and swinging one bare foot, watching a new young female reporter on the news.

"Now she's a class act," her mother said as she dragged on her cigarette. *"I'll bet her mom's real proud of her."*

Corinne had set a course for herself that night, determined to pursue a career in journalism, to reach as high and as far as she could.

She would become that class act. She would make her mother proud. And she would earn the love and acceptance she desperately sought.

She hadn't deviated from that course, either, not even for Toby. She'd pushed herself as hard as she could. She owed it to her mother, after all. She'd built her own ladder of dreams, and touched every rung.

And in achieving those dreams, she'd been shown what an utter fool she was.

She wasn't going to dream again. All hope, all anticipation died inside her that day in the hospital, the day she'd learned of her husband's betrayal; the same day she'd learned that even getting shot wasn't enough to gain her mother's attention.

If she did nothing else in this lifetime, she was going to make certain hope never came back to life inside her.

It was too late for her and Toby.

It was much too late for her.

Chapter 2

The third time Corinne found herself rummaging through her closet, she knew she was in trouble. Obsessing over her clothes for a simple evening with an old friend was not a good sign. Toby was just coming over for dinner. No, not dinner. Just coming over to fix the water heater. Dinner was secondary.

The outfit she had on would be fine, she told herself as she smoothed the front of the lightweight jumper. She'd chosen it because it was cool and comfortable, not because it was green and that happened to be Toby's favorite color. She added lipstick and polished her nails because...well, there was no point in being uncivilized.

His knock on the front door started an uncomfortable pounding of her heart. She checked the mirror over the couch.

After a year of facing a reflection that showed little or no emotion at all, it was something of a shock to see her cheeks flushed and her eyes bright. She scowled at her image. Don't, she warned herself. Don't even get started. She'd come to Aloma for peace and quiet. Any kind of relationship with Toby definitely fell outside those boundaries.

She almost jumped when he rapped on the door again. Patience had never been his strong suit. It was just nerves, she told herself as she stubbornly waited before opening the door. She'd locked herself away at her aunt's house in Dallas for a year, not speaking to anyone unless it was necessary, not getting close to anyone. She would be nervous no matter who was coming over for dinner. Her jittery stomach had nothing to do with Toby. She said a quick, silent prayer that she would make it through the evening without a panic attack.

She took a deep breath and opened the door. Toby stood on her front porch in worn jeans that hugged his hips and a black T-shirt with the sleeves rolled up over his firm rounded biceps. A tool belt hung low around his hips. Dark sunglasses hid his eyes.

"Water heater repairman, ma'am," he said solemnly when she opened the door. "Got an emergency call you needed heating up."

"That I do," she said with a light smile. Toby had always had the ability to make her smile when she least expected to. She stepped back and let him into the room. "The water heater is back here," she said over her shoulder as she walked to the kitchen.

"Whoa there. Slow down a bit. I told you I'd expect partial payment up front, didn't I?"

"No, you didn't. Do you want your sandwich now?"

"The sandwich can wait. I want the beer."

She pulled a beer and a bottle of chardonnay from the refrigerator. He popped the top of his beer and drained half of it before he put it down. She raised an eyebrow as she sipped her wine. "Hard day?"

"I've had better. Old lady Kirby called three times."

"I saw Luke over there."

"It was his day to deal with her."

"His day?"

"We rotate Kirby duty."

"What major crime did she have to report?"

"She got her phone bill today. It seems someone broke in and used her phone forty-three times last month."

Corinne sipped her wine and leaned against the counter. "I

guess she hasn't changed much. When I was a kid, it was always me she thought was out to get her.''

"The thing is, all forty-three calls were to her son in Phoenix. But she didn't make them. Someone must have broken in and done it.''

"And the Aloma County Sheriff's Department is hot on the case,'' she said dryly.

"We've got a few leads.'' Toby grinned.

"What were the other two crimes?''

"Let me see. Someone broke in and stole her canned beets. And the other thing was just the standard 'My neighbor is building a bomb in his basement' thing.''

"Routine stuff.'' She nodded with a smile.

He nodded and took another pull on the beer. He turned the can around and around in his hand.

"I had to take Mr. Davis's driver's license away from him a few hours ago.''

"You're kidding.'' Mr. Davis had been the Aloma High School English teacher for thirty years, until his mandatory retirement three years ago. "Is his eyesight that bad?''

"His sight is fine. It's everything else that's gone haywire. I think he may have Alzheimer's.''

"Oh, Toby. That's terrible.''

"I know. I got a call from the Taylor County Sheriff's Department. He got over to Abilene and couldn't remember how to get home. He scared some poor woman to death because he kept saying she stole his car.''

"That's sad. He was so sharp. Doesn't he have anyone he can live with?''

Toby shook his head and studied the tiles on the kitchen floor. "His wife died, remember? They never had any kids. I think teaching was the only thing that kept him going. And now he doesn't have that.''

"That's sad,'' Corinne said, shaking her head. "He's going to have to be institutionalized.''

Toby's head jerked up. "What?''

"Institutionalized. Like a nursing home. One that specializes in Alzheimer's patients, hopefully."

Toby shook his head. "No way. He'd hate that."

"Toby, he'll have to be. He's a danger to himself and everyone else. What happens if he's driving along and suddenly forgets how to drive?"

"I just told you, I took his driver's license away."

"So? If he can't remember how to get home, what makes you think he's going to remember he's not supposed to drive?"

"He will, okay?" Toby set the beer on the counter and jammed his hands in his pockets.

"I really think you should talk to someone at mental health services."

Toby shook his head. "I couldn't do that. Turn him over to someone who doesn't even know him? Lock him up in some sterile hospital room? That would kill him."

Apparently nothing had changed in Aloma. Mrs. Kirby still thought everyone was out to get her, and Toby still thought that if he said something would be okay, it automatically would.

Toby rubbed the back of his neck, hooking his hand there and staring at the floor in thought. The gesture was at once so endearingly familiar to Corinne, it reached across the span of a decade and squeezed her heart. Whenever he was the most disturbed and lost, Toby rubbed the back of his neck. She didn't think he was aware of it himself, but she remembered. She rolled her lips together and fought the urge to cross the floor and wrap her arms around him.

"If you want, I can make a few phone calls. I know a woman at mental health services in Abilene. She might give you some advice—"

"I said I'm not putting him in a rest home!"

From the look on his face, his harsh tone surprised even him. He returned the beer to the counter with a soft metallic clank. He took a deep breath and spoke calmly. "I can handle this. This is my town. I'm the one who needs to decide what to do about him."

"Toby, you're the sheriff," she said quietly. "You didn't get elected God."

"I know that."

"What makes you think you're going to be able to stop something that devastating?"

"I know I can't stop it, Corinne. I know how it is. But I don't walk away from my responsibilities."

Whether he intended it or not, Corinne felt accusation in his tone. They weren't arguing over Mr. Davis, she realized; they were rehashing an age-old disagreement. Toby had been taught from a young age by his father that it was his responsibility to stay in Aloma and make sure it thrived, to do everything in his power to halt the flow of the town's young people to the city. It was more than civic pride for Toby to follow in his father's footsteps and be sheriff—it was familial duty.

But then, Toby had been raised that way—with a strong sense of family. Corinne had no such thing.

Toby sighed and ran a hand roughly through his hair. "I'm sorry. Let's just drop it, okay? I'm not going to put him in a rest home, and that's all there is to it."

"What would John have done if he were here?" The moment Corinne asked the question, she wished it back. She should have known Toby had already asked himself the same question. From the taut look on his face, he had not found an answer.

"Knowing him," Toby said, "he would have told Mr. D. he didn't have time for this nonsense. He would have ordered him in no uncertain terms to cut it out. And that would be that."

Corinne noted yet another thing that hadn't changed—Toby still considered John Haskell to be a god. A god he would continually measure himself against. And continually fall short.

Corinne almost crossed the room a second time to comfort him, to reassure him that whatever decision he made, it would be in Mr. Davis's best interest. But then she remembered *she* had changed.

"And that would be that," she agreed.

Toby drained the rest of the beer. She took the can from him and dropped it into the recycle bin by the door, her face carefully blank.

When she turned back, his fists were planted on his hips, his mouth a grim flat line. "Where's the water heater?"

She leaned against the counter and despite herself, felt her lips curve.

"Well?" he demanded.

"You're sweet, Toby."

His eyes grew wide. "Sweet? What the hell is that supposed to mean?"

"I just think it's nice, that's all. It's sweet that you care so much about his welfare. Of course, I also think you're intentionally deaf, dumb and blind. But sweet."

He sighed and rubbed the back of his neck. "I still can't keep up with you. Where's the water heater?"

Still smiling slightly, she opened the closet door. He was acting mad, but she could tell anger from fluster, and this was fluster. They were back on even ground. "Voilà."

She stepped back and watched as he leaned around the heater, checking it out from all angles. He knelt on the floor and looked at something underneath. He checked the tools hanging from his belt. He sat back on his haunches and studied the heater, scratching his chin with his eyes narrowed.

"You didn't tell me this was a gas heater," he said.

"Does that make a difference?"

"Just a little. I'd feel better if you waited outside. Close to the back fence. Your mom has insurance, right?"

"Why? Is it dangerous?"

"Not really. No. It's not."

"Then why do you want me to go outside?"

"Just to be safe. It never hurts to be cautious when you're dealing with gas."

"Toby, I can call a repairman, someone more qualified—"

"I'm qualified. I can handle it. But I'd feel better if you'd wait outside."

"I don't know—"

"Just go, okay. I'll be fine."

Corinne hesitated for a long time, then picked up her glass and walked toward the door. "You're sure you'll be okay?"

"I'm positive. It'll take about fifteen minutes. Just go tend to your garden or something."

"There is no garden. Mom isn't the type—"

"Then you should think about planting one. Backyard's no good without a garden."

"You're sure you'll be okay? You don't have to—"

"Just go."

"I'm going."

Toby watched her walk out the door, a worried look on her face.

He made sure she couldn't see through the windows, then turned the temperature knob up a few degrees. He didn't touch his tool belt.

That left him fourteen and a half minutes to nose around a little. He thought he'd seen some interesting items in the fridge. He opened the door and, sure enough, there were two chicken breasts marinating in some kind of spicy-looking sauce. Fresh vegetables lay on the shelf beside a bottle of salad dressing, and a bowl full of sliced peaches sat on the shelf below. Not a cheese sandwich in sight.

Mmm-hmm. Fresh rolls in the bread box. It was beginning to look as if Corinne had put some time and energy into this casual meal between just-friends. He flipped back the edge of a plastic bag on the counter.

Well, now. Two candles lay inside. He licked his lips and dusted off his hands. Candles, eh? What did that mean?

He edged up to the window and peeked around the fringe of the curtain. Corinne stood by the fence, chewing on her lip. Served her right. Deaf, dumb and blind, huh? Didn't get elected God?

The soft evening sunlight played off the glints in her hair, sparking here and there the way it would play off water.

It was the tightness in his throat, the way his hands itched to touch her, that brought him to his senses.

What was he doing? Setting himself up to be put through the wringer all over again?

He stepped back from the window. Hadn't he learned? He knew

firsthand how easily she could walk out of his life without a backward glance.

He went back to the counter and looked at the candles again. Two sticks of colored wax—they didn't mean a thing. None of it really meant anything—not her coming back, not her asking him over the first time they talked.

He tamped down on what he realized was hope flickering in his chest. He'd hoped before. Hoped, prayed and begged, as a matter of fact.

And she'd gone off and married someone else.

The memory felt bitter even now, all these years later. She'd listened to his vows of love, let him declare like an idiot that they were meant for each other, put on the earth to be together forever. And then she'd left, and pledged to spend her life with another man.

He leaned against the counter, his jaw tight, the memory of that time in his life like a block of ice in his stomach. He must be a fool to think for a second of going through that again. He shoved the candles back in the bag and pushed it to the back of the counter.

Corinne probably assumed he was still in love with her—hell, the rest of the town did, simply because he hadn't gotten serious about any one girl since she'd left town. But he'd been busy in the years since then, focused on his career, on the duties of his position. What he did for this county was important, a big responsibility he was proud to shoulder. His life was full and busy. He was perfectly content, dammit.

Toby swallowed the lump in his throat. Watching Corinne move around the backyard, he was struck by the sense of loss he felt at the thought of her leaving again.

But of course he would feel that way, he told himself irritably as he shoved his thumbs in his pockets. Things had been very intense between him and Corinne once. He hadn't realized it at the time, because he'd been eighteen and unable to see past his own hormones, but the connection between him and Corinne had been immediate...and physical. Though they'd had their share of disagreements, physically...Toby shook his head as he remembered. He'd been no monk in the years since Corinne left, but he hadn't experienced anything like that again, either.

He realized with relief that what he wanted, what he *really* wanted, was not to fall in love with Corinne again, but to explore the physical connection they'd shared before. What he needed was to get her out of his system, once and for all. The way she'd left—without a word, without calling or sending even a card, without coming back even once—hadn't allowed for closure. *That* was why he felt this obsession—no, rather like a preoccupation—with her.

He wasn't going to fall for her again. What kind of jerk would he be to do that? But to have her in his arms again, to feel that passion and heat again...that was what he'd wanted from the second he saw her running down the high school track.

She wanted it, too, he thought, though she'd choke before she admitted it. Why else would she have invited him over the first time she saw him? Why else would she have gone to all the trouble of making a nice dinner? And bought candles?

He might have been wrong about what was in Corinne's heart a decade ago, and he might not have a clue what was in her heart now, but she remembered the chemistry between them, and felt it now, too. That much he was sure of.

Rumor had it she would stay in town until the semester break. If so, he had a few months to get her back into his bed. After that...well, after that, she'd be out of his system for good. Maybe this time, he'd be the one to break it off, just to even things out. Even if he didn't, though, when she left again—which she undoubtedly would—it would cause no more than a ripple in his life. He'd make damn sure of that.

He stood around for a few more minutes, relieved to find that he wasn't actually in danger of falling for Corinne again. He peered around the edge of the curtain once more. She looked antsy. She shifted on her feet and tried to get a glimpse through the window.

No, he wouldn't hope again, he thought as he watched the soft evening wind gently tease a strand of her hair at her collarbone. Thank God he was a little older, and a lot wiser.

He walked out onto the small porch and breathed a deep sigh of relief. "All set," he said, rolling his shoulders inside his T-shirt, as if to ease sore muscles.

"Is everything okay?"

"Right as rain. You'll have a hot shower tonight or your money back."

"Thanks, Toby," she said. She still looked a little worried.

"It was nothing. I mean it." He gave her his patented drop-dead, crooked grin.

"I didn't realize it was going to be such a hassle."

"No hassle. I guess I'll just take my sandwich now and be on my way."

"I'm not going to make you eat a cheese sandwich on the porch, Toby. I have food. I've already started dinner."

He tried to look awkward and glanced at his watch. "Oh," he said. "That's not necessary," he mumbled. "Really. I was just kidding about the sandwich, anyway. I have a few things to do."

"I've already started it, Toby. It won't take that long to cook. Can't you stay, just for a while?"

He wrinkled his brow and looked off, as if he were thinking hard. "Well," he said slowly, chewing his lip. Then he looked at his watch again. "Can I borrow your phone?"

"Sure." She led him back into the kitchen. "Right there," she said, pointing to the bar.

She turned away and began taking the chicken out of the refrigerator. Damn, she wasn't going to leave the room. He was really going to have to call someone.

He dialed the station. Luke answered.

"It's me," Toby said shortly. "What's going on?"

"What do you mean?"

"I mean, what's happening?"

"Happening? Here?"

"Yes, there!"

"It's Tuesday night, Haskell. Nothing's happening."

"Good." Whatever Corinne was doing, it smelled wonderful.

"I'm at Corinne Maxwell's. I'll be here for a while, if you need me."

"Why would I need you?"

"Get a pen and write down her number."

"It's on the Rolodex right here, Haskell. Why are you calling? You already told me you were going over there."

"Why is her number on your Rolodex?" Toby snapped.

"The whole damn town's on the Rolodex. Dutch got bored one day and copied the entire phone book. I don't know why. What's going on? Do you want me to call you or something?"

"That won't be necessary," Toby said quickly. Corinne was leaning over the open oven door. She wore some kind of one-piece shorts thing, loose and filmy and flowing. She'd always looked dynamite in green. His gaze trailed up the curve of her calf, to the tender skin at the back of her knee. He clenched his fists and forced his mind back to Luke.

"Just wanted to let you know where I am, if you need to reach me."

"Why would I need to reach you?"

"Or if I'm not here, you can reach me on the radio."

"I repeat, why would I need to reach you?"

"That's right. And keep an eye on the situation out west of town."

"What the hell—" Luke's voice broke off, and Toby heard the sound of his chair hitting the floor. "I get it. You're trying to act like a big shot in front of your lady-friend."

"That's confirmed, officer."

"You want me to start talking about some important official business, make you sound impressive?"

"Go ahead and run that by me."

"Mr. Davis called and wanted to know when you were going to give his driver's license back. He's got to go to the package store and they might want to see some proof that he's over twenty-one."

"Don't let that man drive. Or drink."

"Don't worry, I'm keeping an eye on him." Luke laughed. "Sorry, but I don't have anything juicier than that."

"You'll need to get started on that, then."

"I can go down to the bingo parlor and see if anyone's interested in inciting a riot you can bust up."

"Get right on that, officer. You know where to reach me."

"You've told me five times now. I think I know. Over and out, chief. And Toby?"

"Yeah?"

"Good luck."

Toby hung up, and turned back to Corinne. She was tossing the salad.

"Exciting things going down at the station?" she asked.

"Actually, it's pretty quiet at the moment." He walked closer to her and leaned against the counter. He stole a cherry tomato and popped it into his mouth.

"You've got to be kidding," she said dryly.

"I rule this town with an iron fist, I told you. No one dares step out of line."

Corinne rolled her eyes and turned back to the refrigerator. She leaned over, retrieving something from the crisper, and Toby caught a great profile of the curve at the top of her thigh. He grabbed a celery stalk and snapped it in half.

"Don't knock it," he said. "It's the whole reason you moved back, and you know it. Nothing ever happens here."

She just smiled that little smile of hers and said, "You're right."

Toby shook his head and heaved a dramatic sigh. "You never used to let me win an argument."

"Lots of things have changed." Her face grew serious as she chopped vegetables. "Check on the chicken, will you?"

He opened the oven door and looked, but didn't know exactly what he was looking for. "It turned into a ham."

She threw him a confused look, and he grinned. "Just kidding."

She gave him a slightly exasperated smile. Good. She'd been getting that closed look again, shutting him out. Hell, he didn't want to get into any deep discussions, either. Just have a little fun, while he could.

Something in him had to push.

"That is why you came back, isn't it, Corinne?"

She was silent for a few seconds, then she turned to him, echoing his words. "Nothing ever happens here."

She went about the dinner preparations in silence, almost oblivious to him. She raked one hand through her hair, drawing it back, and the movement nearly took his breath away.

Toby cleared his throat and lifted the corner of the bag on the counter. "Oh, hey. Candles. I'll put them on the table."

He didn't give her a chance to argue, telling himself that if he intended to get her back into bed, a little ambience wouldn't hurt. He found holders in a sideboard and set them in the middle of the table as she brought the food over. She carefully avoided looking at him as he got matches from the kitchen and lit the candles.

"You nervous?" he asked from behind her.

She jumped as if he'd touched her with one of the matches. "Of course not. I believe I can handle you, Toby Haskell."

He grinned crookedly. "Don't bet on it, sweetheart. And I was referring to teaching. Are you nervous about your first day teaching?"

She was really something when she blushed. Her skin got all hot and rosy, and her lips pursed up.

"I'm not nervous about that, either. They're just kids. I've dealt with worse, believe me."

Toby shook his head. "Fools rush in," he mumbled. "So tell me again where that idea came from? I never saw you as an English teacher."

"From where did the idea come, Sheriff." She raised one eyebrow as she pulled back her chair and sat at the head of the table.

He sat on the corner, close enough that he could reach out and take her hand in his if he wanted. "Okay, so you'll be a great English teacher. Whose idea was it?"

"Aunt Muriel's." She took the tongs and filled her plate with salad, and he could see her weighing her words. That much hadn't changed; she'd never been one to speak before she thought things through first.

"I was moping around her house, hiding out from reporters and cameramen. I guess she got tired of me feeling sorry for myself."

"I have a hard time picturing you doing that."

Corinne shrugged. "I don't know. The doctor said I was mildly depressed. I didn't feel depressed. I didn't intend to mope around for the rest of my life. I knew I should start doing something, anything. It's just that...I don't know. It just seemed easier not to think about anything."

She looked off for a moment, lost in thought. Toby fought the urge to reach out and take her hand. Though he was sitting three feet from her, she looked more alone than anyone he'd ever seen.

She turned her attention back to him and smiled wanly.

"Mom called and said the school needed an English teacher until the end of the semester. Aunt Muriel decided I was the perfect candidate for the job, since it was only temporary and in my hometown. The school board was desperate enough for a fill-in, they didn't mind that I didn't have a teaching certificate or any experience. So here I am."

Toby frowned. It was hard to picture Corinne letting other people make decisions for her. "So just like that? You're a teacher?"

She shrugged. "Till the end of the semester."

"What about after that? Are you going back to reporting?"

Her expression became solemn. She was getting that look on her face altogether too often. He realized he was holding his breath waiting for her to answer, and he took a big bite of his chicken. It might have been delicious; he didn't know. It stuck in his throat.

Finally, she shook her head. "No, I'm not going back to reporting."

Good. Now he didn't have to tell her that he'd lock her in his jail cell before he let her put herself in danger again.

But he'd made a couple of decisions in the few minutes since they sat down at her little table. One, he didn't like that dead look in her eyes. Having her spitting mad at him was preferable to this lifeless look. And two, she did feel what was between them, whether she wanted to or not. He could feel it, could see it in the way she looked at his hands, at his mouth, then looked away. He could see it in the way she jumped when he got too close to her.

The second item might take a while to put into action, so to speak, but the first... He could irritate her at the drop of a hat.

"I'm kind of surprised to hear that, sweetheart. I didn't figure you for a quitter."

Her fork froze halfway to her mouth. "A quitter?"

"Yeah. Reporting was all you ever wanted to do. You were going straight for the networks, you told me. I figured it would take more than a little gun to change your mind."

"How about I shoot you in the face, Sheriff, and see how it affects your outlook on life?"

He grinned, knowing it infuriated her more. "I'm just wondering if I'm seeing the whole picture, that's all. You said getting shot wasn't the only reason you came back. Now most people would do just what you did. They'd throw in the towel—"

"Throw in the towel?" Corinne's knuckles went white as she gripped her fork. "What do you think, Toby, that I fell off my bike or something? That I need to walk it off? For God's sake, Toby, I got shot!"

"I know. I saw." For a moment, his voice was as cold as hers was hot. His gaze met hers seriously. "And for most people, that would be enough. And they'd run home, too. They'd run scared."

Her fork clattered to her plate and she leaned back, a look of disbelief on her face.

"But you," he continued, ignoring the murderous look she gave him. "You I figured for a fighter."

"You're about to see just how right you are."

He waggled his eyebrows. "Promise?"

She sighed and ran her tongue over her teeth. "Okay, Sheriff, you win."

"Already?"

"Already. I have no idea why, but you're trying to hack me off. You win. Now, can we please get back to our meal?"

"Nope. I still want to know what you're doing here."

"You know good and well. I'm filling in at the school until they find a replacement."

"What are your plans after that?"

She simply shook her head. "I don't have any."

He choked again. "None? None at all?"

She arched her brows. "Nope."

"You've had your whole life mapped out since fifth grade."

She shrugged and chewed carefully on her chicken. "Maps get torn up." She warned him with her eyes to drop the subject.

He'd never been good at taking orders.

"You have to have some plans, some idea."

"I don't make plans anymore."

"Everyone makes plans of some kind. You have to have some idea of what you're going to do next, sweetheart."

"No," she said calmly, almost as if her eyes were not snapping fire. "No, I don't. Making plans means having hopes. It implies aspirations. And I have learned to live one day at a time. I've learned to focus on today and let tomorrow take care of itself."

It was a nice, sentimental load of bull.

"Yeah, right. You just don't want to talk to me about it."

"Yes, that's it." She took a bite of her chicken.

"So basically you're saying that you'll be staying at least a few months, but possibly no more than that."

"That's correct."

"Good. Because I *do* have aspirations."

"Good for you," she said quietly, chewing thoughtfully on a piece of roll.

"What, you ask? If you must know, I have aspirations that concern you."

She arched her brow again and gave him that look that was supposed to convince him she didn't care.

"I just needed to know how much time I had."

"Time for what?"

"To get you into bed."

Her jaw dropped, then closed with a clamp. Her eyes blazed with cold fury. At least she was showing some emotion, even if it was anger.

"I mean it. I wasn't going to say anything, but what the hell. I want you, Corinne, and I intend to have you. I just need to know how much time I have. Is it going to be slow and sweet? Or is it going to be a full-court press? I'll let you decide."

"Pretty sure of yourself, aren't you?"

"I've been honing my skills while you were gone," he said

seriously, tearing off a piece of his roll. Then he grinned again as her eyes flared. Jealousy, perhaps?

"Don't be crass, Toby."

"I'm not being crass. I'm being honest. You should try it sometime."

"I never lied to you."

"You're lying right now. You're lying to yourself—have been all along." He pointed at her with a piece of bread, then popped it into his mouth. "You said you came back because nothing ever happens here. Because you had nothing better to do. Because your aunt asked you to. Everything but the truth. And the truth is, you came back because you belong here. You always have. Your pride won't let you admit you were wrong."

"I wasn't wrong. I left because I had to. No matter what happened while I was away, I was not wrong for going."

He shook his head and tsked. "That stubborn pride isn't going to get you anywhere, sweetheart."

"Get out," she said coolly.

He stood. "I had a feeling you were going to end up saying that. I'm going. But I'll be back." He winked.

She followed him to the door, her arms folded tightly over her chest. Her voice held just a hint of a tremor.

"I watched you stand in front of your dresser mirror practicing that wink so you could charm Mrs. Hobbs out of giving us homework, Toby. It never worked on me."

"No, but this always did."

He spun on his heel. She was close enough behind him that he didn't have to reach. He simply opened his arms and cornered her.

She made a small gasp of surprise, her eyes wide. He tightened his arms around her. She opened her mouth to protest, but he didn't give her a chance. Just before his lips touched hers, he saw her eyelids flutter closed.

Excitement—something Corinne had thought was long gone for her—flared in her chest. She let her mind swim. She thought she'd run out of feelings. Thought that Don and the gunman had killed her spirit.

She wasn't prepared for how good it felt to be overwhelmed.

A small part of her warned that this was exactly what she *didn't* want. She wasn't interested in this complication.

But a larger part knew that she hadn't had physical contact—barring a few haircuts and a teeth cleaning—in a year. That part of her drank in the feel of Toby's lips on hers, his arms around her, like dry, cracked earth drank in summer rain.

He tasted different now, felt different—older, more male, and infinitely more dangerous. She could almost taste it as his tongue slid boldly past the seam of her lips and against her own.

It was he, not she, who pulled away, with a little nibble at her lower lip and a gleam of hunger in his eye.

"Go away, Toby," Corinne whispered. She looked away, then cleared her throat and repeated the order with more force. "Go home."

"Aw, now don't look like that. It couldn't have been that bad."

"Go away."

"I'm going." He stepped to the door and opened it. "But I'll be back."

Chapter 3

Toby was half a block from Corinne's house when he began to mentally kick himself. "You're a jerk, Haskell. A real jerk."

He never did have any control when it came to Corinne.

He pulled up to the station, but sat in the Jeep with one arm draped over the steering wheel for a long time, wondering if he should go back and apologize.

Finally he dragged himself into the office. Luke was watching a program on the television that sat on top of a file cabinet in the corner, his booted feet propped on his desk. He didn't acknowledge Toby's unexpected appearance.

Toby leaned back in the chair across from Luke's desk. He folded his hands over his belt buckle and glowered at the wall. What did he have to apologize for? All he'd done was state the truth—something Corinne never had been able to do.

In his mind he saw her stricken face, the flare of panic in her eyes when he'd turned on her. He didn't know who he hated more—the gunman, for shooting her, or her ex-husband, for failing to protect her.

Or himself, for scaring her again. He swore under his breath.

"So," Luke said, looking up during a commercial. "Early night?"

"Shut up."

"Enjoy your dinner?"

"Kiss my butt." Toby picked up the stapler on Luke's desk and toyed with it. "I didn't even make it through dinner."

"I think there's a cheese sandwich in the fridge."

Toby snorted then stood to pace the room. It was too late to go anywhere, too early to go home. And he couldn't seem to think of anything to do with himself.

"If you want, Haskell, I can just shoot you now and get it over with."

"You're a real pal."

"I'm serious. If you're just going to go through all this again, you might as well let me put you out of your misery. I'd have to dig my bullets out." With a lazy groan, Luke dropped his feet to the floor and started rummaging through drawers. "I think they're here in the file cabinet somewhere...."

"If I'm going to go through all *what* again?"

"This thing with Corinne."

"What *thing?*"

"She led you around by the nose from the time you were eleven years old. It was painful to watch. It's going to be even more humiliating now that you're supposedly grown-up."

"She's not leading me around by anything. I just went over there to fix her water heater."

"Uh-huh," Luke said, turning his attention back to the television.

After a moment Luke said, "She's only here for a few months, you know."

"I know that."

"She never did like this town. Couldn't wait to get out. Probably getting stir-crazy already."

Luke was right. It was irritating as all hell. "Is this leading up to something?"

"I'm just saying," Luke said philosophically, "that I don't see any point in getting all worked up when you know she's not going to stay."

Toby decided he wasn't the only jerk in the room. "I know she's not going to stay. Believe me, I know. And who says I'm getting worked up?"

"Everybody. Since she came back to town, you decided we had to start using Tootsie Rolls instead of money in the weekly poker game. And just when I was starting a winning streak. You chewed out Joe Avedo because his dogs were running loose downtown. You've given out four speeding tickets in the past week. That's more than you wrote all last year."

"You know, gossiping is a feminine trait."

"I'm not gossiping. I'm simply passing on necessary information so my best friend doesn't make a complete ass of himself and go falling for the wrong girl. Again."

"I'm not falling for her again. I got over her a long time ago."

"Sure."

"Of course I did. What kind of idiot would carry a torch for over ten years? So she came back. I looked her up. We talked. No big deal." He leaned back against his desk and tapped his toe restlessly. "Besides, look who's giving me advice on my love life."

"You could do worse."

"Worse than listen to the guy who thinks true love is a myth?"

"I don't think it's a myth. I just think it's as rare as a white Christmas is around here."

"It's not that rare. My parents loved each other."

"Your parents were one in a million. I just don't see why everyone makes themselves miserable looking for this thing that's supposed to make them happy. It doesn't make sense."

"See, Luke, the thing is, you're just expecting everybody to live down to your standards. It's kind of a 'Can't win, don't try' thing with you."

Luke shrugged. "Which one of us is enjoying a nice, relaxing evening and which of us is moping around because he got shot down?"

"I'm not moping. And I didn't get shot down."

"Up until a few weeks ago, you were fine. And since she came back, you've been walking around looking like you were about to get shot out of a cannon."

"It's serious business, getting a woman into bed."

"Is that all it is?"

"Of course." Of course, he repeated silently. "What more would it be?"

"You can't kid me. I'm the one who held your head when you got puking drunk when she married that guy."

"Just for the record, you were the one who got me puking drunk in the first place." His casual laugh sounded forced even to his own ears. "Look, that was a long time ago. I'm not crazy in love with her anymore. I know she's going to take off as soon as this substitute teaching gig is up. And if she doesn't, she made it clear years ago that I'm not her idea of the perfect mate. I know what I'm getting into."

"I hope so. You want to go out to The Corral tonight, get a steak and maybe stick around for the dance? That redhead was there again last week. Why don't you try heating up her water?"

Toby shook his head. He could practically hear his father, chastising him for letting Corinne distract him from his duties for even a second. "Nah. I think I'll stick around here, maybe go check on Mr. Davis in a while. Catch up on the paperwork."

Luke sighed and stood, taking his hat off the rack by the door. "Suit yourself. But remember, the offer's still open."

"I will. Maybe I'll head out to The Corral later."

"I wasn't talking about that. I meant the offer to shoot you. Somebody needs to put you out of your misery." He patted his holster and grinned at Toby's one-fingered gesture.

"Hello?"

Corinne looked up from her desk to see a pretty woman standing in the door of her classroom. She wore a floral print dress in a flowing fabric. Her long curly hair was pulled back in a loose ponytail at the nape of her neck. She held two cups of coffee.

"I thought you might like some company," the woman said, smiling as she entered the room.

"That would be great," Corinne answered, pulling up another chair beside the desk. "Have a seat."

Corinne had noticed the woman the day before at the teachers' in-service meeting, thinking that they were about the same age.

"I remember my first day," the woman said as she handed Corinne a cup. "I was a nervous wreck. You probably haven't had that problem, though."

"What makes you think I'm immune to nerves?" Corinne asked as she sipped her coffee.

"You always seemed so...I don't know. Together, I guess. I didn't figure you'd get anxious about something this simple, after all you've done."

Corinne murmured something noncommittal. As much as she disliked the thought, she knew she was something of a local celebrity after her years on television and her dramatic departure from the media. She didn't want to talk about her reporting career, though. She'd shut that door, and she intended to see that it stayed shut.

"But then, you never worried about anything, even when we were kids. You always had plenty of confidence."

At the blank look on Corinne's face, the woman laughed. "You don't remember me, do you?"

"I'm embarrassed to say I don't. Did we—"

"That's okay. I'm not exactly upset that I don't still look like that same mousy little wallflower. I'm Becca Danvers."

Corinne couldn't hide her surprise. "Becca! I don't believe it. You look so...different."

The Becca that Corinne remembered was painfully shy, always looking as if she were trying to blend in with the wall.

"I hope so. I look at those old school pictures and—ugh."

"You weren't ugly. You were just—"

"Too shy?"

"Too shy." Corinne laughed. "You've come out of that, though."

Becca shrugged. "I had to get over my shyness if I was going to be a teacher. I could just see myself standing in front of a class and being so nervous I squeaked."

Corinne made a face. "Don't give me something else to worry about."

"Has anyone prepared you for the nightmares?" When Corinne's eyebrows shot up questioningly, Becca nodded and leaned a hip on the edge of Corinne's desk, stirring her coffee with a plastic straw. "I teach all the math classes. I dream all the time that I've lost my grade book. Or that I can't remember the lesson. Or I don't *understand* the lesson. One night last week I dreamed I was trapped inside the quadratic formula and couldn't get out." She sighed and shook her head. "I was stuck. It was horrible."

It was something of a surprise to hear the sound of her own easy laughter. What an entertaining idea, to have her nightmares of gunmen and murder replaced by ones of incomplete lesson plans. As if teaching could ever mean enough to her to actually give her nightmares.

"Don't worry. You'll be great. You always were the best at whatever you did."

"There you are! Good, I can give both of you your grade books now."

Corinne looked up to see Mrs. Meddlar standing at the door.

Mrs. Meddlar had been the school secretary since anyone could remember. She was still as energetic as she'd been when Corinne walked the halls as a student. She was Aloma High School's source of transcripts, hall passes and, most importantly, gossip.

"I don't know if Mr. Sammons had time to give you the complete details of your responsibilities when he hired you to sub," Mrs. Meddlar said briskly. "I've compiled a list of the duties the English teacher generally performs."

Corinne scanned the list quickly. "I'm the senior class advisor? What does that entail?"

"You help them fill out college applications, counsel them if they need it, things like that."

"I can't counsel anyone." Corinne cast Becca a worried glance. "I'm not remotely qualified."

"Relax, sweetie, it's nothing. The students hardly ever ask, and when they do, it's the same old thing. You know." Mrs. Meddlar bent in close and raised her eyebrows knowingly. "Sex," she stage-whispered. "And if you ask me, just skip that safe sex nonsense and tell them to keep their pants on and their knees together."

Becca smothered her laugh with a cough and tried to turn away. Corinne warned her with her eyes not to desert her now before she moved discreetly on to the next item on the list. "I'm also in charge of senior class fund-raisers. What's all that about?"

"The senior class always does the Haunted Hayride at the Halloween carnival. They put on the Christmas play, too. There's one more big fund-raiser after spring break. But then, I guess you'll be gone by then." She stopped and eyed Corinne keenly. "Probably back to Dallas, eh?"

Corinne ignored Mrs. Meddlar's thinly veiled dig for gossip and sat heavily in her chair with a sigh. She'd wanted a job that would be time-consuming. It looked as if she'd found it.

"I also brought you a list of all the students you'll have in your classes. That way you can go ahead and fill out this grade book." She plopped the book on Corinne's desk.

"Good," Corinne said, her eyes scanning the list. She wanted to get started learning their names. "Becca, if you don't mind, maybe you could look over this list with me and tell me what you know about each one."

"Sure." Becca smoothed her hair back from her forehead and leaned over the desk to look at the list. "What do you want to know?"

Mrs. Meddlar couldn't resist the opportunity to gossip and she came behind the desk to look over Corinne's shoulder. One by one, the women went through the names, while Corinne jotted notes. It was much the same as the research she'd once done before she interviewed someone.

"Blake Handley. He's a good student, but he has a real problem with spelling and punctuation," Becca said. "You might want to keep an eye on him in that area."

"His father works at the cotton oil mill," Mrs. Meddlar added helpfully. "And his mother drove her Jeep Cherokee into the side of Mrs. Haney's gift shop last year, right after they got into that quarrel about those Easter egg baskets. She told everyone it was an accident, but..." She let her voice trail off and raised her eyebrows.

"Carl Buchanan. One of the many Buchanans, of course," Becca continued. Half of Aloma was either a Buchanan or related to them in some way. "You know, he's the only boy now. They had a run of females in the family for a while, much to their dismay, I'm sure." Becca smiled. "He's got about fourteen girl cousins in this school. He's basically a good kid, but he likes to cut up in class a little."

"Do you know his father paid over forty thousand dollars for that car he's driving?" Mrs. Meddlar asked Becca. "Forty thousand dollars! Of course, considering he owns half the town, I suppose he can afford it. He gave Carl his old pickup. Although it really wasn't old. Two years, hardly long enough to wear the tread off the tires..."

They went through the list of names, with Becca remarking on each student. Corinne could tell the young teacher was trying to give each of the teenagers an honest reference. But she had a hard time saying anything bad about any of them. At worst, she'd say they needed improvement in some area, or might need a little extra help with some things.

Mrs. Meddlar had no such qualms. "That little heathen has stolen my stapler at least ten times," she said when they got to one name. "She wears her jeans much too tight," she said about another girl.

"Jeremy Huckaby." Becca shook her head as she read the name and sighed.

Corinne raised her eyebrows and looked at the name on the list of seniors. This was as close to a bad reference as any of the students got from Becca.

Mrs. Meddlar tsked. "Sad," was all she'd say.

"What?" Corinne laughed uneasily. "What is he, some kind of demon?"

Corinne was teasing, but Becca's face remained serious.

"He's a very angry young man. He's been in a lot of trouble lately."

Mrs. Meddlar nodded, her curls flopping. "Every day it seems like I hear some new kind of mischief he's gotten into. He stole all the letters off the Dairy Queen sign. He took the garbage cans from the park and dumped them into Hank Edwards' water tank. He's just looking for trouble.''

"Why is he like that?" Corinne asked, then silently cursed the reporter's instinct in her that had to eternally question everything.

"You haven't heard about his father? Surely your mother told you about Pete Huckaby. He owned that little trucking company about five miles out of town?"

Corinne shook her head. It was highly unlikely that she and her mother would ever engage in a gossip session about the goings-on in Aloma. "No. What happened? Did he have an accident or something?"

Becca shook her head and started to speak, but Mrs. Meddlar interrupted her. "He went to the state pen. He was using his business to transport...illegal substances," she whispered.

Mrs. Meddlar's eyes were bright with a morbid excitement, while Becca's held reluctance.

"What kind of illegal substances?" Corinne asked uneasily.

"Drugs." Again Mrs. Meddlar stage-whispered her response.

Becca nodded hesitantly. "He was selling drugs out of his truck, trying to make some extra money. Toby arrested him last winter."

"No wonder his son is so angry."

"He's a good kid, Corinne. But you're liable to have your hands full with him."

"Don't worry about it too much, honey." Mrs. Meddlar patted Corinne on the arm. "You're only here for a few months. No one expects you to be a real teacher."

Corinne lifted her eyebrows in surprise. *She* expected it. "I intend to do my best by the students."

"Of course you do, and you will. But no one expects perfection. If the kids give you too much trouble, just send them to detention. Get them out of your hair."

Becca left a few minutes later, after promising to help Corinne in any way she could.

Mrs. Meddlar lingered. "She certainly has changed, hasn't

she?'' She nodded in the direction of the door Becca had just walked through.

Corinne murmured agreement and shuffled through papers on her desk.

"She was always such a wallflower. Who would have thought she was so pretty?''

"She was never ugly.''

"No, but she was never pretty, either. Her mother made her wear those plain dresses that hung so loose on her. She never got to style her hair like the other girls.'' Mrs. Meddlar sighed and shook her head. "Her mother thought it was a sin to care about how you look. She used to lock that poor girl in the closet and make her pray on her knees for hours at a time. But since the hateful old bat died, Becca's finally getting to spread her wings a little.''

Corinne raised her head in surprise. "Her mother died? When?''

"Oh, lands, it's been about a year and a half, I guess.''

Corinne didn't want to get into a gossip session about Becca. For one thing, no one had ever confirmed the rumors about Mrs. Danvers and her fanatical religious practices. And for another, Corinne knew what it felt like to have a less-than-desirable relationship with her parents.

Like Becca, Corinne's father left when she was very young— in Corinne's case, right before her second birthday. Corinne's mother, Linda, had made it plain, in deed and in word, that Corinne's conception was an accident. She'd told anyone who would listen that if she hadn't gotten pregnant at the age of seventeen, her life would have taken a far better path.

Corinne learned early on that she was a mistake, and in her guilt had done her best to make amends to her mother for that mistake. To prove to her mother and to herself that, though she hadn't been planned or wanted, she still had a lot to contribute to the world. She realized now that she'd been looking for her mother's approval and acceptance all her life. In that, too, she had failed.

Even the day of her shooting, with the eyes of the world on her, waiting to learn if she would recover from her injuries, Linda had done nothing more than call to see if she was okay. Unable to talk, Corinne had nodded to her aunt Muriel, who told her mother that she was indeed fine. A card from her mother had been in Corinne's mail when she was released from the hospital. Alone, she'd cried silently that a two-dollar card was her mother's only sign of concern when she'd been so close to death. But Corinne had kept that card with her everywhere she went for six months. Now it was tucked safely away in her dictionary at home.

Corinne had been extremely careful to make sure no one knew about the distant relationship she had with her mother. Her guilt and shame were no one else's business. She was sure—if the rumors about Becca and her mother were true—Becca would feel the same way.

Corinne made a noncommittal noise and continued to shuffle through her papers.

Mrs. Meddlar didn't get the hint. "Now she just needs to find herself a good man—like you—and she'll be happy."

Corinne snorted. A good man. Now that was a joke. "I guess you haven't heard. I'm divorced."

"Oh, I wasn't talking about *that*. I meant Toby Haskell. Now that you're back in town, you two are together again."

"Who said we were together again?"

"Everybody. He was with you at the track last week. And Mrs. Kirby said you had a nice dinner together the other night. About time, too. You two were meant for each other."

Corinne sighed. She had little doubt that whatever she said next would be repeated and translated across countless telephone wires throughout Aloma county tonight.

"I don't know how these rumors get started," Corinne said, shaking her head. Of course, she knew very well how they got started, and the source was standing right in front of her. She slid the papers into her briefcase.

Mrs. Meddlar frowned and shook her head. "You mean it's not true? Well, that was just what I heard, you know."

"You know how people will talk, whether they know what they're talking about or not," Corinne said.

Mrs. Meddlar nodded her head and clucked her tongue. "It's a shame."

"At least you and I know the truth."

"Mmm-hmm... Hmm?"

Corinne drained the last of her coffee and snapped the latches shut on her briefcase. "I'm glad at least you and I can have a discussion without it getting twisted and exaggerated as it's passed all over town. Toby and I were talking at the track the other night because he was welcoming me back to town. Mom's house had been empty for a while, and he wanted to know if I needed help with anything. Which I did, so he came over the next night to look at the hot-water heater. But of course, you know small-town gossips. I've seen him twice, and the next thing you know they'll be running our engagement announcement in the newspaper."

"Some people just have too much time on their hands," Mrs. Meddlar said as she followed Corinne out of the classroom.

Corinne nodded her head in agreement. "Some people are more interested in a good story than they are in the truth. But you and I know the truth—that it was over between Toby and me years ago. We're friends now, and that's all we are. I'm glad, too. He's a good friend to have."

"That's nice. I'm happy for you two, that you can get past the...well, the past. It's nice when you can—"

Mrs. Meddlar turned left to her office. Corinne hooked a sharp right to the book room. "I'm sorry, I have to check out my manuals. But we'll talk later." She flashed Mrs. Meddlar a dazzling smile—the one she had once used quite effectively on reluctant interviewees—and nodded as if Mrs. Meddlar had been the one to suggest it. "It was great seeing you again."

Corinne stood in front of the shelves of books a few seconds later and blew out a great sigh. The last thing she wanted to face every time she went to the grocery store or the gas station was speculation about her and Toby. Her cheeks grew warm at the memory of Toby's kiss, and at her immediate response to it. She hoped Mrs. Kirby wasn't peering through her window at that particular moment, or all Corinne's protestations would be added fuel to the flames. The thought of people thinking of Toby and her as a couple didn't sit well. She felt suddenly, irrationally, as if she were the only person on a losing team. All of Aloma was on the other side, and Toby was their team captain.

Perhaps the absurd conversation she'd just had with Mrs. Meddlar would steer the gossip in another direction at least. People would stop talking when they learned there was really nothing to talk about.

She realized the naiveté of that assumption a few minutes later as she walked by the school secretary's office and overheard the conversation Mrs. Meddlar was having on the phone.

"That's what she said, Helen. She told him flat out, she just wanted to be friends. Well, of course he was upset. You know how he's always been crazy about her. But if you ask me, if he just bides his time... Yeah, me too. She came back for a reason, and it sure wasn't to teach English.... I don't know. Her own mother hasn't even been to see her. But then, they've never been what you'd call close. Me, too. I've got to go, Helen, so I can get home and put the beans on. Call me later."

The sight of Corinne walking down the long hallway in his direction hit Toby like a fist in the gut. She looked tired. She gazed absently at the floor in front of her as she walked, her lower lip caught between her teeth.

He ducked around the corner and pressed against the wall, then peeked back. Her heels clicked and the sound echoed off the walls. She was wearing a maroon pencil-slim skirt and a white blouse, all pressed and polished. She reminded him of a present wrapped in thick, shiny white paper—all class, and hiding untold treasures.

"Hey there," he said smoothly and reached out a hand as she walked by.

He was met with a fist solidly planted in his midsection.

"Uh," was all he could say as he attempted to stand straight and face the murderous rage on Corinne's face.

"Toby Haskell, you idiot!" She swiped her hair back from her face and clenched her teeth. "What do you think you're doing, scaring me like that?"

"Uh," he said again, trying to inhale.

"When are you going to grow up?"

She glared at him and drew herself up to her full height of five foot ten, a good four inches shorter than he. She somehow managed to look down her nose at him.

He held a hand out to stop her tirade. "Sorry," he managed to wheeze. He put his hand to his ribs and gingerly checked them.

"Are you okay?" she asked finally, calming a little.

"I will be. I think."

"I'm sorry. But you shouldn't have done that."

"Believe me, I won't do it again."

The sound of voices and footsteps came from the end of the hallway Corinne had just walked down. Mrs. Meddlar was talking to Mr. Sammons, the principal.

She took a deep breath and blew it out. After their conversation, there was no way she was going to have Mrs. Meddlar catch her talking to Toby.

"Uh-oh," Toby groaned, still testing his ribs. "Quick, in here."

Before she could protest, he pulled her through a doorway into the dark auditorium.

Chapter 4

"Toby!" she whispered in the darkness of the auditorium. "What are you doing?"

"I don't want to talk to Mrs. Meddlar right now."

"Neither do I, but I'm too old to be hiding out with you."

"If you go out now, you're just going to have to explain what you're doing in a dark auditorium with your boyfriend."

He had a point. She decided to stay put.

"You are not my boyfriend," she argued.

"Maybe not, but that's what the town will be calling me as soon as Mrs. Meddlar catches you in here with me."

"I just got through telling her—shh!"

The voices grew louder.

Corinne took a deep breath and tried to ignore the pressing of the dark around her. She would not have a panic attack in front of Toby. She mentally began counting down from five hundred, another technique her doctor had taught her to focus her attention on something besides her growing anxiety.

Almost as disconcerting, however, was the warm feel of Toby

at her side. But at least his presence was something else to focus on.

"What are you doing here, anyway?" she whispered.

"I came up here to look at you for a while."

She didn't realize how close he was until his knuckle brushed lightly against her collarbone. She jumped and took a step back.

"You're jumpy today," he said.

"I'm not jumpy!" she snapped, then took another deep breath and smoothed her hands on her skirt. "I just...wasn't expecting that."

"Sorry," he said. "As a matter of fact, I guess I should apologize for the other night, too."

More than a little startled by that admission, Corinne couldn't think of anything to say except, "Yes, you should."

"I was out of line. I know. And I ought to be sorry."

"Ought to be?"

It was too dark to see, but she knew he was grinning. "But I'm not."

"Why am I not surprised?"

"I was, believe it or not. I felt bad when I left your house. I was pretty crude."

"And overbearing. And rude."

"I should have taken my time, courted you a little."

"And assuming. And boorish."

"So I do apologize. But I'm not really sorry."

"Excuse me. Is that supposed to make sense?"

"I apologize for upsetting you. But I enjoyed it too much to be sorry for it."

Corinne shook her head. "You're something else, Toby."

"As a matter of fact, I felt bad enough that I told myself I was going to stay away from you."

"What a great idea."

"But I can't."

She felt his breath on her cheek a half second before his lips lowered to hers. His lips were firm. Not demanding, but insistent. Not harsh, but gently thoughtful. Not heated, but calmly determined.

His knuckles slowly trailed against her sides. He opened his hands and cupped her rib cage, his thumbs resting just under her breasts.

Where was all her indignant resistance? Where was her cool aloofness, the surety that her response to Toby's kiss the other night had been a fluke, a moment of weakness? It was all swept away with barely more than a token sound of protest, as his lips covered hers, and his strength seeped into her with the feeling of slipping into a warm bath. She didn't have what it took to stop him—or if she did have it, she wasn't interested enough at the moment to dredge it up. Her blood pounded and a dozen tiny explosions touched off through her body.

Toby moaned and slanted his head, and the sound pierced straight through Corinne like a sharp needle.

He pulled his head up. She took a deep breath and put her hand to his chest, lightly pushing him away.

"Stop," she said.

"I will if you really want me to."

"I want you to." In the dark he wouldn't see it was a lie.

He took a half step back, his hands trailing down her arms. Taking her hands, he lifted them to his mouth and kissed the palms, then her wrists.

Even in the dark, Corinne could feel his eyes on her, could taste the self-satisfied smile on his lips.

"Okay, I'll stop. For now."

"I mean it, Toby. I don't want to start anything with you."

"The hell you don't." His thumbs played in the palms of her hands, caressing. His breath was ragged, and she struggled to keep hers from sounding the same. "You put as much into that kiss as I did, Corinne."

She knew she couldn't argue with him, but that still didn't make it right. "So what? So you've proved that you can kiss me and I enjoy it. It's purely physical, Toby. It changes nothing. It means nothing."

"Means plenty to me. I happen to like *purely physical*. As a matter of fact, purely physical is one of my favorite things in life."

He lifted her hands again and nibbled softly at the base of her thumb.

She pulled her hands away, and stifled mild disappointment when he let her.

"I'm not interested in physical or anything else, Toby."

"The hell you're not," he said again, quite cheerfully. "This is me, Corinne. Remember? I was your first in every way. You want me as much as I want you. Don't bother denying it. I can feel it from here."

His hand reached out and softly covered her breast, his thumb lightly caressing the tip. With a gasp she pressed back against the wall.

"See, they're hard as little pebbles. You want me as much as I want you. You're just afraid to admit it."

The crack echoed through the deserted auditorium as she slapped his face. His breath drew in with a hiss.

"I'm not afraid of you or anything else." The indignation in her voice was as much for herself as for him. In a frightfully short time, he'd managed to push all her buttons. And she'd stood right there like an idiot and let him.

After his initial moment of shock, he went on as if he hadn't felt her anger. "You remember how it was between us. You know you do. You said it yourself." His voice slipped over her, easy-going and calm, as if they were talking about the price of tomatoes. She could feel his breath on her neck. So close. But not touching.

"You remember how it was. That was heat. We couldn't have stopped ourselves back then if we'd wanted to. Remember that night, out at the peach orchard? I do. You were wearing a red-and-black sweater. For a while, anyway. Our song was on the radio. Remember, Corinne?" His voice was soft, hypnotic. The memories swirled, making Corinne feel as if she were about to pitch forward. She hugged the wall behind her, her throat closed against the words of protest she should be uttering.

"Remember? How I made you feel? We had something special. A connection. It's still there, sweetheart, and it's stronger than ever. All you gotta do is say the word."

He stepped back then, and Corinne slumped against the wall, feeling drained.

Mrs. Meddlar was long gone by now. Corinne knew she could leave the auditorium without anyone seeing. But she stood there, fighting to get her composure back before she stepped into the light and Toby saw just how much he affected her.

She dragged a shaky hand through her hair and pressed her lips tightly together. "Listen, Toby," she said, angry at how tremulous her voice sounded. "Listen," she said again, with more force. "We're going to be bumping into each other a lot—"

"I plan on it."

"And this is not going to happen again. You can't just come in here and...and—"

"Relax, Corinne. Believe it or not, I didn't come here to hassle you. I'm here on official business. This was just a perk."

"Don't do this again. I don't have the time or the inclination to get involved with you. I've never denied that I was attracted to you. And that what we had once was special to me. But I'm not the same person I was back then."

Beside her, he steeled. "So, are you afraid you won't be cold-blooded enough to walk away without a backward glance this time?"

If the bitterness wasn't so raw in his voice, she might have laughed. *Without a backward glance.* If he only knew.

She'd been anything but cold-blooded back then. She'd been desperate, determined. She was going to prove to her mother—and herself—that she was not a mistake. She was going to change the world and show them both that she was worthy of love and respect. It had almost killed her to leave Toby, and the only way she'd been able to do it was because she *hadn't* looked back, hadn't dared. If she had, she would have been back in his arms before the sun set.

She hadn't been cold back then. But she was now, she reminded herself. She could thank her ex-husband for that. He'd taught her to be cold—cold enough to use the bitterness in Toby's voice against him. "Of course I'm not worried about that. No matter what happens—or doesn't happen—between me and you, I'll be leaving Aloma when this job is over. I'd prefer not to have to sneak out of town like I did last time, though.''

Beside her, she heard him step away, *felt* the hurt her hateful words had caused. She wanted to reach out, to hug him and take the words back.

Maybe she wasn't as cold as she'd thought.

They stood in silence for a tense moment. Then she heard Toby give a soft chuckle, one totally devoid of humor. ''It didn't exactly have a happy ending last time, did it? But then, last time, I admit, I wanted you to stay forever. This time, I just want...well, you know what I want.''

''And I know it won't happen.''

''Maybe not. God knows I have enough on my plate without spending all my time sniffing after you.'' He sighed, and she got the feeling the weariness in his voice had nothing to do with her. ''But you're here for five months. And that's a long time for you to keep lying to yourself. We'll see if you can last that long. Or if the memories don't haunt you, too, and you decide a little 'purely physical' is just what you need.''

''Don't hold your breath, Sheriff.''

He opened the door and a sliver of light pierced the darkness, illuminating his wicked smile. ''I could be holding more than my breath before too long, sweetheart.''

Corinne closed her eyes and sighed in exasperation, smoothing her clothes before she followed Toby out of the auditorium. She held her head high and determinedly put one foot in front of the other, heading for the front door. She was almost there when she turned.

''Toby?''

He spun on one booted foot and faced her, his eyebrow raised.

''You said you were here on official business. Is something wrong?''

His face instantly grew grim. ''Jeremy Huckaby was busted for shoplifting in Abilene this morning.''

Corinne caught herself pacing nervously in front of the desk and stopped. She'd made it through the entire first day—almost.

Her feet ached, her head pounded, and her stomach twisted. She faced the final period. Senior English Composition—the class she dreaded most.

This case of nerves wasn't a surprise, but it did rankle her to feel agitated. She hadn't felt jittery like this since her first days as a reporter, when she'd felt the intense need to prove herself. She'd gotten over the nerves—though not the need to prove herself—as she worked her way up, and thought she'd earned some respect in the business.

That was before an enraged viewer had shot her. Before her ex-husband had shown her the respect she thought she'd earned was a sham. Before she'd learned that everything she'd put her life into, her energy and heart, had been for nothing.

The thought of Don put starch back in her spine. He might have taken everything else, but she'd be damned if she let him take this simple challenge from her.

She leaned back against the desk and feigned confidence. She'd learned in the trenches of investigative journalism that faked confidence was every bit as intimidating as the real thing.

She'd been bombarded with questions about the shooting from her other classes. She preferred not to talk about it, but after the third class she realized she didn't have much choice. She would have to face the issue head-on, get the questions and remarks out of the way. Then maybe she could get on with the business of teaching. Sooner or later, the students would get used to her and wouldn't see her as "the reporter who got shot on television."

As soon as she'd introduced herself as an alumna of Aloma High, she tackled the inevitable.

"As some of you may have already heard, until about a year ago, I worked as a reporter for Channel 27 in Dallas. Following the verdict of a trial I had been covering for the station, a riot broke out in downtown Dallas. We covered the riot live, and in the midst of all the pandemonium, a man with a gun grabbed me." Corinne stated the facts as coldly and plainly as possible, hoping that if she avoided any secrecy, the mystique would wear off sooner.

"He wanted to get the man who'd been convicted released,

which, of course, was not possible. The gun went off, and the bullet struck me here—'' she pointed at her jawline, then moved her finger down to her chin ''—and came out here.''

"The police killed that guy, didn't they?" a girl in the front row asked.

The girl—Corinne was pretty sure her name was Monica—knew good and well the police had killed the man who shot her. The scene was played over and over again on every station in the country. Even doing her best to avoid it, Corinne had seen it herself several times. "Yes, the police shot him immediately after he shot me. He was killed instantly."

"My mom said they had to wire your jaw back together."

"That's true. The doctors did a good job of patching me up."

"Did you get any of his blood on you?"

Corinne had to stand up to see the boy slumped in the back row. It was Jeremy Huckaby, the troublemaker Becca warned her about.

Funny, he didn't look that dangerous. He was thin, with lank black hair that hung down in his eyes and ragged clothes that hung loosely from his body. He didn't look very clean, but he certainly wasn't intimidating.

Several of the kids laughed nervously, and a few groaned. "You're gross," a girl said.

Corinne gave the boy a bland look and didn't answer. That was enough for now, she thought. "If you have any *serious* questions, I'll be happy to answer them now. Then we can get on to more interesting things. Such as what's in your textbooks."

Most of the students wore bored expressions, she noticed with relief. Seniors were much too cool to be interested in a teacher's life.

She grabbed her book and told them to turn to a poem on page twelve.

The students exchanged glances of disbelief before they opened their books. Apparently they hadn't expected that she would make them work on the first day of school.

She'd lectured all day, and her throat was sore. But she wanted to get started off on the right foot. She didn't want the students to think she was going to be an easy teacher simply because she was a sub. They discussed a few poems, with her doing most of the discussing, until there were only about five minutes left.

"Okay. For tomorrow, I want you to write a two-page essay. The subject is your choice. It's due at the beginning of class tomorrow."

Monica raised her hand. "Miss Maxwell?"

"Yes, Monica?"

"We don't usually have homework on the first day of school."

Her comment was met with several murmurs of agreement. Evidently the new teacher needed to learn how things were done around here.

"Then we'll be pioneers. Years from now students will talk about this class and how it blazed new trails in the learning world, set precedents for future generations to aspire to."

Blank stares met her.

"We're going to work in here today," she clarified.

That announcement was met with grumbles and the slaps of notebooks onto desks, new packages of writing paper being ripped open.

"What do we write about?"

"Any subject you desire."

Desire was an unfortunate choice of words, Corinne realized as soon as it was out of her mouth.

"Any subject *I* desire?" Josh Baxter asked, and was rewarded with the anticipated snickers and hoots.

Becca had warned her about him. *He's the quintessential class clown, Corinne. Whatever you do, never laugh at him. If you do, you might as well kiss the control of your class goodbye.*

"Is it okay if I write about how much I desire Cindy Wells?" he asked, an exaggerated expression of wide-eyed innocence on his face.

"You certainly may," Corinne answered, determined to keep the upper hand. "As long as you keep in mind that your parents are free to read these papers at any time."

The object of Josh's desire had definite feelings about his choice of topics. "Write about something else," Cindy said with a toss of her flaming red hair.

Josh was undeterred by her attitude or the teasing of his classmates.

"I don't get it."

Corinne didn't have to check the chart to know who was talking. Carl Buchanan, all-around jock. He was the captain of the football team and the biggest kid Corinne had ever seen. Carl's father had been in high school when Corinne was in elementary school, but she still remembered the awe the rest of the students had of him. Carl was following closely in his father's footsteps.

"What don't you get, Carl?"

"What are we supposed to write about?"

"Whatever you want to write about. The subject is your choice. I just want to get an idea of what kind of writers you are, see where we stand in this class."

"So, what do I write about?"

Corinne stared him down. She knew the boy wasn't stupid, just trying to act that way. But he didn't know who he was up against. Corinne had fought hard during her years of investigative journalism, and she knew how to win. She'd won an interview with a writer notorious for avoiding the press. She'd elbowed aside more than one reporter competing for the same story. She'd made a televangelist break down and confess to embezzling while the cameras were rolling. She could handle a high school punk.

She didn't get a chance to do it, though.

"Why don't you write about how you lost last year's district championship game?" Jeremy said from the back of the room.

The class oohed. Carl stood beside his chair.

"Why don't I write about how I'm going to rearrange your face?"

Jeremy wasn't intimidated. He sneered at Carl and made no move to get up. "Of course, it wouldn't take two pages to talk about that game. 'I ran the wrong way' doesn't take up much space."

Carl took two steps toward Jeremy, his fists raised.

"Get up!"

"Sit down!"

The class froze at once, Carl included. Corinne had also learned that her voice could be surprisingly strong when she wanted it to be.

"There will be no fighting in this classroom, period. Now, I want complete silence while everyone works on their essays. These papers are due at the beginning of class tomorrow. There will not be another word uttered until the bell rings."

"But we don't—"

"Not another word."

Corinne's voice was deadly calm. Carl glared at Jeremy one more time and dropped sullenly into his chair.

Carl was probably planning what he was going to do to Jeremy as soon as the last bell rang. Corinne tried to think of some way to stop it, but she didn't know how. The only thing she could control was what went on in her room.

She stifled a sigh and sat down behind the desk. She rotated her sore ankles where no one could see her and wondered how Jeremy was going to live through the pounding he was surely going to get. She hoped he was a fast runner.

The bell rang and the room emptied in a matter of seconds, with everyone bloodthirsty for the impending fight.

She went to Mr. Sammons's office, hoping he would be able to do something to stop it. He wasn't in his office, nor was he in the break room or the supply closet when she looked there. Not that it would do much good if she did find him, she thought as she walked back to her deserted classroom. He could get them off the schoolgrounds, but the boys would find a place to fight.

She picked up the armload of books she was taking home and walked out to the parking lot. Toby stood beside her car, his hand clamped firmly on Carl Buchanan's shoulder. They were both looking at her back tire.

"Hi, Corinne. Looks like you've got a flat one there."

Corinne looked at the deflated tire. "I can't believe this. I just bought those tires."

"That's a shame. Carl here said he'd be happy to take this one down to Johnny's service station and have it aired back up, check for leaks.''

Carl cut his eyes over to Toby and frowned, but he didn't disagree.

''Are you sure you don't mind, Carl?'' Corinne asked. Back in Dallas, she'd have called the auto club and hailed a cab to take her home. In Aloma, there was no such option.

''I don't mind,'' he said, his sullen tone stating clearly that he did indeed mind. ''It'll take a few minutes.'' He took her keys and opened the trunk.

''Mmm. How many minutes, do you think?''

Carl shrugged. ''I dunno. Forty-five, maybe an hour.''

Corinne bit back a sigh. She was grateful for the boy's help, even though she knew Toby was practically forcing him into it. But the thought of standing around in this unbearable August heat for another hour was disheartening. And she didn't really want to go back to her classroom, either. She wanted to go home.

''Buchanan, you take care of the tire and I'll take Miss Maxwell home. We'll bring her car home later.''

''You don't have to take me, Toby. I can walk.''

''Sure you can, you've got two legs. But there's no sense in you walking when I can drive you.''

''It's only a few blocks,'' Corinne said lamely. Actually, it was six blocks, which wouldn't have bothered her at all if her arches weren't killing her and if she hadn't already started sweating just standing in the heat.

''I'm going by there anyway.''

She didn't want to make a scene in front of a student, but there was no way she was going to be alone with Toby Haskell again. ''You really don't have to—''

''You said that already. I'm a public servant, you're the public. I'm going to serve you.''

He ignored the look she threw his way and climbed in the Jeep. With a cocky grin, he started it.

Corinne stood between the two cars, undecided.

Toby rolled down his window.

''Come on, Corinne, let's go.''

The sound of the engine dropped as he clicked on the air conditioner. Even the sound of it was cool. But still, the last time she'd been alone with Toby...

She started walking. "No thank you, Toby. It's a nice day for a walk."

He kept the Jeep even with her and rolled down the passenger window. "You might as well get in," he called.

"No, thank you." She tossed him a frozen smile over gritted teeth, and kept walking.

"Suit yourself," he called. "So long as you know, I'm going to follow you the whole way. And someone will probably see us. Within fifteen minutes the new teacher will be the talk of the town."

Corinne cut him a scathing look and kept walking, her heels sinking slightly into the hot tar of the road. Perspiration beaded and ran down the small of her back.

"A little thing like this could turn into a big scandal in just a few hours. What kind of story do you think all those ladies will come up with, trying to figure out why I was following you home at—" he glanced down at the speedometer "—three miles an hour."

Corinne refused to be intimidated. For half a block. With an angry moan, she jerked the passenger door open and tossed her books onto the seat. "You're a jerk," she said as she sat down.

Toby grinned and pressed the accelerator to the floor. The Jeep rocketed forward.

"Whoa," Corinne said, regaining her balance and searching for her seat belt.

"Sorry," Toby muttered as he rounded a corner. "I just have to round up the other member of this little feud."

Corinne had no idea what he was talking about until she saw Jeremy slinking down the alley behind the old movie theatre, his hands stuffed in his pockets.

Toby headed the Jeep into the alley behind him. Jeremy whirled around. Fear flickered across the boy's face before he had a chance to mask it. The fear was quickly replaced with annoyance when he saw it was them and not Carl.

Toby stopped the Jeep and opened the door, then stood with one foot on the floorboard. "You need a ride to see your probation officer, Huckaby?" He didn't give the boy a chance to answer. "Good deal, get in."

Jeremy muttered something and turned away, but Toby's voice stopped him. "I said, get in."

This time Jeremy's mutter was audible, but he turned back and walked to the Jeep. Corinne stifled a smile and nodded politely to Jeremy when he flounced into the back seat and swiped hair out of his eyes.

"I was afraid you might forget you had a meeting this afternoon, Huckaby. Good to see you're staying on track." Toby flashed a grin into the rearview mirror and then laughed good-naturedly at the sour look on Jeremy's face. Jeremy remained silent and looked out the window.

Toby drove to the courthouse and parked the Jeep by a side door. "Go through that door and down the hall on your left. It's the second door on the right."

Jeremy remained silent as he got out. He walked up the sidewalk, his hands again in his pockets and his shoulders slumped. Toby left the Jeep in Park and watched him.

Jeremy's steps slowed the closer he got to the door. He glanced back surreptitiously to see if they were still there. Toby grinned and waved. "I'll be waiting here when you get out," he called.

Corinne didn't have to be a lip reader to understand the words Jeremy used before he finally gave up and entered the building. Toby just smiled and shook his head. He waited a few more minutes before he put the Jeep into reverse.

"For a second, I thought I was going to have to drag the boy in there."

"I did, too. He's safer in there than he is out here, though. Carl Buchanan is ready to flay him alive."

"I know. I drove by the school and the entire student body was heading for the alley. My natural law-enforcement instinct kicked in," he said with a devilish dimpled grin, "probably because they looked so bloodthirsty. One of the kids told me Jeremy was mouthing off again and Buchanan was going to kill him."

Corinne wasn't surprised that one of the students felt it was okay to confide in Toby. To them he was more of a friend than an authority figure. He was one of them—a feeling Corinne was sure Toby had cultivated. He'd always wanted to be as well-liked and respected as his father had been.

Toby drove the car with the ease of someone who drove often, and within minutes they were on her street. Corinne searched the floorboard for the shoes she didn't remember taking off.

"So, I collared Carl and convinced him he should help me with the tire first."

"That was convenient, wasn't it? That my tire just happened to be flat right when you needed it to be." She glanced sideways at Toby.

"Yeah, convenient." He cut his gaze over at her and she saw the muscles in his face working to hide a smile. "But I would have found something else, if I had to."

Corinne studied him for a moment, trying to decide if that was a guilty grin on his face or just a plain old grin. With Toby, it was hard to tell.

"You know, you've already got the worst reputation of any teacher in the history of Aloma. Homework on the very first day, Corinne? What kind of monster are you?"

Corinne laughed. That was the bad thing about Toby. He was fun to be around. It made her forget the need to be cautious.

"Jeremy made some remark about Carl losing last year's championship game."

Toby winced. "That kid must have a death wish. If there's one thing you don't joke about around here, it's football."

"I remember. Football is the number one priority in life. The only reason he'd say something like that is if he really did want to get into a fight. He knew how Carl was going to react, and surely he knew there was no way he was going to best that ox in a fight."

"He's been that way ever since that mess last winter with his dad. You heard about that?"

Corinne nodded. "I heard. He's headed for trouble, one way or another. It's written all over his face."

"Maybe not," Toby said, pulling up in front of her house.

"I hope you're right. But I think he's destined to spend major time in some kind of correctional facility."

"You're just a jaded old reporter. You don't see any good in the world."

Corinne started to make some kind of retort, but decided not to bother. It was true. "You're right about that. But if you'd seen the things I've seen, you'd be jaded, too."

"If you'd stayed here like I asked you to, you could be ignorant and content like me." He grinned and sighed deeply as if to demonstrate his satisfaction with life.

She couldn't get mad at him, not with that dimple winking and his eyes twinkling somewhere between merriment and devilment. But she didn't have to sit here and be reminded of her faults. He reached out a hand to stop her when she moved to get out.

"Seriously, Corinne, you ought to give the kid a chance. He was a decent boy, before I arrested his dad. At first, a lot of the other parents wouldn't let their kids have anything to do with him. Like this kid they've known all their lives has instantly become evil," he said, his voice suddenly tinged with disgust. "That made him more defensive, and he started living up to his reputation."

"I'm not trying to give him a hard time, Toby. I've seen this kind of thing more than you have, though. He isn't interested in improving his attitude."

"He will be. He's been through a lot in the past few months. He needs some time to work it out in his head."

Corinne shook her head. Toby could afford to be idealistic. He'd lived all his life sheltered in Aloma. She'd learned the folly of trusting in the supposed goodness of basic human nature.

She opened the door, then stopped. "I know you think you can solve all of Aloma's problems single-handedly, Toby. But I think this one's out of your league."

Toby rubbed the back of his neck and looked at the steering wheel. "You may be right. But I still have to try, don't I?"

Of course he would try, Corinne thought. If anyone in his jurisdiction had a problem, Toby Haskell was going to do his best to make it right. From the strain in his voice, the situation with Jeremy wasn't as simple to handle as the one with Mrs. Kirby, and it bothered him a great deal more.

"It would help, *Miss* Maxwell, if you'd keep an eye out for him at school."

"What do you expect me to do, Toby? I have classes to teach. I'm not a baby-sitter."

"Just keep an eye out. Let me know what's going on with him. Between the two of us, we can keep him on track and make sure he doesn't do something he's going to regret later."

"Why? You go so far above the call of duty, it's not even funny. He obviously doesn't want your help, or anyone else's."

Toby's expression grew serious, and he looked her in the eye. "If you could have seen the look on his face, Corinne, when I arrested his father, you'd understand perfectly."

Corinne frowned. Was that actually *guilt* on his face? "Toby, you were just doing your job. You're not to blame for the situation. Jeremy's father is."

"I know that. I knew Pete was guilty, but that didn't stop me from feeling like I was responsible for destroying Jeremy's life. That does something to a person, Corinne. At least, it does to a person who hasn't made themselves too hard to feel anything."

The sting of his words bit into her as she moved to close the door behind her. But that was what she wanted, wasn't it? To be too hard to feel anything?

"Besides, he *is* my responsibility, in a way. The people of the county elected me sheriff, and that means a lot. One day Jeremy will quit being mad at the world, and he'll want to get on with his life. I don't want him to have anything hanging over his head when the time comes."

Corinne shook her head at his naiveté all the way up her sidewalk and into the house. She was kicking off her shoes when she realized Toby hadn't tried to touch her. Not once.

Chapter 5

The words on the paper were graphic and violent. Corinne peeked over the edge of the paper she was reading. The sophomore students were focused on work; they weren't interested in the flood of color to her face.

She read on, grateful not to feel the tingling that signaled the beginning of a panic attack. Jeremy Huckaby's paper was one of the most disturbing things she'd ever read. Her own words came back to haunt her: *any subject you choose.*

Jeremy chose a subject of violence. Violence against her. It was the story of a reporter getting shot while covering a race riot. There was no doubt it was meant to portray her.

It was an unapologetically angry piece. And meant to frighten her. It was painfully clear how much pleasure he got at the thought of her being victimized.

Corinne bit down her initial reaction and tried to look at the situation from a broader perspective. It was difficult, though. She felt as if she were going through the ordeal all over again. And once again, someone was looking on and getting benefit from her pain.

She glanced down at Josh Baxter's paper at her elbow. Two pages of why he loved Cindy Wells. She'd corrected his grammar and told him to look in the thesaurus for an alternative to *beautiful.* It was so easy. She didn't feel as if she were holding the boy's psyche in her hands.

The bell rang and Corinne jumped. It was lunchtime.

She cornered Becca in the teachers' lounge as soon as she saw her. "Do you have a minute?"

Corinne led Becca back to her classroom and pulled the paper out of the bottom drawer of her desk. Once she had it, though, she hesitated in giving it to Becca.

"I probably shouldn't bother you with this," she said, the pages in her hand. "I'm sure it's nothing. It just caught me a little off guard, I guess, and I might need some advice—"

"Corinne, hand it over," Becca said, her hand out. She grimaced as she read the first paragraph. "This is..." She darted a quick look at Corinne and continued reading. "How horrible." She made a face. "Good at painting a mental picture, isn't he?" she said ruefully.

She looked at Corinne and her brow furrowed. "Corinne, I'm so sorry. Why in the world would he write something like this?"

"I told the class to write a two-page paper on any subject they chose. This is Jeremy Huckaby's choice."

"Serves you right," Becca muttered, then laughed at Corinne's stricken expression. "I'm just kidding. I'm so sorry you had to read this. It must not be very pleasant for you."

Becca's sympathy was obvious on her face. Seeing it stiffened Corinne's spine. She'd had enough sympathy to last her a lifetime. "It wasn't pleasant, but not traumatic, either," she denied. "I'm sure it's just a play for attention. But what should I do about it? How much trouble will he get into if I tell Mr. Sammons about this?"

Becca shrugged. "He's on thin ice right now. He was causing trouble all summer, and then with getting caught shoplifting... There's talk that if he gets into any more trouble, he'll have to go to school at The Project."

Corinne nodded. The Project was the school inside the county youth correctional facility. Some kids just went to school there and were free to go home at night; others had to live in the facility until their sentence was served.

"Something like this might not be enough to get him sent there, but it wouldn't do him any good, either. And with the county facility being an hour's drive away, he might end up staying there full time, instead of just attending classes."

Corinne paced in front of her desk. "I did a story on one of those places one time. Sometimes they're more of a breeding ground for criminals than a reform system. They stick all the problem kids together and they learn how to be even tougher."

She remembered what Toby said, about wanting Jeremy to have a clean slate when he got ready to move on with his life. Juvenile hall, even for a few months, would definitely not be a clean slate.

Becca nodded. "I know. But what else are you going to do? If he's a threat to the other students..."

Corinne took the paper back. "I don't think Jeremy is a threat to the other kids. I don't think he's a threat to anyone but himself."

"I agree with you there. If you could have seen him a year ago, Corinne. He was such a sweet kid, very sensitive. The other kids teased him for being so sensitive. Now he's just angry."

"You know, I'm wondering if that's what he wants. To get sent away, I mean. He won't have anything to do with the other kids. He acts like he hates all of them, and resents being here."

She pictured Jeremy with some of the street toughs she'd seen in Dallas, the type of person he'd be sharing quarters with. The type of person who'd grown up with violence and anger. Jeremy wouldn't stand a chance.

Corinne tapped the paper against her jaw. "Maybe I should call his mother and have a conference with her."

"Maybe."

"I hate to bother her right now, though. She's got enough on her mind without worrying about what kind of mess I'm making with her son."

"Corinne, Jeremy was a mess before you ever got to town."

Corinne smiled sadly. "I know. I don't think I'm going to tell Mr. Sammons, or Mrs. Huckaby."

"I think that's a good idea. You can just sit him down and have a talk with him yourself. Maybe get him to write you another paper."

Corinne shook her head. "No. I think I'm just going to grade it and hand it back to him."

"And not say anything?"

Corinne nodded. "I'm going to grade it like any other paper. He's looking for a reaction. I'm not going to give him one. Wouldn't I be rewarding him, if I did?"

"I'm not a psychologist, Corinne. I don't know. But that seems kind of risky."

"Risky, how?"

"Letting him think he can get away with unacceptable behavior, for one thing. And what if one of the other students finds out what he wrote about, and that you did nothing to correct him? You could be setting yourself up as a victim in their eyes if you don't at least say something."

Corinne read through the paper again and dragged a hand through her hair. "I don't know. He doesn't seem the type to brag to the other kids. I think I'm going to let it pass by. If I act outraged, he's going to know he succeeded."

Becca shrugged. "If it's any consolation, I wouldn't take it personally. He's been lashing out." She looked at the paper again and sighed. "I can't believe this is the same kid I saw take his little brother trick-or-treating last year."

"Mmm," Corinne murmured. "Toby asked me to keep an eye on him. He thinks there's something there to salvage."

"There's always something there to salvage, Corinne. No one is all bad. Are you going to tell Toby about this?"

"No. There's no point."

"He wants to help Jeremy. He might want to talk to him."

"Toby wants to help the world, or at least this little corner of it. He thinks *sheriff* is synonymous with *Divine Protector*."

Becca laughed. "I think you should tell him anyway."

"Jeremy hasn't broken any laws here."

"Still, he cares about the boy and wants to help him."

Jeremy would probably feel betrayed if she went to Toby about school business. He'd feel that everyone was ganging up on him.

This was stupid, she told herself. Jeremy was the one who'd done something wrong, not her. She didn't have to treat him with kid gloves.

So, why was she going to? she asked herself. Because she didn't want him to think she was intimidated by his essay? Because she didn't want to acknowledge that anything anyone could say or think about the shooting could affect her?

Or because she thought she might know what he was going through, having his whole world bottom out in one moment?

She wrinkled her nose and shook her head. "No. That really would be making too big a deal out of it, getting the law involved."

Becca shrugged. "Okay. But if anything else comes up, let me know. We teachers have to stick together, you know."

Corinne laughed lightly. "I'm not a teacher. I'm just a sub who doesn't have a clue what's going on."

"I'll let you in on a little secret. Sometimes none of us can figure out what's going on. You ready to grab some lunch?"

Corinne decided early on that since she wasn't staying long in Aloma, she wouldn't socialize with the other teachers. She had only entered the teachers' lounge today to grab a quick cup of coffee and to find Becca. "I brought something from home. I'll just eat at my desk and grade papers. Besides, I don't have much of an appetite left."

"I'm not going to argue with a woman who forgoes frozen fish sticks and Mrs. Meddlar's long-winded opinion of the decline of rural civilization."

Corinne sat at her desk as Becca left. She sighed and leaned back, trying to read the essay in front of her from an editor's standpoint. An editor with a strong stomach.

Actually, the writing was quite good, if she overlooked the theme. There were no glaring grammatical errors. It flowed well, and he stayed focused on the theme, gruesome as it was. And it was accurate, she knew that for a fact. She said so at the bottom of the page, complimenting Jeremy on his use of active verbs and descriptive adjectives. She even went so far as to say he had a good imagination and should think about entering some of the school writing contests. The only real criticism she gave was that he should try to think of a more original topic.

She chewed her lip, wondering if she'd done the right thing.

And she thought this job was going to be easier on her mind than investigative journalism. What a joke.

Toby was having a bad day. First thing in the morning, Clyde Cummings had called to say someone had stolen his riding lawn mower. Toby knew damn well no one had stolen his lawn mower, and was about to tell Clyde that, when he looked out the window and saw Mr. Davis riding it down the street.

So he'd had to chase Mr. Davis down the road. Mr. Davis acted as if it were the most logical thing in the world to be driving someone else's lawn mower down the street.

"You are the one who forbade me to drive, Mr. Haskell. How do you expect me to get around?" Mr. Davis had asked imperiously.

"Why would you steal Clyde's lawn mower, though?" Toby countered as he led Mr. Davis back to his home.

"Because I have a push mower. No point in even trying to ride that thing." Mr. D. had looked at Toby as if he were a bit slow.

After that episode and two trips to Mrs. Kirby's house, reassuring her that no one had any reason to break into her house and adjust the color on her television set, he had gone to the feed store. Inside, Billy Malone and Scott Tooley were arguing hotly about which feed was better for Herefords. Toby had walked up just in time to mediate.

"Tell that ignorant SOB he couldn't ranch his way out of a paper bag!" Billy had told Toby.

"You tell him that if he's so damn smart, why's all his cows look like they been dragged behind an 18-wheeler for twenty miles?" Scott yelled.

Billy swung at Scott. Scott swung back. Toby got so sick of the idiots that he'd arrested them both for disturbing the peace. It took fifteen minutes to convince them both he was serious.

Now, five hours later, he sat with his elbows on his desk, massaging his temples and trying to ignore the ruckus the two men were putting up in the cell.

"You let me out of here right now, Haskell, or I'll call my lawyer."

Toby leaned back in his swivel chair and propped his booted feet on the scarred desktop. He picked up a letter opener and began tapping it against his knee.

"You don't have a lawyer, Malone, so just shut up. Your wife makes the bail, I'll be happy to get rid of your whiny butt."

The problem was, neither Billy's nor Scott's wives seemed particularly interested in bailing the guys out. In fact, they rather liked the idea of a night without the men.

One good thing had come out of the mess: the two men in the cell now had a common enemy and were in the process of working out their differences.

It was really starting to hack Toby off. His official title ought to be Baby-sitter, not Sheriff. He couldn't even convince his inmates he was serious. First, Mr. Davis, then Mrs. Kirby. And now these two jokers, who were more amazed that he'd have the nerve to actually arrest them than they were intimidated at his power.

It was no wonder Corinne didn't take him seriously. No one did. In all the years his father had been sheriff, Toby couldn't remember anyone laughing at him when he told them they were under arrest.

Toby tossed a deck of cards into the cell and went out to the Dairy Queen to get them some dinner.

He was still thinking about Corinne as he drove down the quiet Aloma streets. That big shot producer she'd married probably had all kinds of power and prestige. Aside from the fact that he was undoubtedly a jerk—a judgment Toby felt perfectly qualified to make even though he'd never laid eyes on the man—Corinne had probably been impressed with his position. After all, he didn't go around all day trying to coddle old ladies and busting up fights between men old enough to know better.

He was driving back with three orders of steak fingers when he saw Carl Buchanan and his gang hanging out in the grocery store parking lot. They were loud, but the store was closed and they weren't loud enough to be bothering anyone. He started to pass them by.

A few of them yelled a greeting and waved to him. He sourly tossed back a wave and kept driving.

Then, from the corner of his eye, he saw a beer bottle being tossed into the bed of a pickup.

He turned the Jeep around and headed back.

"You guys having a good time?" He put his Stetson on and stepped out of the Jeep. There were probably fifteen guys in all, and a couple of girls. All of them were kids Toby knew well. They weren't afraid of him. They were too drunk to care much about anything. Hell, most of them didn't even bother to hide their bottles.

Carl nodded. "We're doing okay, how 'bout you?"

Toby nodded. "I'm doing pretty good, 'cept I'm gonna have to bust you all for drinking. Anybody here not a minor, raise your hand."

The group snickered. A couple of hands were raised, but Toby knew they were all under eighteen.

"Okay, you're all under arrest for drinking in a public parking lot, minors in possession of an alcoholic substance, et cetera. We'll work out the details at the station. You guys wait here while I call Luke."

Carl chuckled and stood ramrod straight. "Aye-aye, Captain." He saluted.

Toby nodded and went back to his Jeep. They didn't even try to run. They laughed and started making up prison nicknames for each other.

Toby called Luke from the car phone. "I need some help. I raided a beer party in the grocery store parking lot."

Luke groaned and said, "Couldn't you do that some other night? I've got a date."

Toby's temper snapped. "Get down here! And bring your mom's minivan." He walked back to the group. "I want you five in the Jeep." Still giggling, they climbed clumsily into the Jeep.

"I wanna run the siren! Can I run the siren, Toby?" one of the boys asked as he climbed in.

Luke showed up ten minutes later.

"Buchanan, get in Luke's van. Come on, everybody in." He shooed them into the van, ignoring Luke's dubious expression.

Somehow they managed to make it to the station with everyone still in one piece, but the steak fingers were devoured somewhere in the three minutes it took to get there.

"Everyone follow me," he called as he walked up the steps.

The kids snickered behind him, making jokes and pushing each other around.

"Good news, boys," Toby told Billy and Scott as he unlocked the cell door. "Due to prison overcrowding, you're getting an early release."

Billy and Scott looked at each other, puzzled. "What about our steak fingers?"

Toby rolled his eyes and motioned them both to leave. Scott picked up the cards and the two men agreed to continue their game down at the Dairy Queen.

"Okay, everybody line up at this door. As you get to the front of the line, give me your name and phone number."

It was all a joke to them. They didn't even act nervous. Most of them gave fake names, but he knew who they all were anyway.

When the kids were all inside, Toby slammed the door behind them and sat down at his desk.

"You had Billy and Scott in there, too? What is this, a crime spree?" Luke asked with a laugh. He tossed his hat onto the rack by the door. Toby just glared.

"Listen, Haskell. I need to ask you a question." Luke leaned casually on the edge of the desk. "What the hell are you doing?"

"I busted them," Toby said shortly. "They were drinking."

"I know what you're doing. I just want to know why. We've caught kids drinking before. We take them home, give them the lecture. The parents ground them and they mow the courthouse grass for a few weeks. That's what we've always done, since your old man was sheriff. This is one hell of a mess."

"We were wrong." He wasn't about to say his father was wrong. "We shouldn't let them get away with it."

Luke shrugged. "I know you're right. I just don't understand why all of a sudden you decide to get so technical."

Toby cradled the phone and leaned back in his chair. "I realized we were wrong, not to be more professional in this job. This isn't some little problem. Those kids were drinking. Some of them would have been driving. It's time we all get a little more technical."

"And after all, big-city police wouldn't let them get away with it."

Toby shot him a look. "No. They wouldn't."

Inside the cell, a few of the boys started singing drunkenly, hanging on the bars. "Nobody knows the trouble I've seeeen...."

Luke shook his head. "You've got the mayor's son in there, Haskell."

"I'm aware of that."

"You've got the banker's daughter in there."

"I know that, too."

"You've got half the football team in there. Homecoming is in four weeks. This is going to get ugly."

Toby picked up the phone and started dialing. "I know that."

A couple of the kids were beginning to realize this was no joke. "Hey, Toby. Let us out, okay, man?"

"Okay," Luke told Toby. "It's your job. If you want to hack off the whole town and lose your job just to impress Corinne with your authority, go ahead. It's your neck."

"Sheriff?" one of the girls asked. "You're not really going to call my dad, are you? He'll kill me."

Another one chimed in. "I need to go home, okay? You can let me out now." The laughs that followed were edged with growing nervousness.

"Right," Toby said to Luke. "It's my neck. Try to remember that, would you?" he suggested as he listened to the ringing.

Inside the cell, nervousness was giving way to anger and fear. One of the boys started crying. Carl Buchanan told him to shut up.

"You're not calling my old man," Carl said angrily. "He'll have your job. You're not calling my old man."

Toby covered one ear with his hand and continued calling parents.

Corinne swept her gaze over the classroom, trying to gauge the reactions of the students. She'd just passed back their first essays.

Of course, at the moment everyone was too caught up in last night's scandal to worry about grades. And the rumor that just started in the past hour—that the boys arrested might not be able to participate in any extracurricular activities—only fanned the flames of the controversy.

Even Jeremy was interested, though in a more gruesome way than the rest of the kids. He didn't play football. He thought it was so funny that guys like Carl Buchanan would get arrested, he'd worn a half smile all day. It was the happiest Corinne had seen him.

She sneaked a peek at him over the lid of her open satchel. He was studying his essay, but she couldn't read the expression on his face. Was he glad? Disappointed that she hadn't acted in outrage? It was impossible to tell.

The bell rang not long after that. She gathered her things and walked out into the crush of students in the hall.

The kids were gathered in the hallway outside the principal's office, murmuring in hushed tones. She couldn't make out the words, but the students had all the earmarks of an angry mob.

It wasn't hard to determine who they were angry at. Toby strode from the outer doorway, through the crowd toward Mr. Sammons's office. With a smile, Corinne recognized the tan shoulder of Toby's uniform, and the curve of his Stetson. He nodded to the students coolly, as if he routinely walked through lynch mobs.

Mr. Sammons opened the door for him and eyed the crowd. Corinne got a quick glimpse of Dan Buchanan, Carl's father. Behind him was Coach Steck and a few others. Mr. Sammons closed the door behind Toby. With a quick snap of his wrist he closed the blinds over his window.

Corinne edged behind the students and entered the hallway. She circled around to the teachers' lounge, which led directly to Mr. Sammons's other door.

Corinne figured that no one in the history of Aloma was more hated than Toby at this moment. After all, he had the unmitigated gall to actually think those laws applied to *them,* the stars of Aloma High, the native sons.

Corinne poured a cup of coffee from the pot in the lounge and edged up to Mr. Sammons's door, putting her ear to it.

Inside the office, Toby nodded politely at the men and sat down in a chair facing the desk.

"I'm sure you know why we asked you to meet with us today, Toby."

"I'm sure I do," Toby said.

"We're all concerned, of course, with the terrible thing our boys have done," Dan Buchanan said. Toby could feel the man's booming voice through the soles of his feet. "We want to cooperate in any way we can."

It was a decidedly different attitude than the one the man had shown last night when he was bailing Carl out of jail, but Toby didn't push the issue. "That's good. Concerned parents are important in situations like this. Of course, it's up to the courts to decide what the terms of their punishment will be."

Coach Steck cleared his throat and cast Dan a look. "We aren't sure that filing charges against the boys is the best way to go."

"It's the only way to go, Coach," Toby said companionably. "I took care of the paperwork this morning."

"We'd like you to hear us out, Toby, before you go any further," Mr. Sammons said. His leather chair squeaked as he leaned back, all studied nonchalance. Though admittedly it had been a while since Toby's last visit to the principal's office, he could still read the signs.

"I'd be happy to hear whatever you have to say, Claude." Toby made sure his voice was firm. He got a kick out of using the old guy's first name. "I'm not going to promise you anything, though."

"We're not asking for that, of course. We're not asking for you to do anything except listen. It occurred to us that perhaps there would be a better way of dealing with this situation. A way that might be less, well, less harsh. Just as effective, mind you, but not as harsh.''

''I can assure you the boys won't do hard time,'' Toby said wryly.

Dan Buchanan forced a laugh. ''Of course they won't. But there are bound to be ramifications from this that would punish them far into the future. In light of the fact that the boys are so young—''

''Old enough to know better,'' Toby interjected.

''And as this is their first offense, we thought it might be better to—''

''What we thought, Toby,'' Mr. Sammons interrupted, leaning forward and meeting Toby's eye intently, ''is that this situation is bigger than just the law that was broken.''

''I agree completely. Teenage drinking is a big problem, and could lead to adult alcoholism.''

''That's why we feel this would be a good time for us to band together, pool our resources and make sure we do right by those boys. You see, Sheriff,'' he bowed his head deferentially ''we envision the school, the law, the families, all as part of a team, a community. Not unlike the way your father used to think, I should say.'' Mr. Sammons laced his fingers together in demonstration. ''In fact, I've received over thirty phone calls today, all about this very issue. The people are concerned about those kids, as they have a right to be. There are many facets to this problem.''

''You folks are more than welcome to handle this matter any way you want. The law, of course, won't be stepping back.''

''We aren't asking you to do that—no, not at all,'' the coach said earnestly. ''We're simply thinking that if the punishment were kept more...in the family, say, the boys will learn a greater lesson—''

''We want you to drop the charges,'' Dan Buchanan said.

Sammons glared at him before turning back to Toby.

''No,'' Toby said.

''We aren't asking that the deed go unpunished. We'll work

something out. The boys can do community service. The parents will have their own ways of dealing with the kids at home—''

"We believe that together we can make sure these boys are given the proper guidance," Steck added. "We've decided to call a meeting of all the parents, and decide on a course of action. We were thinking we could arrange a community service schedule—''

"We're not dropping the charges," Toby said stonily.

"There's more at stake here than these boys—''

"I know what you're getting at, Claude, and we're not dropping the charges." Toby moved to stand up.

"If you press charges against these boys, I'll be forced to put them on academic suspension. They won't be allowed to participate in any extracurricular activities."

"Like I said, I know what you're getting at. But I happen to think there are more important things in a boy's life than football."

"There are damn few things more important in my boy's life than football right now, and I don't mind saying so," Dan Buchanan boomed. Coach Steck shot him a sharp look, and Mr. Sammons put out a hand to silence him, but Dan went on. "I'm putting it to you straight, Haskell. This is my boy's chance to win a scholarship to college. We've got men all over the state courting him. An old boy from Southern Methodist is supposed to be here in two weeks. Six games missed would blow his chances."

Corinne opened the door and stepped into the office. "Good afternoon," she said to the men gaping at her. "I was outside the door, and I couldn't help overhearing. I'd like to add my opinion, if you don't mind." She took a seat beside Toby. She didn't care if anyone minded.

Toby looked at her as if she had two heads.

"I think Mr. Haskell made an excellent decision," Corinne said. She smiled at Dan Buchanan. "It's important for the kids to know that this type of behavior is completely unacceptable on every level."

Dan Buchanan finally closed his mouth, then opened it again. "We can handle this just fine on our own."

"I'm sure you can. No one here wants to sell these kids short. And, if I might add, there were girls there, too. Not just football players.'' She smiled widely again, the same smile she'd given the CEO of the retail chain right after she'd proven on camera that he was buying sweatshop merchandise from third world countries and putting Made In America tags on them.

The men just stared.

Corinne took their silence as permission to continue. ''Everyone in this room is more concerned about the total welfare of the kids than they are about, say, a relatively trivial thing like football.''

''Miss Maxwell,'' Mr. Sammons said evenly. ''We appreciate your input. But perhaps you should let us handle this.''

''But, Mr. Sammons, we're all a part of this team,'' she echoed his words. ''The school, the law, the families, all working together. These boys are my students.'' She put an open hand to her chest and looked around the room, wide-eyed. ''This situation concerns all of us. Now, Mr. Buchanan, there are more ways to get into a good college besides football. I think the thing to do now would be to focus on Carl's grades.''

''Carl is no brain and everyone knows it.'' Dan's face grew redder with each passing moment. ''He's not a student, he's an athlete. He was put on this earth to play football. That is, if you don't bungle it up for him.''

''If he ends up dead in a drunk driving accident, or in prison because he killed someone else, he won't be playing anything,'' Toby said.

''Mr. Haskell is right, Mr. Buchanan. I realize that it will be a sacrifice to Carl and to your family if he doesn't get to play. But these boys need to know that there are consequences to their actions. And this is a much easier way to learn that lesson than if we wait until someone gets hurt.''

''Little lady, you need to butt out. I know you get a thrill out of stirring things up. And if I remember right, that little habit of yours got you into trouble before.''

Corinne could feel Toby bristling beside her. She put a hand out. ''No one is trying to stir up anything, Mr. Buchanan. We're simply having a civilized discussion.''

Dan stepped closer, his face flushed with anger. For half a second, Corinne's heart leapt in fear. Before she could stop, she found herself shrinking back.

"You'd better watch your mouth, little girl, or you're going to find yourself in trouble again. Butt out!"

Toby bolted to his feet. "Back off, Buchanan."

"You need to remember who you work for here, kid," Dan snarled.

"Is that supposed to be a threat?" Toby stopped two inches from Dan's nose.

"You're here to serve the town. It so happens that what would best serve the town right now is for you to drop those charges and let these boys play ball. We've got the homecoming game coming up in a few weeks. My boy is not going to miss that game!" Dan's voice boomed off the walls. Corinne realized with a cringe that all the students could hear him.

"He's welcome to come to the game," Toby said easily. "But he won't be playing."

"Toby, Dan, please sit down. We can work this out in a reasonable manner." Mr. Sammons stood and tried to calm them both.

"I've heard enough," Toby said, putting his hat on. "Meeting's adjourned."

Toby took Corinne's arm and led her out of the room. She followed silently, hustling to keep up.

His stride was stiff and angry. Neither of them spoke until they were in the parking lot. The afternoon sun was bright; Toby brought his Stetson down lower over his eyes, his jaw clenched in frustration.

"What the hell were you doing in there?" he growled when they got to her car.

She gaped at him. "I was supporting you. Didn't you hear?"

"And now everyone's going to hate you, too."

"So?"

"So, didn't you hear that idiot? That wasn't the wisest thing you could have done, sweetheart. I can handle this. I don't need you standing up for me."

"I wasn't standing up for you. I was standing up for the right decision." She shook her head. "Why are you mad at me? I'm one of the few people who agree with you on this."

"And I appreciate that. But you shouldn't have come in there. Now you're going to be the bad guy, too. All the students are going to hate you."

Corinne laughed lightly. "They already do, and I've barely completed a week of teaching. Don't worry about it. I don't mind being the dragon lady."

"Buchanan looked like he was ready to hit you."

Corinne shrugged it off. "He's not going to do anything to me. He can't. Quite worrying about it, okay? This will all blow over in a couple of weeks. On the other hand, say you hadn't arrested them. Say one of them went out and got themselves killed. Right now we'd be planning a funeral. That wouldn't blow over. Ever."

"I wish you hadn't come in there."

"I had to, Toby. We have to stick together on this." She reached up and put a hand to his cheek, then pulled it quickly away when she realized what she was doing. She took a step back. "You look exhausted. Did you get any sleep last night?"

His eyebrows pulled together in concentration. "Last night? Let me see. Between listening to whining kids and yelling fathers, answering phone calls from every gossip in town, and being threatened by the mayor, the banker and about fifteen farmers, I don't think I fit in any sleep."

Corinne's mouth curved in a halfhearted smile. "If it means anything, Toby, I'm really proud of you. You did the right thing last night. And the right thing just now."

Toby wasn't so sure. His dad wouldn't have handled it like this, that much he knew for sure. But for the first time, he was coming to accept the fact that no matter how hard he tried, he wasn't John Haskell. He smiled wanly and took her hand. He kissed her palm. He was the town villain all of a sudden, and he would take comfort from anywhere he could get it.

As Toby watched her drive away a few moments later, he realized that her approval did mean something to him. In fact, it meant everything. Finally, he'd done something to impress Corinne Maxwell. And it had only taken alienating the entire town to do it.

Hell, if he arrested them all, she might just kiss him without slapping him.

Chapter 6

"Dear God, you look incredible."

Corinne fought the instant surge of pleasure Toby's words brought. She should have known better than to agree to this. She smothered her smile and pursed her lips, feigning immunity to his charm.

She looked down at the green wool dress that draped across her shoulders and hugged her hips. "It's just a dress, Toby."

"I'm not talking about the dress. I'm talking about you." He sighed and put one hand over his heart, thumping it dramatically.

Corinne simply rolled her eyes and stepped back from the door to let him in. She turned away so he wouldn't see the slow heat of pleasure creep into her face. The man was dangerous.

And devastatingly handsome. He wore his uniform, and Corinne wondered weakly if that theory about women loving a man in uniform applied to her, too. She'd never noticed the affliction with any other man. But then, most men didn't fill out a button-down tan shirt and pants the way Toby did.

"I thought you were off duty tonight," she said. "Why are you wearing your uniform?"

"For a purely physical reason—because I know you can't resist it." With a flourish he whipped out a box he'd been holding behind his back. He held it in front of her.

It was a fat white homecoming mum, complete with about fifty yards of dangling ribbon, tiny cowbells and football ornaments. Their graduating year was in green numbers made from pipe cleaners, glued to the middle of the fake flower.

"You idiot." She laughed.

It had been one of their biggest arguments when they were seniors in high school. She'd let him know in no uncertain terms that she didn't like the tradition of the homecoming mum. She thought it was silly and ostentatious, and not at all attractive. Why any woman would want to wear a fake white flower pinned to her chest was beyond her, but it was a Texas tradition.

She couldn't believe it when, in their senior year, he showed up on her doorstep with the biggest one she'd ever seen. And then had the nerve to be angry when she refused to wear it.

"You have to wear it. It cost me a fortune."

"Toby Haskell, I'm not your prize. You are not going to show the rest of the town what a great guy you are because you bought me the biggest mum in town." She looked down at the green-and-white monstrosity in the plastic florist's box. *"Besides, it's huge. I'd feel like a float in a parade."*

"You have to wear it, Corinne." When Toby couldn't think of another point to argue his case, he simply held on to the one he had like a bulldog.

"I told you, Toby, these things are a status symbol. All the guys try to outdo each other and get the biggest, gaudiest-looking thing they can find, and the girls stick them on their chests so they can show the world their worth. It's archaic, and we don't want to be a part of that, do we?"

"I do."

It had been an intense fight, but Corinne remembered the reconciliation afterward, at their favorite parking spot, also being particularly intense. Intense and...hot. Like the room had become.

Corinne swallowed against a suddenly dry mouth and wondered if Toby was remembering the same thing. She looked up at him.

His gray eyes were charcoal dark. He remembered. She cleared her throat and pursed her lips.

"Don't even think that's going to work again." She arched her brows. "And I'm not wearing that."

"You have to. It cost me a fortune."

He grinned wickedly at her, and her heart did a slow flip. She stared at him for a moment, hating the way her heart always pounded when he looked at her like that, heaven and hell wrapped up in a sexy smile. Finally, she took the box from his hand and laid it on the table.

"What are you doing?"

"I'm putting it on."

He looked disappointed. "I liked it better when you put up a fight."

"You liked it better when we made up, after the fight," she said, struggling with the long pin the florist provided. "Help me with this, will you?"

He jumped at the chance. His fingers were long and strong as they pierced the pin through her dress and around the stem of the mum. She stared, fascinated despite herself, at the ridges of his knuckles, the blue vein that swooped over the back of his broad hand.

His warm breath fanned her cheek as she stared at the silver star on his chest. Surely it wasn't necessary for him to get this close. The spicy scent of his cologne teased lightly at the edge of her senses.

But the greatest assault of all was him, just him. The presence of his body inches from hers.

"Aren't you done yet?" she snapped.

He laughed. "No, not yet."

She stepped away. "That will have to do." She looked down at the mum, smoothed her dress, did anything she could to keep from looking at him.

"Well," she said, dusting her hands. "I'm ready if you are."

"I'll say. I've been looking forward to this all day. Our first official date."

"I've told you a dozen times, this is not a date. Aren't you nervous?"

"Nah. I never got nervous when I played the game. I see no reason to be now that I'm just a spectator."

"I'm not talking about the game. I'm talking about the mob of angry parents and suspended players who are threatening to string you up by your ears and hang you from the flagpole."

"Oh, that," he said as he led her out the front door. He held the screen as she locked the door, then shrugged. "Why should I be nervous? They're just blowing steam. It's just talk, Corinne. Nothing's going to happen."

"I hope you're right. The whole Buchanan clan is calling for your blood."

"I'm right. Besides, who'd mess with me tonight?" He puffed his chest out in exaggerated masculinity. "I'm the sheriff, and I've got the best-looking date in town. And, I might add, I bought her the biggest mum in three states."

"I'm not your date," Corinne said automatically as he opened the car door for her and she sat down inside.

He grinned at her as he shut the door, whistling tunelessly as he moved to his side of the Jeep.

"Seriously, Toby," she continued her one-sided debate as he got in. "I don't want you to think I'm inviting...anything between us tonight. I just think it's important for the school to show unity on this issue. This whole mess has been a controversy from day one, and I think that's a terrible message to be sending the students."

"Uh-huh," Toby said as he pulled the Jeep into the street.

"I think the students need to see all the authority figures united in concern over the main issue, and that's their safety and well-being. Attending the game with you is my way of showing that I agree with you, and support your decision not to be too lenient on those boys."

"Sure, yeah."

"I hate it that so many of the Buchanans—and the rest of the parents, too—are openly disagreeing with you about the arrests.

They're not doing their kids justice in the long run. Those kids need to learn now that there are consequences to their actions.''

"Yep."

"They need to learn now that their parents aren't always going to bail them out. Some of them might want to leave Aloma and get out into the real world. It won't matter then if they play football or who their daddy is. Did you know Dan Buchanan had the nerve to call me at home? He wanted me to talk to you because he thinks that you and I...that we...that we're..."

"Dating?"

"Yes. He wanted me to try to talk some sense into you, he said. He rambled on and on about 'boys will be boys.' And about how you're 'an elected official who needs to learn how to serve the concerns of the voters.'"

"He told you that?"

"Yes! Can you believe that?"

"Did he sound threatening? Did he make you nervous?"

"Of course not." Corinne denied the flicker of fear she'd felt during and after that conversation. She'd come to Aloma to get away from fear. She wasn't about to let some redneck father take her security away from her. She was never going to let that happen again.

She took a deep breath and smoothed the skirt of her dress as they pulled up to the football grounds. "So anyway, Toby, I just want to make it plain once again that tonight is strictly platonic. I know you've expressed a...a desire to move our friendship to another—"

"Corinne." Toby laid his arm on the seat back and leaned toward her. His fingers toyed idly with her hair, and his gaze captured hers. She found it impossible to look away.

"Y-yes?" She cleared her throat and fought the shiver that ran up her arm when his finger brushed lightly against her neck.

"You go to awfully great lengths to deny this is a date."

"This isn't a—"

He covered her mouth lightly with the backs of his fingers.

"I'm glad you're concerned about the kids," he said. He smiled and licked his lower lip.

"Of course I'm concerned about them. They're my students. And this *isn't*—"

He was already out of the car and moving around to open her door. She sighed and slumped in her seat, looking down at the gaudy flower pinned to her chest.

It was going to be a long night.

It was humiliating. It was brutal. And as painful as it must have been for the boys, Corinne decided it was even more excruciating to watch.

The Aloma Bulldogs—what was left of them—played with heart, played with determination and soul. And got stomped all over the field.

Through it all she and Toby stood on the sidelines, cheering the second string boys along. Corinne willed her boys to play better. She prayed for some luck. She crossed her fingers and wished for them to get the ball, to hang on to it. Finally she beseeched God for an end to the demolition.

Three times she felt pain in her hands and looked down to see her nails biting into her palms. She wanted to jump the fence and help the team.

Toby remained optimistic throughout the pounding. He yelled, he cheered, he clapped and even rattled a cowbell, showing his support. But Corinne knew he had to be aware of the animosity from the crowd. The anger was palpable in the air. Every few minutes someone would walk by muttering, just loudly enough for them to overhear, that this was all Haskell's fault.

"We'd win this game if Deputy Dawg over there would mind his own business."

Corinne looked over her shoulder at the small group of men. They stood with their arms crossed at their chests, glaring at Toby. She recognized most of them as Buchanans. She didn't know which of them spoke, but it didn't matter. They all looked capable. Dan and Carl Buchanan were conspicuously absent, though.

She looked back to see if Toby heard. He was grinning, but she caught the glint of steel in his eyes as he faced the belligerent crowd.

"Evenin', guys." He nodded and turned back to the game.

Corinne couldn't toss it off that easily. She looked repeatedly over her shoulder, waiting for the moment when the glares and barely audible remarks became more serious.

Toward the end of the game, Luke stepped beside Corinne and pretended interest in the mismatch on the field.

"How's it look?" Toby asked under his breath, still watching the field.

"Everything checks out so far. Dutch is at your mom's house, and I just left your place. Nothing yet."

"Told you. It was just talk. There won't be any trouble."

Corinne's nerves sang. "What are you two talking about? Toby, have you been threatened?"

Toby cut his gaze over to her, silently warning her to lower her voice.

"We heard rumors that Toby would pay if the Bulldogs don't win this game," Luke said quietly. "Somebody's been calling the station and describing what they're going to do to Toby and his mother and—" He cut off abruptly when Toby held his hand up.

"It's just talk." Toby scowled at Luke. "Rumors. Don't worry."

"Don't worry?" she said, her voice rising. "You're posting *guards,* for crying out loud!" She took a deep breath and cast a glance at the group behind them. "And I'm not supposed to worry," she said through clenched teeth.

"I've got it under control," Toby insisted.

She stared at him, realization dawning. "You're here to guard me," she said flatly. "That's why you asked me to come with you. They made threats against me, too, so you wanted to keep an eye on me."

He put his hand on her shoulder. "Listen, sweetheart, it isn't that big a deal—"

She swatted his hand away and stalked off.

It was anger she felt, she told herself. Not fear. Righteous anger that made her heart pound and her blood run alternately hot and cold.

Anger at a town that would be more concerned about a football game than their own children's health and safety. Angry at Toby for thinking he could control everything. As if she would just sit back and trust him to take care of her, to see to her safety. As if she'd ever let anyone do that again.

She'd come here to get away from fear, she reminded herself as she moved quickly through the crowd. She had been sickened by herself after the shooting, at how terrified she was of every little noise, every unexpected move around her. The panic attacks had shamed her. She hadn't had one in over a month, and she wasn't going to be like that again.

Footsteps sounded behind her. She whirled, saw it was Toby, and turned back toward home. He stepped in front of her.

"Move," she said, sidestepping him.

He matched her step. "Car's over there."

"I'm not riding with you."

"Oh, but you are," he said easily.

"I'm walking home."

"You're riding with me. I'm taking you home, and when I get there, I'm going to stay."

People slowed down to watch them argue. Corinne glared at him and clenched her teeth. "Like hell you are."

She edged her way past him and made it to the middle of the street before he caught up and stepped in front of her again. Corinne turned and began walking down the middle of the road.

Toby pivoted and blocked her way again. Faces inside the passing cars stared unabashedly at their strange behavior.

"You're making a big scene, Toby, and I don't appreciate it."

"You're the one being pigheaded." She could swear he was getting a kick out of this. "It's my duty to protect and to serve. Whether you want it or not."

"I'm warning you, Toby. You really don't want to be around me right now."

She stepped around him, directly into the path of a pickup.

Her gasp was drowned out by the screech of the pickup's tires and Toby's angry oath.

"Dammit, Corinne!"

Corinne was so stunned by her near miss that she didn't have the presence of mind to protest when Toby put an arm around her shoulder. But when he put the other arm behind her knees, she came to her senses.

"Toby," she shrieked as he scooped her into his arms.

He tightened his grip. "Be still."

"Put me down. Now!"

Toby ignored her. It was embarrassing, being lugged across the street. The people in passing cars really gawked now, pointing and laughing to boot.

Corinne pushed against his chest. It was no use—she couldn't get any leverage. It was ridiculous, especially considering the fact that she wasn't exactly a petite damsel in distress. Toby shifted her close to his chest and her legs flopped ungracefully.

"I'm going to kill you for this," she said calmly as he carried her to the Jeep.

He wasn't content to set her beside the passenger door. He dug his keys out of his pocket and unlocked the door without putting her down. When he got the door open, he dumped her inside, shoved the lock down, and slammed the door.

"I hope you're happy," she said when he got behind the wheel. "You have now created the biggest scene in the history of Aloma. We'll be the talk of the town."

Still he was silent.

"I'm probably going to get fired for this, I hope you know. In fifteen minutes, this is going to be blown all out of proportion. People will say you were arresting me for public intoxication or something. I'll be run out of town."

"Good. The same thing is going to happen to me after that game. Wanna go together?"

"You know where you can go," she said pointedly as he pulled the Jeep in front of her house.

Corinne bit her tongue, determined not to talk to him. For about three seconds.

"Why didn't you tell me?" she asked him. "Why didn't you tell me you thought I might be in danger?"

"You were never in any danger, Corinne. You know those guys. They're just a bunch of blowhards."

"And yet you wanted to keep an eye on me? If I'm not in danger, why did you pick me up and lug me across the parking lot? That was ridiculous."

Toby at least had the good grace to look sheepish. Corinne glared at him in the glow of the dashboard light and decided she didn't care how sheepish he looked.

"I didn't want anyone to say anything to you. I didn't want you to run into any of those guys. They watched you walk away from me. They knew you were alone." He killed the lights, throwing his face into darkness.

"I'm not afraid of them, Toby," she said vehemently, knowing she was lying.

"I just wanted you to have a nice evening. I didn't want you to worry."

"Toby, you can't go around trying to take care of the whole town. I have a right to know...." Her voice trailed off as she realized he wasn't listening to her. He was staring intently at the front of her house.

"Stay in the Jeep," he said shortly, slamming the door behind him. He trotted up the sidewalk.

She ignored him. She closed her door quietly behind her and pulled her shoes off before she tiptoed up the walk behind him.

One of the living room windows was broken. Corinne's eyes quickly scanned the front of the house, but she could see no other damage.

Toby leaned down and looked through the window. Corinne tiptoed closer behind him.

"Do you think—"

"Ahh!" Toby jumped at the sound of her voice, and Corinne started at his reaction.

"Dammit, Corinne!" He lowered his voice to an angry whisper. "What the hell are you doing? I told you to stay in the Jeep!"

"No!" she argued. Adrenaline pumped through her system, and her heart pounded. "Do you think anyone's in there?"

"I don't know. Wait in the car, and I'll check."

"No," she said again. "It's my house. I'm going inside."

Toby took a deep breath and his jaw tightened. Corinne could see him mentally struggling to maintain control. ''Go back to the car, lock the door, and I'll let you know when it's safe.''

Right. She was just going to sit passively in the car and wait, while who knew what was going on inside her house.

Not likely.

She didn't bother arguing with Toby. She turned on her heel and marched up the front steps.

Chapter 7

Toby's feet thudded loudly up the sidewalk behind her.

"At least give me the keys and let me go in first," he said, stepping in front of her. After a moment's hesitation, Corinne silently complied.

Toby unlocked the door and swung it inward quickly, scanning the room. From behind him, Corinne did the same. There was no one in the living room.

Toby motioned for her to stay quiet, and he moved silently into the hallway. Corinne stood rooted to the floor, staring at the rock lying amid the broken glass on the floor.

Until that moment, Corinne had been going on anger and adrenaline. The anger she felt at Toby for lying to her. The outrage at the townspeople for not supporting Toby. The complete disbelief that someone would lash out at her for supporting him. All these emotions served to keep her from acknowledging the panic building within her.

But as she stood there staring at the rock, hearing the blood pounding in her ears, Corinne knew the panic was about to get out of control.

The strength drained from her legs. She sat heavily on the couch, still staring at the rock. Inside herself, she warred with the fear. She was not going to lose control, she told herself. She wasn't going to give them control over her. She would not whimper. She would not shake. She would not cry. Never again.

She grabbed her wrist and started counting.

She didn't hear Toby walk back into the room until he spoke. "It's empty," he said.

He squatted and picked up the rock. "At least there's not a note," he said, a weak grin on his face.

Corinne's nostrils flared and her lips curled in derision. "Too cowardly to leave one, I'm sure. That's okay. We know who it is."

"I'll call Luke. We'll find out."

"Don't." Corinne's voice was deadly calm. Once again, the counting worked. She knew the difference between normal agitation and a panic attack—knew it well. She stared at the rock, feeling the panic slowly being replaced by control.

"Don't call Luke? Why not?"

Corinne shook her head and finally looked at him. "Don't call anyone. I don't want anyone to know about this."

Toby studied her for a moment, then moved to sit beside her on the couch. "Are you okay?"

Corinne rose and locked her knees to keep from pacing. She crossed her arms over her chest. "I'm fine, and I'm going to remain fine. But I'm serious, Toby. I don't want anyone to hear about this. Those jackasses are expecting me to run scared and make a big deal out of this. I'm not going to give them the satisfaction."

Hearing her own words reminded Corinne of Jeremy. There had been another incident with him just this afternoon. She'd walked into her classroom and caught him rummaging through the drawers in her desk. The funny thing was, she got the impression he intended for her to catch him.

She'd finally met Jeremy's mother a few days before in the hopes of learning some way to reach Jeremy. JoAnn Huckaby told Corinne that he refused to talk about his father and his crimes.

Corinne thought that maybe Jeremy wanted to run from the situation, and this was his way of doing it.

Once again, she'd elected to handle the situation without outside help.

Over the past few weeks, she'd come to agree with Toby and Becca that Jeremy really wasn't a danger to her or anyone else. But staring at the rock now in Toby's hands, she wondered if she was wrong.

As if reading her thoughts, Toby said, "We don't know for sure this is about the football players."

"Of course we do. What else would it be about?"

She didn't bother to answer her own question. The strain of trying to keep still became too much for her. She went into the kitchen to put water on the stove for tea.

Toby followed her. Robotically she removed mugs from the cabinet, and tea bags from the pantry. Toby watched her silently.

"I have to make a report, Corinne," he said finally. His voice was calm, but she knew he wanted to say more. She didn't care.

"So, make it. Just make sure no one else ever knows about it."

Toby closed his eyes and shook his head. "I'm sorry this happened."

"Don't be."

"I promise you, no one is going to hurt you."

"I know."

"They're just mad, trying to get at me."

"I know."

"Dammit, would you say something!"

Toby crossed the room in three short strides. He took her by the forearms and studied her face. "Are you okay? Say something."

"I'm fine, I told you. I'm not upset."

"That's what's got me worried. You should be mad or upset or—or something."

"Well, I'm not," she said firmly. "And I'm not going to be. That's what they want. I'm not playing their games."

The teakettle whistled and Corinne busied herself pouring the steaming water.

"I'll stay here tonight," Toby said, swirling his tea bag around the mug.

"No, you won't," Corinne said calmly.

"Don't worry, I'm not going to try anything. But I want to keep an eye on you. I'll stay on the couch."

"No, you won't."

"Corinne, I'm not going to leave you here alone after this."

Corinne's jaw tensed, but her eyes remained cold. "You aren't staying here. I can take care of myself."

He reached out and traced the silvery scar that ran down her chin. "No, you can't," he said softly. "I'm not letting anything happen to you again."

She jerked her head away and spoke through clenched teeth. "I will handle it. Myself."

"How the hell do you plan to do that? What if we're both wrong? What if it's not just talk and blowing steam? What if one of those idiots really wants to hurt you? What if they all go out and get drunk and decide to do more than talk?"

He stood and began to pace, rubbing the back of his neck. Watching his agitation, Corinne felt herself grow even more calm. It was as if an icy numbness was born in the pit of her stomach, and slowly radiated from there.

"Look, I don't want to scare you—"

"I'm not scared."

"—but I think we should think about this. When you walked away, some of those guys said some things. I don't think they were serious, but just to be on the safe side..."

"You have to go now."

"I'm not leaving."

"Yes, you are. Go fill out your report. If I need to sign anything, I'll do it tomorrow."

"This is stupid. We need to talk about this, decide how we're going to handle it."

"I told you, I'm going to handle it alone."

"You don't have to be some kind of hero here, Corinne. Don't tell me this doesn't affect you. Don't tell me it doesn't bring up bad memories."

"How can you even begin to compare a broken window to what happened to me? How can you even presume to know—"

"I know it's not the same thing, Corinne. But this is also violence, and it's directed at you. You have to talk about it, honey. You have to talk about what you're feeling."

"See, Toby, that's the thing. I *don't* have to talk about it. I don't have to, and I'm not going to."

"At least let me call your mother—"

"Don't you dare!" The vehemence in her voice surprised even her. "I said you are not to tell anyone. I will not be the talk of this town. I will not be known as a victim here. I will not!"

She clamped her mouth shut against a further outburst. Her breath came in small, staccato bursts. Toby watched her, his eyes full of a sadness that she couldn't stand to look at. She set her mug on the counter with a thud and went to the front door.

She held the door open in an obvious gesture.

Toby stared silently at her for a moment, hurt in his eyes. "It doesn't have to be this way, Corinne. I could help you."

"Go."

He opened his mouth to speak again, then shut it. He shook his head and sighed. He walked past her without a word, without looking at her, and left.

Toby shifted uncomfortably in his seat. Moments like this, he was more glad than ever he'd decided to stay in Aloma. Big-city cops had to do stakeouts all the time. What a pain.

He was parked half a block away from Corinne's house, barely out of sight. Dutch was watching the other side of the house at Toby's request. Corinne would be furious if she knew she was being watched, but he didn't care. He wasn't about to go off and let her deal with everything alone.

The thing was, he didn't really believe she was in any danger. What he was worried about most was the one thing he could do nothing about—the thoughts that must be going through Corinne's mind.

In the past year, he'd beaten himself up over the fact that he hadn't been there for her. He still felt a sense of responsibility for her, but he hadn't been able to stop what happened to her. Never mind that he was hundreds of miles away when she was shot. Never mind that it had been her choice to be in the situation she was in, not his. Never mind that there was probably nothing he could have done even if he *had* been there, instead of watching the drama unfold on television with the rest of the country.

The scene played itself out in his mind a million times in the past year. He knew the memories had to be worse for her. The thing was, he knew he could help her now, if she'd let him. And he knew that helping her would make him feel better, too.

He'd watched from the car as she cleaned up the broken glass and nailed a sheet up over the broken window in her mother's living room. The light in her bedroom went out half an hour later. He hoped she was getting some sleep. He figured, though, that more likely she was sitting in the dark, going over old terrors in her mind. He could be in there with her, talking it out, dealing with it together. Holding her. But instead, she had to be her usual stubborn self and tackle everything single-handedly.

He shifted in the seat, trying to stretch. The car was quickly becoming too small for his long body.

He kept his eyes trained on the house, remembering the old days. Remembering how he used to stay up nights thinking about Corinne Maxwell. Whispering her name to himself, going over every word she'd ever said to him, dreaming of things he would say to her, someday. His golden girl.

He'd been a fool back then. He craned his neck from side to side and wondered if he was really any smarter now. She'd stood there in that kitchen, pretending she wasn't shaking, pretending she had it all under control, and all he'd wanted to do was take her in his arms and make her forget all of it.

He was still a fool. And even a fool could see, things weren't going to turn out any different this time around.

Corinne screamed.

Toby was out of the car and running for the house before the faint sound stopped. Reaching the front porch, he swung open the screen and kicked in the door. He raised the pistol he had drawn.

Moonlight spilled in the living room through one window. No one was in that room.

Dutch bounded up the front porch behind him.

"Check the back," Toby told him. "Corinne!" he yelled.

She didn't answer.

Toby's heart thundered in his chest. He made his way carefully down the hall past her mother's bedroom, gripping the pistol in both hands, pointed at the ceiling.

"Corinne!" he yelled again. The door to her bedroom was slightly ajar.

Toby kicked it open. He leveled the pistol. He swept it around the room.

Corinne was crouched on the bed, her eyes glazed and wide with fright. She stared through him.

"Corinne! What is it? Is someone here?"

The room filled with the sound of her terrified gasps—huge, painful gulps of air, over and over. One hand clutched at her chest, the other groping for something she couldn't find. She pressed back against the bed and stared at him in terror.

His eyes swept the room quickly, checking the side of the bed, behind the chest. The room was empty.

"What's wrong, honey?" he asked, fighting to keep her from hearing the panic in his voice. "Tell me what happened."

As he talked, he crossed the room again and flung the closet door open, expecting someone to leap out at him. It was empty.

He looked back at the bed. Corinne still stared at the door, her eyes unfocused, every muscle in her body tense with fear, her chest heaving. Dear God, was she having a heart attack?

She didn't see him rush to the bed until he was beside her, his weight on the bed shifting her.

"Corinne," he said softly, placing a hand on her arm.

She gasped and started, jerking away and really seeing him for the first time. "No!"

"Corinne, sweetheart, are you okay? What happened? Is someone here?"

She stared at him, her brow wrinkled, and she edged away more, still gasping. "Toby?" Her voice was hoarse from sleep, or from screaming. She wiped a hand across her face, then rubbed her eyes. "Toby, what's wrong? What are you doing here?"

"You tell me. I heard you scream. What happened? Are you okay? I'm going to call an ambulance."

"No!" She rolled from the bed and cradled her head in her hands. Her breathing was still hard, but it was starting to ease a little. She looked around the room, then back at him. "I had a nightmare."

Toby heard a noise in the hall. He rose and raised his pistol. It was Dutch.

"No one out back," Dutch said as he entered the room. He looked at Corinne on the bed and tactfully turned away.

"Dutch? What are you doing here?" Corinne asked, pulling the sheet up to her neck.

"I think it was just a nightmare," Toby told Dutch quietly, motioning with his head for Dutch to leave. He led the young deputy into the hall and pulled the bedroom door softly shut behind him. "Go ahead and check out the rest of the house," he whispered. "If everything looks okay, just go on home."

Dutch nodded and began checking the other rooms.

"Toby?" Corinne's voice was stronger now. Toby took a deep breath and braced himself.

When he walked back into the room, she stood, pulling on her bathrobe. To his immense relief, she no longer gasped for air.

"What happened? What are you doing here?"

"We heard you scream. Sweetheart, are you okay?"

"You heard me scream? At the courthouse?" Her brows drew low over her eyes and she raked a hand through her hair. She looked so small and confused. Toby wanted nothing more than to take her into his arms and hold her.

He hesitated, measuring her state. Her hands fumbled clumsily with the belt of her robe, her hair tumbled in her face. She was fighting a losing battle with her composure.

"Not at the station. In my car. Down the street."

Corinne's hands froze. She stared at him silently for a moment, her mouth slightly open in disbelief. Toby decided the best defense was a good offense.

He sat on the bed, making sure his voice was calm and controlled. "I know you wanted to handle this situation, and I respect your desire to be alone. But protecting the citizens of this county is my job, and you are one of those citizens. I had reason to believe you might be harassed—"

His voice cut off as Corinne reached out, shoved him hard in the chest—hard enough to rock him backward—and stomped out of the room.

Toby lay on his back for a moment, staring at the ceiling. It could have gone worse, he supposed.

Corinne slammed two coffee mugs onto the counter, then stopped. She put one back into the cabinet.

She stuck the teakettle under the faucet and wrenched the hot water tap on. After a moment she heard Toby's boots on the wooden floor of the dining room. She didn't turn around.

She dropped the kettle onto the stove burner with a wet clang and flicked the burner switch to high. She could feel Toby behind her. The tension in the room was thick enough to smell. It gave her something to concentrate on besides the fear still clinging to her insides. The humiliation of being rescued from her own mind.

Corinne's cheeks burned with anger and indignity. It was bad enough when she woke herself with her screaming, bad enough to hear her own tortured breathing. No one else had a right or a reason to hear.

But now someone else had heard. Now someone else knew the scenes that haunted her sleep and reduced her to a senseless, pathetic quivering heap. Damn him!

Silently she spooned hot chocolate mix into her mug. Toby shifted behind her, the rustle of his clothes loud in the silent room.

Even Dutch had heard. She wanted to ask how far away they'd been parked, but she didn't want to talk to Toby. What she wanted to do was kick him out, but she knew he wouldn't leave without a fight. He considered himself to be the brave knight, ready to slay dragons for her. She was just too drained to make him see she didn't need him to comfort and take care of her.

The thought flitted across her mind that it felt good to have someone else there. That when she did awake, she was not alone.

She banished the thought along with the memories of the nightmare.

The teakettle shrieked through the heavy silence, and Corinne poured steaming water into her mug. Toby silently removed a mug from the cabinet. Her back to him, she edged over to the bar between the kitchen and dining room and stirred her chocolate. She heard him remove a spoon from the drawer and prepare his own mug. He stirred the spoon inside the mug, making more noise than was necessary, she thought rather irritably.

He could do whatever he wanted. She didn't have the energy to argue with him.

"Got any marshmallows?"

Corinne ignored him.

"'Cause this would be great with marshmallows."

She tightened the belt of her robe and blew on her chocolate.

"Or maybe some tuna. Got any tuna?"

She looked up at him, startled. He grinned. "I knew you weren't ignoring me."

"Yes, I am." She turned away.

"No, you're not."

One brow cocked, Corinne silently turned back to the bar.

"Sweetheart, what was that in there?"

"I told you. It was a nightmare. Haven't you ever had a nightmare?"

"Not one like that."

"No? And what's your worst nightmare, Toby?" Her voice dripped with sarcasm. "What horrible mistakes have you made that keep you up at night?" Corinne closed her eyes and ran a hand through her hair, scratched the back of her neck. "Look, I'm sorry. Just...I need to be alone. Just finish your drink and go."

"Is that what you think is going to happen? Because that's not how it's going to go."

"Oh, really?" She faced him again with one hand on her hip.

"Really." He took one step toward her. She backed up, the edge of the bar pressing into the small of her back.

"I'll tell you how it's going to go." Toby's voice was low and controlled, his eyes intent, never wavering from hers. "First, you're going to put the mug down. Then I'm going to put my arms around you.''

He took another step toward her. Corinne's mouth went dry.

"You're going to fight me at first, because that's how you are. You have to feel in control at all times. But pretty soon you'll relax and realize how right I am.''

"In your dreams.'' Corinne's voice was thin and shaky to her own ears. She edged down the bar.

"Yes,'' Toby agreed. "In my dreams.'' He took another step closer, so near now she could touch his chest, if she reached her hand up a little. Instead, she remained frozen, trapped by Toby's eyes like a butterfly pinned to a board.

"You're going to relax and let me take care of you. Because you'll realize that it feels good to be held. That it makes you feel better to be comforted. That you don't have to be alone, you don't have to go through everything by yourself. That you can talk to me, and you can tell me how you feel, and it doesn't make you weaker. It makes you stronger.''

He reached out, his long fingers wrapping around her mug. Her grip tightened. He set his own mug on the counter and began prying her fingers loose one at a time. His gentle coaxing continued, low, slow and hypnotic.

"You're going to realize that you feel better not pushing me away. That I can help you. You're going to realize that this is what you need—to face your demons with someone who cares about you. You're going to realize that even though I can't go back and change what happened, I can make you feel better now. I can keep what happened a year ago from haunting you now. I can keep it from haunting you from now on.''

He was wrong. When he got the mug out of her hand, he wrapped his arms around her. But she didn't fight it. She stood stiffly against him, her body unaccustomed to the feel of another so close. He was warm, and she felt as if she'd been frozen in a block of ice for a year. He was strong, and she felt too weak to raise a hand. He was solid, and she felt she would dissolve into vapor and float away.

The bad thing about Toby was, he knew about basic human

instinct. He knew the power of a touch. He knew that when she felt the security wrap around her, she would be unable to pull away.

His arms tightened on her shoulders, and she felt herself slowly relax despite herself. His chin rested lightly on her shoulder, and he cupped the back of her head, pulling it to rest against his own shoulder.

His breath lightly fanned against her ear, and she lay her cheek against his shoulder, letting go. She ignored the voice that said this was wrong, this was dangerous. It was just a hug. A hug couldn't hurt anyone. Not a hug that felt this good.

"See," he whispered in her ear. "It's okay. It's going to be okay. I'm not going to let anything happen to you. Right here, right now, you're safe."

Until he said the words, Corinne didn't realize how much on her guard she'd been. For the first time in a year, she felt truly safe. She took a deep breath, feeling the tension go out of her arms. Relaxation spread down her torso and into her legs, a warm, liquid sensation. Her mind searched idly for a moment in the past year when she'd been relaxed. There was none.

His hand stroked the back of her head, smoothing and soothing. He lifted her hair and cupped the back of her neck, his skin warm against hers. Corinne sighed and leaned closer into him.

"See," he said again. "I told you."

She knew he was trying to get a reaction from her. She didn't care. She smiled against his shoulder.

"You're a know-it-all," she said.

"You're just now figuring that out?"

She laughed lightly and pulled away. She put a hand to his chest and pushed him gently away from her. "Okay, Sheriff, you win. You were right. That felt nice. I feel better now. Are you happy?"

He cupped her chin. "I am, as a matter of fact. But I'm not done yet. I said you were going to talk to me. I'm not leaving until you spill your guts."

He was out of luck, she thought as she raised her mug for another sip of her chocolate. There was a limit to her weakness.

"If you don't mind, I'm not much in the mood for gut spilling tonight. Perhaps some other time."

"Nope." He lifted his mug in one hand, took her hand in the other, and led her into the living room.

"Toby, really, I appreciate what you're trying to do. And as angry as I am that you openly defied my wishes and stayed when I asked you to leave, I'm glad you were here. You were right. I feel much better."

"Good," he said. He sat on the couch and pulled her down beside him. "But not good enough. Spill it."

"I'm not going to spill anything." She didn't want to argue with him, didn't want to break the soft bubble of good feeling she was carrying around her after their embrace. But she wasn't going to give him what he wanted. "Seriously, Toby, I'm fine now. You can consider me both protected and served, okay?"

"Nope. You need to talk."

"That's where you're wrong. I don't have to, and I'm not going to. It wasn't that big a deal, Toby. It's not as if I went to war or anything. I got shot. I just happened to be on national television when it happened to me."

"And you just happen to be the only woman I ever—" His voice broke off suddenly, and she turned to study his face.

He wore a strange expression, one she couldn't quite name. Then suddenly it was gone. The old Toby was back, looking a little too sure of himself, as usual. "I know you don't want to hear this. But you really ought to see a doctor about those nightmares."

Corinne fingered the edge of her robe. She wasn't going to tell him anything, really. But then, the words just came out. "I've already seen a doctor."

"And?"

"And...you know what an anxiety attack is?"

"I think so."

"It's when your body thinks you're in danger, even when you aren't, and reacts accordingly. Dumps all this adrenaline into your system—enough to outrun a charging bull, it feels like—except there's really nothing threatening you."

Toby shook his head and ran one large hand through her hair. "It looked scary as hell, sweetheart. How often does this happen?"

"I think I'm about over it, really. I hardly ever have them anymore."

"Anymore?"

Corinne sighed. She should have known he'd keep digging. But then, he'd already seen the worst, so there was no point in trying to keep secrets. "I had them more frequently, right after... Well, more after the divorce, really, than after the shooting. Aunt Muriel made me see this shrink a few times. He said it was all hitting me too hard—the shooting, ending my career, ending my marriage. That I felt attacked and unsafe. But you know shrinks. Maybe he knew what he was talking about, maybe not. Really, Toby, it was just a temporary thing. And tonight...you know, with the rock through the window, and the new job and all." She hugged her elbows and rubbed her hands briskly over her arms. "Anyway, tonight was an aberration. If you hadn't come charging in here, no one would even have known. I might have just gone back to sleep and not even known myself."

"Are they dangerous, these attacks? I mean, it looked like you were having a heart attack or something."

Corinne edged away. "No, they're not dangerous. I'm fine."

"Well, do you think the doctor was right? Did it bother you that much, leaving your job and...and your husband?"

Corinne shrugged. "Who knows. What difference does it make?"

"It makes a lot of difference, if it makes you feel like that."

"I'm fine, I told you!" Corinne turned her cup in her hand and watched the tan-and-brown liquid swirl together. "And it doesn't matter, because what's done is done. If I made a mistake, it's my own fault." She thought about making him leave, but she wasn't ready to be alone again. Not just yet.

Toby studied her for a moment. "Talk to me, Corinne. Tell me about that time in your life."

"This isn't necessary, Toby."

"Yes, it is. If you don't talk, it's just going to build inside you until you go crazy."

Corinne rolled her eyes. "Thank you, Dr. Haskell," she said dryly. "You guys watch too many talk shows at the station."

"We try to be enlightened. You're the one being stubborn. What else did the good doctor say?"

Corinne shrugged. "I just saw him a couple of times. He told me I wasn't going to die like I thought I was, and he told me how to ride out the panic attacks. Since then, I haven't really needed to see anyone."

"After an ordeal like you went through, I'd think you'd want to have extensive therapy."

"I didn't *need* extensive therapy. And I wish you wouldn't call it an ordeal. The whole thing only took nine minutes, from the moment he grabbed me to the moment he shot me."

"It was the longest nine minutes of my life, I can tell you that."

"Your life?" Corinne cut her gaze to the side and scoffed. "You should try being the one with the gun at your head, instead of just watching it."

His face was serious. "I would give anything if it could have been that way. I would've traded places with you in a heartbeat."

Corinne swallowed at the sudden fierceness in his voice. Her nose and eyes were burning with tears she wasn't about to give in to. This was why she didn't want to talk about that day.

"Okay, Toby, so we've talked. I feel better. As a matter of fact, I believe I'm healed. No more nightmares for me ever again. And no more panic attacks. You were right. You've been a big help. Now let's talk about something else."

Toby shook his head and put a hand on her knee. "You're not getting off that easy. You haven't said anything about Sulley, or the trial, or the riot."

"Oh yes, the riot. A perfect example of what I don't want to talk about."

"That must have been scary, even before the guy with the gun showed up."

Corinne ignored him.

"You shouldn't have been there. I thought that bozo you were married to had something to say about what assignments you were given. He shouldn't have let you go.''

Corinne pulled her feet onto the couch and hugged her knees. She couldn't do it. She couldn't make her mind go somewhere else, make herself think about something—anything—else. The more Toby pushed, the more scenes of that day popped into her mind.

''I insisted,'' she said against the skin of her knee. ''Sulley was my story from the first. I wasn't going to let someone else finish my job for me.''

Despite her resolve not to, Corinne found it easy to talk about Sulley. The words came in a soft, steady stream out of her mouth, out of her heart. She didn't raise her head. Somehow it made it easier, talking about Sulley with her head resting on her knees.

Joshua Moon Sulley. The unofficial leader of the African-American community in Dallas. Sulley could always be found on one picket line or another, or at a town meeting, ferreting out racial discrimination of any form. He was the most recognized figure in the city, but definitely not the most well-liked. You never saw Sulley without a picket sign in his hand and an impassioned speech on his lips. He was revered by half the city, reviled by the other half.

The first time Corinne interviewed Sulley, she found him to be an obnoxious grandstander, more interested in spouting his personal grievances than he was in helping anyone. But as she came to know him, she came to admire him for his passion, to respect him for the generous heart he never showed the cameras, and to be amazed at the progress he made when others failed. After a while she counted herself not only as one of Sulley's supporters, but one of his friends as well.

When Sulley's business partner and lifelong friend was murdered, along with Sulley's wife, the first fingers of suspicion pointed at Sulley. They didn't waver until his conviction.

She had covered every aspect of the investigation, every moment of the sensational trial. And with every bit of evidence that mounted against Sulley, Corinne felt her soul wither inside.

She shook her head and forced her mind back to the present.

"This is serving absolutely no purpose, Toby," she told him, her cheek still resting on her knee. Though they weren't touching, she could feel his body close to her own, could feel the heat and strength of him beside her. "Talking isn't going to change anything."

He didn't answer. She jumped a little when she felt his knuckle brush against her neck, rubbing the skin from her shoulder up to her ear.

"A lot of it was probably my fault anyway." Her own voice surprised her. She hadn't meant to say it aloud.

"Your fault? With Sulley?"

Corinne sighed and raised her head. "No, with the riot."

"Oh, yeah," Toby scoffed. "You are single-handedly responsible for race relations in a city of a million people."

"I'm serious. I wanted Sulley to be innocent so badly. I was ready to believe the defense's theory that he'd been framed. I was more than ready. I was anxious for it. I hoped—I actually *hoped*—that he'd been framed. I wanted to see corruption in city officials, corruption in the entire Dallas Police Department, before I wanted him to be guilty."

"You can't feel bad about that, sweetheart. It was a terrible situation all around. There was no way it was going to have a good ending. Either way, someone did a terrible thing. He was your friend. Of course you wanted to support him."

"I should have been a journalist first, not his friend. I should have reported the facts in an objective manner." The words spilled out, though she hadn't before allowed these thoughts to fully form in her mind. All her fears and doubts and regrets about Sulley—about herself—came to the front of her mind, and she knew she'd never be able to get them to recede again.

"My reports were biased. I know they were. I gave those people hope that he'd be acquitted."

"I watched your reports, Corinne. They weren't biased. You presented the facts."

Corinne shook her head. "It was in my heart that he was innocent. Whether it was in my words or not, my beliefs would have come through. I gave them the belief that there was no other possible conclusion, that he was falsely accused. No wonder they rioted when he was convicted. They had the rug pulled out from under them."

"You can't possibly think it was your fault, Corinne. You were one reporter. One. How many other press and television people were there? You weren't the only source of information those people had."

"That's not the point, Toby. My reports reached hundreds of thousands of people, many of whom rioted that day."

She leaned back and rested against the back of the couch, feeling drained. She didn't fight when Toby put his arm around her shoulder and rubbed her arm.

"Corinne, it's not your fault. The guy was guilty."

"I know," she said miserably. "I know he was."

"Those people were rioting because they were as upset as you, and wanted to lash out."

"They were rioting because they believed their leader had been framed for murder and convicted of a crime he didn't commit. And I helped them believe that."

"I can't believe you're blaming yourself for any of it. You didn't do anything wrong."

"I got too close to the situation. I let myself get personally involved."

"If you didn't, you'd be some kind of unfeeling monster."

"No, Toby. I'd be a journalist."

Toby sighed and hugged her closer. "If you ask me, the whole profession is screwed up if that's the way you're supposed to be."

Corinne smiled wanly and bit her lip. "You'd never cut it, Toby. You'd want to single-handedly solve every problem you covered."

"You're right. And I'm not the only one, am I?" He placed his index finger under her chin and lifted it, turning her to face him.

"I guess not," she said quietly.

"Corinne, caring about what happens to people doesn't make you a failure."

"I know that. It's just that, when you're a professional, you separate your personal feelings from the job in front of you."

"Right," Toby said, rolling his eyes.

"It's true. A professional—" Corinne stopped and sighed. "Never mind. I know you can't understand. I wouldn't have understood if I hadn't been in that business."

She hung her head and chewed on her lip.

"Look." He sighed and took her hand, toying idly with her long fingers. "You put your heart and soul into that job, and that's not wrong. You got burned, but that was someone else's fault."

A tear coursed down Corinne's cheek. She breathed shallowly. She didn't want him to know she was crying again.

"You probably didn't know this, but I watched every newscast you ever did."

"You did?" She turned to face him, then turned away quickly and wiped her cheek.

"I did. We get the station on cable, down at the courthouse. I watched throughout the whole business with Sulley, too. And if it counts for anything, I never thought you were biased."

"You don't have to tell me that, Toby. You don't have to make me feel better."

"I'm not saying it to make you feel better. As a matter of fact, if you want to know the truth, I thought you were one cold-blooded woman."

Corinne laughed in surprise and sniffled.

"I'm serious. If I hadn't known you better, I wouldn't have believed you cared about anything—"

"Toby, stop," Corinne laughed. With the heel of her hand, she wiped more tears from her eyes.

He hugged her to him. "I'll bet you could jump right back in there and take up where you left off," he said, his voice tight.

"I don't want to go back."

"Good. I don't want you to, either."

He continued to hold her close, and she let him. Damn him, but he was right. She did feel better. She hadn't voiced her deepest fears about the riot to anyone. Truthfully, she would never know if she was responsible in any way. But in the back of her mind, there had always been that thought, that possibility...

"How did you know it was nine minutes?" Toby asked suddenly.

"What?"

Toby pulled back and studied her face. "You said it was nine minutes, from the moment the guy ran up to you with the gun, till the moment he shot you. How did you know it was nine minutes? You weren't timing it then."

Corinne looked away, and she could feel the closeness they'd just shared slipping away. She didn't know if she was ready to talk to him about the rest. But the words came out anyway. "I watched the tape."

"That was a dumb idea."

"Thanks, Sheriff."

"I mean it. Whose idea was it to let you watch that tape? It was that idiot you married, wasn't it?"

"It wasn't his idea." Her short laugh had a bitter edge. "In fact, he was quite angry when he found out I'd seen it."

"Finally, the guy's showing some common sense."

"Scot, the photographer, brought it to the hospital."

"What were you supposed to do, sit down with the family and watch it over dinner?"

"Don't be mad at Scot. He was doing it for my own good."

"Oh, yeah, a lot of good that's going to do you. Watching yourself get held at gunpoint for almost ten minutes, then shot in the jaw."

"He had a reason. There was something else on the tape he wanted me to...to know about."

Toby would be furious. She knew he would. And a part of her wanted him to be furious. For her. "There's a little more to that day than you know."

Chapter 8

Corinne shifted away from Toby on the couch and took a deep breath. She hadn't told anyone what she was about to tell Toby. Not her aunt, and certainly not her mother.

"What?" Toby's voice was strained, and she realized she still clung to his hand, her fingers twisting in his grip. She thought in a detached way that it must hurt him, but she didn't let go.

"What is it I don't know?" he asked.

She cleared her throat. "Scot brought the video to the hospital. I could tell he wanted to say something, and at first I thought it was just that he felt bad about the shooting."

"You mean the fact that he just stood there and taped the whole thing instead of helping you?"

"He tried to help me. That was him you saw, trying to talk the guy into giving up the gun. He'd put the camera down and someone else picked it up, I don't know who. Anyway, before that, when he still had the camera..."

"What, Corinne?"

"He brought the tape to the hospital so I could watch it. See, there are two channels of audio on a tape. One channel goes out over the air, everything you hear on your television. Then there's the headset audio. That's what the cameraman hears through his headphones. It's the director back at the station, giving him direction.''

''The director? That would be—?''

''That would be Don, my husband.''

''Your ex-husband.''

''Yes.'' She cleared her throat, wondering if she could really do this. ''His voice was on the tape. Scot made me a copy, without anyone knowing. He turned up the headset audio so I could hear what was being said while I...while I was being held hostage.''

Corinne pulled her hand free from his and clasped her hands together in her lap. Toby's hand roamed over her back, warm, soothing, but she wasn't soothed. A year later, she couldn't get rid of the sick feeling in her stomach when she thought about that tape.

''I'll show you.'' She got up and walked robotically to the cabinet where she kept the video. She knew it was gruesome and probably unhealthy of her to keep it, but she'd tried before and couldn't throw it away. A part of her needed to remember.

Her breath caught in her throat, she turned on the television and stuck the tape in the recorder. She pushed Play and sat down beside Toby.

People were running and yelling all around her, throwing bottles, breaking store windows.

Don's voice came on, giving Scot direction, making comments about angles and light.

Toby's hand gripped her knee tightly, but he didn't say anything. Corinne listened, still morbidly fascinated despite herself. The voice she'd once thrilled at the sound of, when she was an idealistic young journalist, carried across the breaking glass and shouting people.

The gunman moved in behind her. Corinne reported the damage being done around the block, unaware of the frustrated maniac nearby.

How pompous she was, she thought as she watched the screen. Acting as if the mayhem around her wasn't affecting her. As if she weren't heartsick over the rioting around her. The picture of the calm, objective reporter. Well, she was about to be taken down a notch or two.

The gunman didn't do anything at first. He stood behind her and stared at the camera, his fists clenched in rage. He darted glances to the chaos going on about them, but his attention fixed mostly on the camera.

Don was the first to notice the gun. His voice came over the audio. "My God, he's got a piece! Scot, close in on that guy behind her."

Corinne didn't know why Scot panned away. She kept her monologue going, cataloging numbly the events happening around her. The moment she realized there was something going on directly behind her, she turned.

He grabbed her roughly, wrapping one arm around her neck. He stuck the gun hard against her throat, screaming in her ear.

Beside Toby on the couch, Corinne felt herself starting to shake. She clamped down on it, but tremors emanated from within her, beyond her control. Toby wrapped his arm around her. He stared at the screen as intently as she did.

The gunman yelled in her ear. The gun dug into the flesh of her neck. He pinned her tightly against his body from the back. At first she was too frightened and stunned to fight back. In a flash of horrified realization, she saw clearly what was happening to her, and she fought to extricate herself. He slammed the heel of the gun against her cheekbone.

"My God, did you see that?" It was Don's voice again. "Scot, is she bleeding? Close in on her face, see if she's bleeding."

The camera panned closer, blurry at first and then focusing on her face. A thin trickle of blood inched down the side of her jaw and onto her neck where the blow from the gun had broken skin.

"Pan back and get the guy's face." Don's voice was broken, but from excitement rather than distress. He shouted something she didn't understand to someone in the control room. "Turn up her audio and get what the guy's saying. Who is this guy, does anybody know?" His voice grew louder.

The gunman jerked her tightly against him, and Corinne's eyes grew wider with panic. She strained to see behind her. She implored Scot with her eyes to save her.

From the safety of her living room, Corinne thought it looked as if she were imploring the national viewing audience for help. She admitted bitterly to herself, it was powerful stuff.

And Don, being the veteran newsman he was, wasn't about to miss this golden opportunity.

The gunman began dragging her backward. In the recesses of her mind, Corinne remembered a self-defense expert recommended going limp in a situation like this. The dead weight would be harder to hold on to. But try as she might, she couldn't force the tension from her body. She scraped her heels on the sidewalk, fighting being dragged back with the man.

He put his back to a wall, and held her in front of him. The camera followed. On the audio, Don's voice yelled, "Catch that look in her eyes, Scot! Close up on Corinne's eyes. Look, her mouth is trembling, pan down to her mouth. Now, back away, slow, get the gun, get him. Great, great, you're doing great. Where the hell are the police?"

Funny, Corinne had been wondering the same thing at that time. A block away, pandemonium ensued, the rioting crowd unaware of her particular drama. Corinne was alone, helpless, without hope.

She pleaded for the man to let her go. Pleaded with him to talk to her, to let her help him work out his frustrations in a better way.

On the couch, she was nauseated to hear herself sounding weak and pathetic.

The gunman knocked her in the head again, and the world went gray for a minute.

She could hear sirens. None headed her direction. There was a mob of people, fifty yards away, but none of them helped her.

Finally, the screen went gray, showing only concrete. Scot set the camera down.

She heard his voice, shaky with fright. "Come on, man, give me the gun. It's okay, we'll work it out. We can talk about it. Just give me the gun, and I'll let you say what you want to say. I'll make sure it gets played on the air. This isn't the way to solve anything. Give me the gun.''

The man screamed in Corinne's ear, and someone else picked up the camera and resumed filming.

"Let him go," the gunman yelled. "Let Sulley go! Talking don't do any good. This is the only thing anybody understands." He jerked Corinne harder against him and brought the gun up to her jaw. He was crying.

"This is the only thing that gets noticed. This is the only thing that works. Not words. Sulley knew it, too. Talking doesn't change a thing. Action does. Let him go! Let him go or the woman gets it." His voice became more panicked, and the terror inside Corinne grew.

She heard shouts, and booted feet running down the sidewalk to her right. Scot looked in that direction, and Corinne knew from the relief on his face that it was the police.

Immediately on the heels of her relief, however, came more terror. The gunman grew hysterical at the sight of the policeman. He began sidling along the wall, dragging her with him. Three policemen ran into the street and drew their guns. Now she had not one, but four guns pointed at her.

"Back off, or I'm gonna blow the girl's brains out! Get Sulley out here. I want to talk to Sulley. Back off!"

Something inside Corinne snapped. Suddenly, even death was preferable to this torment. She slammed an elbow against the gunman's rib, intending to duck out of his embrace.

The gun went off.

In the mayhem that followed, Don's voice could still be heard.

"Oh, my God! He shot her. She's down. Pan down! Pan down! She's on the ground." The camera didn't follow his directions. Two more pops sounded, and the gunman fell.

In one corner of the screen, Scot was trying to push past the police and get to her. "Who the hell's on the camera?" Don screamed. "Where's Mike? Is he out there? Mike, step back and get the whole scene."

The camera remained on her, lying on the sidewalk.

"Who's got the damned camera?" Don demanded. *"That thing's worth a quarter of a million dollars!"*

Corinne's trembling hand reached up, trying to feel her bloody face. A policeman knelt over her, screaming directions. For a moment, the camera panned up and caught the gunman, lying on the ground where he had fallen, shot by the police. Then it came back to her.

"Corinne." Through a fog, Toby's voice drifted into her consciousness. It hovered there for a moment before she acknowledged it.

His hand gripped her shoulder so tightly that it hurt. He was trembling, too. With anger.

She lay against him, drained. It was selfish, she knew, to make him share this with her. But she'd never known how much better it would feel, having someone else to help her carry this.

Toby made a sound, low in his throat. She raised her head and looked at him. His face was a stone mask, his mouth a grim line. But his eyes—his eyes were wild, dark gray embers that sparked with fury.

"Toby?" she asked, uneasy.

"I could kill him."

"Don't bother. He's dead. The police killed him."

"Not the guy with the gun. That jackass. Don. He has to die."

Corinne didn't bother arguing. After watching the tape, she knew she couldn't live with him anymore. Once, she'd practically worshipped Don, idolized his drive, his charisma, the newshound in his blood. He had a great deal of respect in their industry—something she'd so desperately needed for herself. She'd thought that she loved him, but a few months after the divorce, she'd finally admitted to herself that she'd married him for all the wrong reasons. Like the little girl who'd tried so desperately to earn her mother's love and approval, she'd fallen into the same trap with the man who was her husband.

Toby stood and paced the room. Corinne knew he was trying to remain calm for her sake, but frustrated energy poured off him.

"It's funny," she said, shaking her head. She rose and pulled the tape out of the player.

"Yeah, hilarious." His boots clomped across the floor. He pulled the drapes back and looked out, then checked to make sure the sheet was fastened over the window tightly.

"I mean, it's funny that I always strove for emotional detachment in reporting, and I didn't get it. And now, it's easy for me. I'm emotionally detached from everything." Corinne leaned back against the couch, feeling emptied. "I don't feel anything. Every bit of caring and hope and idealism I had in me...well, it died, the moment I saw the tape."

Toby stopped pacing and stood before her.

"Really?" His voice was husky.

"Really. I don't feel anything anymore. I don't care about anything. I'm dead inside." She didn't intend for it to be, but as soon as she spoke the words, she knew they were a warning to Toby—a way of letting him know she would never be able to give him what he wanted.

Toby remained standing for a moment, then sat beside her again and placed a hand on her knee.

"I mean," she continued, comforted by his warm touch, "I don't even know what to believe in anymore. I don't know who are the good guys and who are the bad ones. They all look the same from where I'm standing. I don't know what's real anymore."

Toby leaned back and drew her with him, and Corinne rested in the crook of his shoulder. It was so nice to have someone to talk to, someone who understood, someone who sympathized. She could feel his heart thudding beneath her ear, but his anger seemed to be banked some.

He squeezed her shoulder and kissed the top of her head. "You," he said in a soft, husky voice. "You are such a liar."

"What?" Corinne drew back sharply and placed one hand in the middle of his chest, staring at him.

"You're a liar."

"Is that so?" She put a few inches of space between them on the couch and clenched her jaw.

"You don't care, huh? Bull. I saw you out there tonight, lady. I saw how intent you were on that game. Every muscle in your

HOW TO PLAY

"PINBALL WIZ"

and be eligible to receive

THREE FREE GIFTS!

1. With a coin, carefully scratch the silver circles on the opposite page. Then, including the numbers on the front of this card, count up your total pinball score and check the claim chart to see what we have for you. **2 FREE** books and a **FREE** gift!

2. Send back this card and you'll receive brand-new Silhouette Intimate Moments® novels. These books have a cover price of $4.25 each in the U.S. and $4.75 each in Canada, but they are yours to keep absolutely **FREE**!

3. There's no catch. You're under no obligation to buy anything. We charge you nothing for your first shipment. And you don't have to make a minimum number of purchases — not even one!

4. The fact is, thousands of readers enjoy receiving books by mail from the Silhouette Reader Service®. They like the convenience of home delivery and they like getting the best new novels before they're available in stores...and they love our discount prices!

5. We hope that after receiving your free books you'll want to remain a subscriber. But the choice is yours — to continue or cancel, anytime at all! So why not take us up on our invitation, with no risk of any kind. You'll be glad you did!

FREE
MYSTERY GIFT!

We can't tell you what it is...but we're sure you'll like it! A free gift just for accepting our **NO-RISK** offer!

PLAY

"PINBALL WIZ"
2 FREE BOOKS & A FREE GIFT!

CLAIM CHART

Score 50 or more	**WORTH 2 FREE BOOKS** PLUS A MYSTERY GIFT
Score 40 to 49	**WORTH 2 FREE BOOKS**
Score 30 to 39	**WORTH 1 FREE BOOK**
Score 29 or under	**TRY AGAIN**

YES! I have scratched off the silver circles. Please send me all the gifts for which I qualify. I understand that I am under no obligation to purchase any books, as explained on the back of this card.

345 SDL CPP3   245 SDL CPPT

Name: _____
(PLEASE PRINT)

Address: _____ Apt.#: _____

City: _____ State/Prov.: _____ Postal Zip/Code: _____

DETACH AND MAIL CARD TODAY!

The Silhouette Reader Service® — Here's how it works:

Accepting your 2 free books and mystery gift places you under no obligation to buy anything. You may keep the books and gift and return the shipping statement marked "cancel." If you do not cancel, about a month later we'll send you 6 additional novels and bill you just $3.57 each in the U.S., or $3.96 each in Canada, plus 25¢ delivery per book and applicable taxes if any.* That's the complete price — and compared to the cover price of $4.25 in the U.S. and $4.75 in Canada — it's quite a bargain! You may cancel at any time, but if you choose to continue, every month we'll send you 6 more books, which you may either purchase at the discount price or return to us and cancel your subscription.

*Terms and prices subject to change without notice. Sales tax applicable in N.Y. Canadian residents will be charged applicable provincial taxes and GST.

If offer card is missing write to: Silhouette Reader Service, 3010 Walden Ave., P.O. Box 1867, Buffalo, NY 14240-1867

BUSINESS REPLY MAIL

FIRST-CLASS MAIL   PERMIT NO. 717   BUFFALO, NY

POSTAGE WILL BE PAID BY ADDRESSEE

SILHOUETTE READER SERVICE
3010 WALDEN AVE
PO BOX 1867
BUFFALO NY 14240-9952

NO POSTAGE
NECESSARY
IF MAILED
IN THE
UNITED STATES

body was tense. It was all over your face, how much you wanted those boys to win. I saw how much you cared about the other guys, too, the ones who didn't get to play.''

"Of course I was concerned—"

"If you want to lie to yourself, Corinne, go ahead. But I'm not going to let you lie to me. Maybe you don't want to care. Maybe you want to stay cold and dead inside, and not worry about those kids or feel anything for them. But you do. You know you do.''

Corinne tried to dredge up some self-righteous anger to fight him off. But all she felt was drained and exposed. "Get out," she said tiredly.

Toby smiled, but it wasn't heartfelt. "That's all you ever say to me," he said. "'Get out.' I'm starting to feel unappreciated.''

Corinne moved away and rose from the couch.

"You know it's true." Toby remained seated. "You can't even deny it. You don't want to admit you care, because if you care about something, you run the risk of getting burned again. You poured your whole life into that career, and the only thing they cared about was how many ratings points you got them. And you're not going to go through that again.''

Corinne tried to find the words to deny him, but they lodged in her throat behind a lump. She whirled and moved to stand before the broken window, a vivid reminder of why he couldn't be right.

The night air was chilly shifting around the sheet. Corinne hugged her elbows while Toby's words echoed through her head. She heard Toby rise behind her.

"I'm sorry," he said, placing a hand on her shoulder. His tone was serious. "This must be very frightening for you. You came back to Aloma thinking you could be totally in control, wouldn't have to worry about being afraid, being threatened. And now, the kids are getting under your skin, I'm getting under your skin—"

"Don't flatter yourself."

"And now," he continued heedlessly, "now you're in even more danger than you were then."

Corinne made a sound that she intended to be of disbelief. "I'd hardly say one broken window is more dangerous than getting shot.''

"I wasn't talking about the window, I was talking about you. You, losing your heart. That's a hell of a lot scarier than facing a bullet. It's a hell of a lot scarier than leaving a career you don't care about."

"I cared about my career."

"No, you didn't. You may have cared about the people, about the stories at first. But your heart wasn't in the reporting. I told you, I watched you every night."

He squeezed her shoulder and she shrugged his hand away. It was the emotional upheaval, the tiredness, that kept her from fighting back, from telling him how wrong he was.

"You think you're pretty brilliant, huh, Toby?" she asked, her back still to him as she stepped away.

"I know you."

The words she should be saying to contradict him wouldn't come, because every word he said was true. In the surreal dark of early morning, her delusions were stripped back and reality stared her, stark and raw, in the face.

"I'm not brilliant, though," he said softly. "If I was, I'd figure out a way to make you stay."

Corinne hugged her elbows tighter. "Toby, I...could you just—" She didn't know what to say, what to think. She only knew she didn't want to think about what he was saying.

"Okay, I'll stop." Toby took one quick stride and gathered her in his arms.

For once, Corinne didn't fight his embrace. It took her mind off the thoughts spinning in her head.

She clung to him, focusing on how his body felt, strong and solid against hers. She emptied her mind of everything but the sight, sound and feel of Toby, edging out the words he'd spoken, and the knowledge that they were all too true.

Her face gently pressed to the V of his neck, she breathed in the spicy scent of him. His hold on her tightened. His broad hand smoothed and bunched the terry cloth back of her robe.

He bent his neck and she felt his breath, warm on her ear. She closed her eyes and turned her head to him. Here, here was a way to get lost. Here was a way past thinking.

She lunged greedily at his lips and wrapped her arms tightly around his neck. Toby groaned half in surprise, half in pleasure, and pulled her up to him, molding his lips to hers.

She was hungry, greedy, threading her fingers through his hair. Her fingers caressed his scalp, and Toby moaned again and crushed her tighter against him. She couldn't breathe, but all she wanted to do was get closer.

Fire sparked within her and quickly fanned to a burning flame. She breathed in deeply, feeding the fire with oxygen that smelled of Toby, smelled of his want. She slipped her hands into his collar, her nails scraping lightly along the back of his neck.

Toby caught her face in his hands, his thumbs together under her jaw. His lips were firm on her own, tasting, then suddenly demanding, moving over her cheek, down the line of her jaw.

"Yes," Corinne breathed, tilting her head to give him better access to her throat. She clung to the back of his neck for dear life.

Toby's broad hands smoothed down the curve of her neck, to her shoulder. He parted the robe, and with a moan and a sigh she loosened the belt and helped it to drop to the floor with a quiet swoosh.

Toby's hands were warm on her bare shoulders. His thumbs hooked under the straps of her tank top, rubbing back and forth along her collarbone. Corinne arched against him, aching for the touch of his hands on her, craving the feel of his callused hands against her feverish flesh.

Toby gripped her shoulders and moved the kiss back to her mouth. He thrust his tongue past her lips, and the fire inside Corinne leapt and doubled.

She'd found what she craved, what she needed—mindless, thoughtless sensation. She slipped one hand inside Toby's starched shirt, her palms hot, his chest even hotter, and with the other hand she began to undo the buttons of his shirt. She pulled the shirttails out of his pants with an impatient tug.

Toby pulled his mouth away for a moment, his breathing haggard, his eyes clouded with desire. "Are you—" was all he managed to say before Corinne covered his mouth with her own, making speech impossible.

"Yes," she said shortly against his lips, and as if to offer proof, took his hand in her own and placed it on her breast.

It was all the encouragement he needed. He cupped her breast through the thin cotton of her shirt, caressing it. Corinne moaned and stepped back, taking his other hand and putting it on her other breast. She closed her eyes and let her head hang back, her hands gripping his forearms. She unconsciously arched against his hands, using his hands to increase her pleasure. First pushing them lightly away to barely scrape her nipples, then pulling them back to crush against her.

Toby squeezed her nipples tightly, and Corinne drew in a sharp breath and bit her lower lip. She swallowed hard and dropped her head forward. She stepped closer to Toby, her knees weak and her heart thudding painfully against her ribs. She pushed his shirt back and kissed the center of his chest.

Toby gripped the back of her head, whispering something unintelligible against her crown.

Suddenly he froze. Corinne kissed a trail down his chest while her fingers fumbled with the belt at his waist.

Toby wrenched away, stepping back.

Corinne stumbled at his sudden abandonment. Mindless, her eyes clouded with desire, she reached for him.

"No." He took her hands in his and held her away from him.

"What?" Corinne's mind reeled.

"I'm sorry. I shouldn't have let it go this far. I'm sorry."

She jerked her hands away and tried to steady her heartbeat. "Toby..." Her voice was a warning.

"No, Corinne. Not now. Not like this."

"Not like what?" Corinne hated her voice sounding so shrill, so out of control.

"Not you, trying—" Toby's voice broke off, and he took a deep breath, scrubbing his face with one hand before facing her with bleak eyes. "Not you, trying to forget. You're not going to use me, use this, that way. We'd both regret it."

Corinne glared at him, speechless with rage and humiliation.

''When we do get together—and we will, make no mistake about it—it will be because you want to be with me, not because you're running from something else.''

Corinne raked a hand through her hair, then snatched her robe off the floor and shoved her arms through the sleeves. ''You're right. This was a mistake from the beginning. I was stupid to think for a second that this would work.'' She belted the robe tightly around her waist. Her hands and knees trembled, but her nose was in the air. ''And really, Toby, thank you. Thank you for warning me. Maybe I was getting too close to—to everyone here. Starting to care too much. But, believe me, that will stop. Right now.''

She walked as calmly as she could manage to the front door and opened it. ''You can leave now.''

''I'm going.'' His breath came raggedly. Knowing that this was as hard for him as it was for her gave her no satisfaction. He took his hat from the table, then stood in front of her, turning it around and around in his hands.

''Well? What are you waiting for?'' She stared daggers through him, and the miserable look on his face didn't stop her.

Toby shook his head sadly. ''I was just wishing I wasn't such a damn fool. Good night, Corinne.''

He put on his hat and walked out the door.

Chapter 9

He was a jerk. He was a smug, superior, self-righteous know-it-all.

He was also right.

Oh, she tried to deny it, Corinne thought as she jogged down the deserted blacktop. On Monday morning at school, she'd looked at each of the students, assuring herself that they meant nothing more to her than a job, a task to be accomplished. But before the thought could even finish itself, she found herself wondering if Benny Preston's shoulder hurt from the hard hit he'd taken during the game Friday night. She caught herself wondering if Cindy Wells was impressed with the enthusiasm and heart, if not skill, Josh Baxter had shown during the game.

She even felt sorry for Carl Buchanan, a little. He couldn't help the genes he'd been born with, and it was too bad his father only appreciated his athletic ability. She caught herself planning to find and nurture in him other talents, let him know that he was more than his football stats. Then she remembered that she didn't care.

How did this happen? She'd only been here a little over a month. Two months ago—two weeks ago—she would have sworn she could never feel anything again. And she liked it that way. That was the way she wanted it, dammit!

She hoped Toby was pleased with himself. If he hadn't pointed it out to her, she might not be running down the road now, trying to wear herself out to the point of numbness.

She heard the hum of a car behind her. She moved far onto the shoulder. The car slowed. In a flash, Corinne remembered the rock through her window. The angry, glaring faces at the football game.

She whipped her head around in fear.

It was Toby in the sheriff's Jeep. Corinne breathed a sigh of relief.

He pulled alongside. "Hey there," he called casually through the passenger side window. "Jogging out here? All alone?"

She nodded. Mr. Davis was in the front seat of the Jeep, and Jeremy Huckaby slouched in the back seat, his eyes red-rimmed. "Hello, Mr. Davis. Jeremy," Corinne said, leaning into the window. Mr. Davis sat solemnly, clutching his hat and staring straight ahead. "Where have you guys been?"

"We went to Abilene. Had a few errands to run," Toby said.

Jeremy rolled his eyes and slouched farther down in the seat.

"Maybe you shouldn't be out here all by yourself. Maybe you ought to stay in town."

Corinne shrugged it off. She wasn't going to admit the same thought crossed her mind seconds before. "I was just heading back into town."

"Good. Why don't you ride back with us? I need to talk to you."

Corinne looked at him suspiciously. She didn't want to get into an argument with him in front of the others. Toby cocked his head and opened his eyes wide, looking like an innocent puppy. "Seriously, there's something I need to talk to you about. Can I give you a ride home?"

There was no way she was going to be alone with Toby Haskell again. She lifted her chin and backed away from the window. "You can call me."

"Corinne, it's important."

Corinne looked again through the window into his face. He *was* serious. He'd quit grinning and his eyes held concern. She knew this wasn't about their argument last week.

"Let me take·you home, okay?"

Corinne pursed her lips. How bad could it be, with two other people in the car?

They dropped off Mr. Davis first. Toby walked him to his front door, and Corinne heard him telling the older man, "I'll be back in a few hours. If you need any help, don't hesitate to call the station."

Mr. Davis scowled and turned to the door angrily. "There is no need to treat me as a child, Mr. Haskell. I'm perfectly capable of looking after myself. No matter what that doctor said."

The Huckabys lived on the other end of town, past the railroad trestle and down a dirt road about half a mile. Jeremy wasn't any more receptive to Toby's guardianship than Mr. Davis had been. Toby walked Jeremy to his front door, where Mrs. Huckaby waited. As soon as he got past her, Jeremy tried to duck into the house, but his mother collared him and told him to thank Toby for taking him to his appointment with his counselor.

He glared sullenly at Toby, and Toby waited patiently with his arms crossed over his chest. JoAnn Huckaby turned away sadly when her son refused to speak. Corinne smiled sympathetically at her through the open window of the Jeep.

When JoAnn's back was turned, Toby stuck his tongue out at Jeremy and crossed his eyes. Jeremy was so stunned that the laugh was out of his mouth before he had a chance to clamp down on it. He coughed and sputtered and then turned and spit on the ground, just for good measure, scowling ferociously.

"You're welcome, Jeremy." Toby grinned. "I'll be back here next week at the same time. Maybe we can fit in a trip to the mall after your session."

"You don't gotta baby-sit me," he said.

"Have to," Corinne and Mrs. Huckaby said at the same time. Jeremy rolled his eyes at both of them.

"Is the old geezer going with us again?"

"Yep," Toby said, walking down the steps. "He has another doctor's appointment."

Corinne could have sworn there was pleasure in Jeremy's eyes as he heard that. As soon as he was dismissed, Jeremy fled into the house.

"What was all that about?" Corinne asked as they drove away.

"Jeremy had a session with his counselor, and Mr. Davis had a doctor's appointment. We decided to carpool."

Corinne shook her head, but decided against commenting on Toby's involvement with his constituents. "Jeremy looked like he'd been crying."

"I thought so, too. The session must have been rough. The family went to the prison to visit his dad last week."

"Poor kid," Corinne murmured.

"Poor kid? Weren't you the one convinced he was a derelict without hope for redemption?"

"Don't start with me, Sheriff."

"Sorry."

"What did Mr. Davis's doctor say?"

Toby frowned and shook his head. "He's running tests. He thinks it's Alzheimer's disease, but they have to rule everything else out before they can say that's what it is."

"Maybe it's just a vitamin deficiency or something. Maybe it's not—"

"That sounds like something I'd say. Coming back to Aloma is turning you into an ignorant, hopeful idealist, too."

"I'm just saying—"

"I know. And I hope you're right. But this time, I don't think so. While we were there, he got all depressed and started crying, then he thought we were trying to have him committed and steal all his money. It's bad, Corinne."

Corinne's shoulders slumped. "You're full of good news today."

Toby took a deep breath and gave her a halfhearted smile. "Actually, it's not all bad. He still functions at normal capacity most of the time. Right now he just gets confused and that makes him mad. There's no telling how long it will be before he needs full-time help. We have a while yet."

Corinne watched Toby as he drove, one arm casually thrown

over the steering wheel. There were dark smudges of exhaustion under his eyes and his shoulders slumped. He'd spent his day hearing nothing but bad news. And yet he still managed to remain upbeat, joking with a kid who despised him, confident he could defeat the unbeatable illness of an old man.

Corinne wondered if he'd eaten well lately. She wondered if he'd gotten any sleep in the past week. She could ask him over for dinner, but she knew it would only lead to more arguments. Toby was driving himself to save the world with his bare hands—herself included—and to live up to an unrealistic ideal of his own father. She wondered if he was even aware how great a man he was, or if he still believed he could never measure up.

"What?" Toby turned to see her watching him.

Corinne shook her head and faced forward. "Nothing."

"Why were you looking at me like that?"

"I wasn't looking at you," she said, then added, "Like what?"

"Like I was a puppy abandoned on the side of the road. A really cute puppy."

"I was simply wondering if you were taking care of yourself. Getting enough rest and eating right," she said primly.

Toby laughed. "So, the woman who doesn't care about anybody or anything—"

"I told you not to start with me."

"Sorry, sorry," Toby said contritely. He laughed lightly, then wiped the smile away with his hand when she glared at him.

Corinne stared out the window. They were both silent for the remainder of the drive to her house.

When they pulled up in front of the little frame house, Corinne noticed him giving the house the once-over. "Don't worry. I haven't had any more trouble this week. It was a onetime thing."

Toby nodded silently. He walked her to the front door and unlocked it for her.

"Okay, what was it you wanted to talk to me about?"

He shrugged and cupped the back of his neck, studying the porch for a few seconds. "Just something I've been thinking about, an idea I had this afternoon. I was hoping you could help me."

She stood in the doorway and cocked her head. "What is it?"

"It's about leaving Mr. Davis alone. You know, those kids I arrested were sentenced to community service. I was thinking about seeing if they could work it off, looking after him."

Corinne shook her head doubtfully. "I don't know. That sounds pretty risky. If he really does have Alzheimer's, he'll need professional care."

"Not for a while. He's still doing pretty good, I think. He just needs supervision right now, help keeping his bills paid and making sure he doesn't leave the gas on, things like that."

"Still, those kids haven't shown that they're exactly responsible citizens. Are you sure they can handle it?"

"I think they can. Besides, this would be a good way to teach them responsibility. Like I said, he's okay most of the time. We could schedule hours for them to check on him, make sure he's eating, things like that."

"What are we going to do when the time comes that he does need full-time care?"

Toby looked at her softly for a moment, a slight smile on his lips. She realized then that she'd said "we," not "you."

"I don't know," he admitted finally. "We'll cross that bridge when there's no other way to go."

She nodded. "Well, if you want to give it a try. I don't think the kids will like it too much. And I'm not sure how Mr. Davis will feel, having fifteen baby-sitters."

"See, I think he might like it." Corinne smiled thoughtfully as his eyes grew bright and he gestured with his hands, growing excited about his plan. "I was reading up on the disease, and they say that long-term memory, and something called remote memory, sticks around longer than recent memory does. For instance, he'd remember who was president when he turned eighteen before he'd remember if he paid the water bill. Which means, he's more likely to remember most of the stuff he taught all those years. Especially since he taught the same classes for so long."

Corinne nodded as she realized what he was getting at. "He could help them with their schoolwork."

"Exactly. They wouldn't be baby-sitting him—he'd be teaching again. I don't know, but I really think that will help him more than anything. Don't you think that if someone has something they really care about, they're more likely to be able to fight off disease?''

He looked so optimistic, she didn't have the heart to tell him she didn't think all the hope in the world could stave off this disease.

''One of the kids would tell him the truth.''

''Maybe not.''

''He'd figure it out anyway.''

Toby sighed a little. ''Maybe.''

She didn't like being the lone voice of negativity. ''But even if he did, it would probably be worth it to him, to be able to work with the kids again. I'd be happy to give them extra assignments to work on with him.''

Toby grinned. ''That's my dragon lady. So, you think it will work?''

Corinne shrugged. ''It's worth a try. You're still going to keep an eye on him yourself, though, right?'' It would be necessary, she knew. The students might be able to help, but there was no way she would trust the care of an elderly man to the likes of Carl Buchanan and his bunch.

''Sure. I drop by there every day anyway. And I already talked to Mom about helping out. She was a nurse for thirty-five years, and will know what to do. If it doesn't work out, I'll think of something else.''

And he would. Corinne couldn't help but admire his compassion. If anyone had found their true calling in life, Toby had. It was silly to feel a twinge of envy, but she did. Wherever John Haskell was, she thought, he must be very proud of his son.

''Maybe you could go ahead and arrange to meet with Mr. Davis occasionally, talk about school,'' Toby said. ''I was thinking that if he felt like he was necessary to someone...''

Corinne leaned back against the door. ''Actually, that's not a bad idea. Heaven knows, I could use all the help I can get, and he was the best teacher I ever had.''

Toby nodded, brows arched in innocence.

"And that way I could help you keep an eye on him."

He shrugged, and the corner of his mouth tipped up.

"I don't mind," she said quietly. The setting sun played across Toby's face, highlighting the reddish glints in his hair. At his warm look, Corinne felt her mouth go dry, suddenly remembering with intense clarity the kiss they'd shared.

She cleared her throat and looked down at her feet. "Okay, so I'll be happy to look in on him. Did you have a specific time in mind?"

Toby shook his head silently, his eyes still on her face. Corinne met his gaze tentatively, then looked away again. She kept expecting him to say something smart about last week, but he didn't. Finally she couldn't stand it any longer.

"Listen, Toby, about last week..."

He braced one hand on the door above her head and leaned close, his brows raised in question, a slight smile on his face. "Yes?"

"I just wanted to say...I mean...I've been thinking, and I feel..." The words stuck in her throat, then came pouring out in an awkward tumble. "I'm sorry for the way we...we parted. I'd really rather we didn't fight every time we get around each other."

"So would I."

"I know, but you—"

"It's okay, Corinne. I've already decided to back off. I have a job to do here, a big responsibility that needs all my attention right now. So relax."

She felt foolish, and strangely, a little peeved. Because it would be silly to frown, she smiled. "It's better this way."

"You're right. It is."

"Just friends."

"Yeah, just friends." Toby tapped the porch rail, cleared his throat, and stepped back. "I'll just be going, then."

"Okay."

"Okay." Two more steps back, his eyes still held hers.

"I'll see you."

"Yeah." He halted.

"I'll call Mr. Davis tomorrow."

"Yeah, do that."

"Okay."

He moved another step.

"Toby," she said, moving toward him without intending to.

"No," he said quietly. "Look, you're not the only one who doesn't need a complication right now. You're not the only one who has other things going on in their life."

She wanted so badly to ask him what he meant by that. Was he talking about the situation with the football players? With Mr. Davis, or Jeremy? Or all of it? Were his duties as sheriff catching up to him?

But she didn't ask him, because she didn't feel she had the right. She'd pushed him away; was it any wonder he'd taken the hint?

"Good night, Corinne."

Corinne stood in the doorway and watched him drive away. A slow lump built in her throat and a totally irrational part of her wanted to call him back.

Chapter 10

Maybe it was the chilly October air that invigorated her. Maybe it was the shrieking children, running around the community center in Halloween costumes, playing games and winning prizes and stuffing themselves with candy, that gave her this warm glow of content. It could have been the mingled scents of roasting corn, hot dogs and caramel apples.

But maybe, just maybe, it was the fact that she finally had what she wanted; she had a quiet, peaceful life in Aloma. The students saw her as a teacher and nothing more. She had made sure there were no complications in her life.

Even Toby hadn't talked to her lately except to discuss Mr. Davis and his chaperons.

It was enough to bore a person silly.

The senior class was sponsoring the Haunted Hayride after the Halloween carnival. As she watched the trailer pull into the parking lot of the community center, she heard herself cheering along with the kids. She was pathetically glad to be out of the house and socializing, such as it was. She caught herself smiling at nothing in particular. She was even excited about the ride.

When she was in high school, she had considered the carnival the epitome of small-town corniness. The same people wore the same costumes, pretending fright, pretending not to know who was under the mask.

Now it felt charming, the very picture of Americana. She felt ridiculously warm and cozy about the whole thing, as if she were a part of the excitement. It could only be the result of intense social deprivation.

Either that, or the double-fudge brownie she'd bought from Becca's concession stand a few moments ago.

Corinne was dressed as a Southern belle. Her hair was done in ringlet curls, and she wore a powder blue dress with a skirt wide enough to park a car under. She'd worn the dress in her own senior play, and unearthed it from the attic that afternoon, when she decided it would be fun to dress up, even if it was silly. Besides smelling of dust and being a bit too tight through the chest, it was in decent enough shape for one night.

She gathered up the skirt of her antebellum dress and climbed awkwardly into the back of the trailer, where she sat on a bale of hay and tried to smooth her voluminous skirts out of the way. Students crowded in, lining the edges of the trailer, laughing and teasing each other. Becca climbed in and sat beside Corinne.

"Okay, Miss Maxwell, this had better be good. Carl Buchanan told me it was going to be a lesson in abject terror," Becca said with a dry smile.

"I have no idea what they're up to. I just arranged for the trailer and the hay, and asked Luke Tanner to lead a sing-along. The senior boys are taking care of the scary parts."

"You don't know what they have planned?"

Corinne shook her head. "They said it wouldn't be fair if I knew—I might give it away. They're excited about it, though, so it must be something bad."

"That's frightening in itself," Becca said frankly.

Corinne laughed. "I'm sure it's just something silly like jumping out of the bushes when we ride by, waving fake axes or something. Josh Baxter will probably dress up like Freddy Krueger and scare all the girls."

''Including this one.'' Becca pointed to herself. ''I wish there was at least one adult who knew what was going on. Wait, there's Josh.''

Josh Baxter, wearing a cowboy suit and holding a stick horse, climbed into the back of the trailer, following closely on the heels, as always, of Cindy Wells. Cindy was dressed as a fairy princess, but had opted to wear her own slightly irritated expression.

''Josh, what are you doing here?'' Corinne asked. ''Why aren't you out with the rest of the boys?''

Josh shrugged. ''Buchanan said he's got it all under control. He wants some of us on the trailer so we can stir things up from in here.'' He looked off as he spoke, watching as Cindy sat next to a freshman boy.

''Get up, man. That's my seat.'' Josh motioned to the boy with a toss of his head.

''Find your own seat, Baxter,'' the other boy said. ''I was here first.''

Josh poked the other boy gently but firmly in the leg with his stick horse. ''You're sitting next to my girl, kiddo. Move.''

Cindy said, ''I'm not your girl,'' at the same time the boy said, ''No.''

Josh gave a long-suffering sigh, then leaned over and whispered something in the boy's ear. The boy moved to another bale.

Josh plopped down next to Cindy. ''Hi,'' he said, flashing white teeth. ''You look beautiful, as always.''

Corinne whispered to Becca, ''What did he say to that boy?''

''I have no idea,'' Becca said. She stood and bent over Josh's ear.

After Josh whispered back, Becca sat down. ''He promised the boy twenty bucks when we get back to the community center.''

Corinne laughed. ''Unbelievable, what some guys will do.''

''Yes. They remind me of you and Toby in high school.''

''What?'' Corinne's eyes grew wide with disbelief. ''We were never like that.''

''Sure you were. Toby followed you around like a lovesick puppy dog, and you let him. It was disgusting.''

''I never...'' Corinne let the thought drift off as she watched the bored expression on Cindy's face. Cindy was crazy about Josh; Corinne had watched them from the beginning of the school year. Cindy pretended to be uninterested, but she always made sure she was in a position for Josh to notice her.

Corinne had often felt like shaking Cindy, seeing the two dance around each other day after day. Didn't the girl see what a sweet boy Josh was? A boy like that would grow up to be a steady, dependable man. A man who would cherish her, would be there for her for the rest of his life. Was Cindy too blind to see that?

No, Corinne thought. She saw it. But she took it for granted. She enjoyed the constant adoration, and she didn't have to give anything in return. She was completely safe.

Her thoughts turned, guiltily, to Toby. She had been in love with Toby when she was Cindy's age. He had known that. No, she'd never told him. But he had to have known.

"Speak of the devil," Becca murmured. "I don't believe that phrase has ever been more appropriate."

Corinne looked up, and her breath caught in her throat. A pirate was climbing into the trailer. A very sexy pirate.

"Oh, my God," Corinne murmured to herself. "That's Toby."

"I know," Becca said. By her tone she was as stunned as Corinne was.

From the ground up, he looked every bit the marauding bandit of the high seas. He wore shiny black boots, with black pants tucked into the top of them—pants snug enough to leave little to the imagination. Tucked into the pants was a flowing white shirt with loose sleeves, the front unbuttoned far past the point of decency.

He wore a black patch over one eye. His hair was dyed jet-black.

He stepped onto the trailer and flourished a fake sword. "Shiver me timbers!" he roared. "Are you ready for the adventure of your lives?"

The crowd on the hay bales cheered.

"I warn you, it's not for the squeamish or the faint of heart." Toby walked up the middle of the trailer, swinging the sword smoothly beside him. "I suggest you take this opportunity, this second, before it's too late, to—'' he whirled on a group of fresh-man girls clumped together on one bale ''—run for your lives!'' he growled, thrusting his face into the group.

The girls obligingly squealed in terror and hugged each other. More than one of them gave him frankly admiring looks. The trailer lurched to a forward roll. Toby grinned, a wicked flash of white teeth against tan skin.

Corinne smothered her laugh of delight when Toby's gaze landed on her. He pointed his sword at her. ''Ah-ha! A beautiful damsel, ripe for the plucking.''

Corinne rolled her eyes. He was going to try to embarrass her in front of her students. She pursed her lips and turned away.

And saw her own expression mirrored in the eighteen-year-old face of Cindy Wells.

The recognition hit her like a thunderbolt. *Oh my God. I was like that. I am like that.*

''I believe I'll bundle up this little morsel and carry her back to my secret island cave, safe from the prying eyes of decent human society,'' Toby growled, standing over Corinne with a wicked leer on his face. He waggled his brows suggestively and brandished his sword. The kids around them laughed.

Corinne started to pull up her old standby: aloof disdain. But she couldn't. She just couldn't. This was one of those magical moments that memories were made of—of playing along, of fitting in and joining the group and laughing over silly things. Of not taking herself seriously.

One of those moments she'd always made herself miss out on.

So she squealed and feigned terror. A grown woman, pushing thirty, holding her hands up and squealing like a teenager. She felt like, and knew she looked like, an idiot.

Toby looked at her in surprise. Obviously, hers was not the reaction he'd expected.

''I can't help it,'' she said dryly. ''I don't have a lot of experience at squealing. Sit down.''

He did as he was told. ''It wasn't such a bad squeal, your first time out and all,'' he said, dropping back to his normal voice. He settled beside her as the hayride picked up speed and headed out of town.

"Oh, it was stupid and you know it. I can't pull off the terrified damsel thing."

"That's okay. You gave it your best shot. What are you doing here, anyway? I figured this kind of thing was way too hokey for you." He fiddled with the patch over his eye.

She opened her mouth to retort. She could use her duties as senior class advisor as an excuse. That she was here because she had to be, not because she wanted to be. It would be a familiar response, for both of them.

Instead, she shrugged and smiled weakly. "It's fun, don't you think?"

"Well, sure, I think it's fun. I always loved Halloween. If I recall, though, you said it was a silly holiday for people who couldn't deal with the fact that they were no longer children."

"Okay, okay," Corinne said irritably. "Must you remind me of my faults constantly?"

He drew back in surprise. "Faults? What faults?"

She glowered at his faked innocence. "Okay, so maybe I was wrong—" At his shocked look, she lifted her chin defiantly. "Maybe I was wrong."

He shook his head as if to clear it. "You? Wrong? I—I don't understand."

"You're getting a kick out of this, aren't you?" she said with asperity. "Did you ever stop to think that maybe I was a little insecure back then? That I was afraid of letting my guard down because—because I might make a mistake?"

He remained tactfully blank-faced.

"Maybe I acted like a snob—"

"I never said that," he objected.

"But maybe," she continued, "maybe some people are afraid to relax. Did you ever stop to think about that? They might look stupid, and nobody would have any respect for them. Or they might make a mistake, one they'd regret. So they weigh the consequences before they take action. Some people don't find it as easy as you do, Toby, to just jump right in and let themselves go. Did you ever think of that?''

"Of course I did,'' he said frankly. "Did you?''

She sighed and turned away, plucking a strand of hay from the bale beneath her. She could feel the magic of the moment slipping by her, out of her grasp. "Yes,'' she said glumly, looking at Cindy Wells. "About fifteen seconds ago.''

He followed her gaze, looking first at Cindy, who was pointedly ignoring Josh's attempts to hold her hand, then back at Corinne. "Ahh,'' he said, nodding slowly. "I see.''

"She's missing out on a lot,'' Corinne said, her eyes on Cindy.

Toby nodded. "Yeah, but look at him. He's a complete goof. No wonder she won't give him the time of day.''

"She's crazy about him,'' Corinne said definitely. "She's just afraid to let him know it.''

"How do you know?'' Toby's voice was soft, cutting through all the commotion around them and arrowing straight to her heart.

Corinne was silent for a long time, not looking at Toby. "Just a hunch,'' she said quietly.

She could feel Toby's eyes on her, studying her. She couldn't look at him. After a moment, he took a deep breath. "Obviously, he cares a lot about her, too. Even if she is giving him the cold shoulder.''

"He's made no secret about it,'' she murmured.

"No, he hasn't,'' Toby agreed. The unspoken words sang between them, words neither dared to say. "He's made himself pretty clear. But I have a hunch of my own. He seems like a pretty understanding guy. I'll bet he'd be willing to give her some room. She's probably scared to do anything to encourage him, because she thinks he'll read too much into it. But he'd back off, if that's what she needed. Let her relax a little, have some fun. No strings attached.''

Corinne sorted. "You don't know this guy, Sheriff. He can be very persistent. She smiles at him, and he thinks she's in love with him. She laughs at one of his jokes, and he starts planning their wedding. It's scary. For her,'' she added as an afterthought.

Toby rubbed the back of his neck and sat up straighter, putting his hands on his knees. "It could be that she's the one reading into things. It could be—and this is just a guess—that he wants her to have a little fun and that's all. If she'd just relax and let her guard down for one night, goof around and act silly and just go with the flow for one night, he'd be happy with that."

She faced him, saw Toby through the costume and dyed hair, met his gaze squarely. "No strings attached?"

He smiled, not the one he practiced to charm her, but a tender smile, just for her. "Not everything should have a price. No strings attached."

She felt as if they'd been cocooned in a private world for the past few moments, but with his smile she felt her spirits lift, caught once again the atmosphere of gaiety around them. For some reason she couldn't fathom, she was nervous.

"What if she can't?" she asked him. "What if holding back has become such a habit that she can't let go of it?"

"Of course she can," he said easily. "Look, here's a perfect chance to prove it." He pointed to Luke, who stood at the head of the trailer, hooking his guitar to the strap around his shoulders. "A sing-along."

"Oh, Toby, I can't sing," she protested, forgetting for a moment that they weren't talking about her.

"Sure you can."

"You've never heard me."

Luke Tanner was dressed as Elvis, which wasn't exactly a stretch since he had a lot of the King's facial characteristics anyway. He stood on the floor of the trailer, one foot planted on a hay bale, and started in on "Heartbreak Hotel."

The students joined in. So did Toby and Becca. Corinne glanced at Cindy. She was looking at Luke as if he were the corniest thing she'd ever seen.

Corinne gave a sigh of resignation and braced herself. She was a terrible singer, which was why she never sang. Not even alone in the car, with the radio blaring so loud she couldn't hear herself.

She sang tentatively, cutting Toby an I-hope-you're-happy look. He sang louder, gallantly covering her voice. Toby was worse than she was, but he didn't care. It made it a little easier.

She sang. Off-key and with as much dignity as she could muster singing Elvis songs and ''The Monster Mash.''

No one stopped what they were doing to stare at her. The sky didn't fall. The world didn't stop spinning on its axis.

When Toby scooted closer and cupped her shoulder, she let it pass. When he turned toward her and put one hand on her knee, she barely took the time to give him a perfunctory look, which he ignored.

She had to get out of the house more, she told herself. This was too much fun.

The trailer bumped off the main road and onto a dirt back road. Luke stopped his song and began a story about an escaped murderer, who had once hidden out in the mesquite brush years ago, not far from where they were riding right now.

Several girls giggled nervously and scooted closer to their dates. Toby tightened his hold on Corinne, scooting closer to her. She smiled and kept her face turned toward Luke.

''They say he killed his whole family with his bare hands,'' Luke continued gravely. ''They never found his mother's head. After he broke out of the asylum, there were reports of a man wandering around these parts, carrying what appeared to be a human skull.''

''I'm scared,'' Toby said. ''Maybe you ought to sit in my lap.''

''Hush, Toby, I'm trying to hear Luke's story.''

''One night, about fifteen years ago, a group of kids were out here camping, and one of them heard a noise in the woods. He decided to go check it out. But he made a very big mistake. He went alone. After a while the others got worried about him. They were smarter. They stuck together. They walked through the woods, dark as pitch, all huddled together and shaking. They couldn't find their friend. They heard a noise—''

One of the girls shrieked from pent-up adrenaline. Her friends shushed her. Luke looked around the group and paused dramatically. Toby scooted Corinne closer and took her hand in his. ''Are you okay?'' he asked in a whisper.

Corinne laughed. ''Shh, I want to hear.''

''They heard a noise, a kind of flapping noise.'' Luke leaned forward, his voice lowered for effect. "It was too dark to see more than five feet in front of them. They inched along, calling their friend's name, shaking and scared. The flapping sound got louder. Then all of a sudden, the clouds blew off and the moon shone down, and there, not five feet in front of them, was their friend's head, stuck on a pole!''

Luke yelled and flourished a stick with a dummy head on it. Suddenly there was a slamming against the outside of the trailer, right behind Corinne. She knew it was coming, and still she screamed and clung to Toby for dear life, falling into the bed of the trailer.

He dragged her back up. The trailer stopped. All around them, girls were screaming and laughing. Boys dressed in gruesome costumes ran from the bushes and surrounded the trailer. They waved fake weapons and dummies' heads and yelled at the top of their lungs.

Corinne collapsed in laughter against Toby, knowing it was fake but not able to keep from being caught up in the moment. She wrapped her arms through Toby's and clung to him, laughing and shrieking like one of her students when the monsters ran by and grabbed at her.

"Oh, Toby, can you believe—"

One of the monsters dragged her backward over the side.

This time her scream was genuine. Her petticoat flounced up and into her face. Strong arms wrapped around her, holding her arms pinned. She was dragged backward, struggling and screaming in earnest.

A hand clamped over her mouth, and another arm tightened around her chest, restricting her breath. She kicked, and hooked her heel on a ruffle of her petticoat.

Toby leapt over the side of the trailer and pounded after them. "Let her go!" he roared. "Now!"

He grabbed at the mask the attacker was wearing and ripped at it. Corinne was dumped unceremoniously as the boy fled into the brush. She fell to the ground and fought for her breath.

Toby jogged a couple of feet after the boy, but came back

quickly to Corinne. He lifted her off the ground and studied her face.

"Sweetheart, are you okay?"

They stood behind a mesquite tree, fifteen yards from the trailer. The others were oblivious to the situation. For a bizarre moment it was too like another moment, when she'd been helpless and alone amid a group of people.

She tried to stand upright, but sagged against Toby, her knees weak and shaking. Her heart hammered, and she could feel herself about to lose control. Memories of being dragged into violence by a crazed man flooded her.

It was the memories, too, that brought her back.

Because this wasn't like that time. She was okay now. Toby was here. She was fine. It was just a joke.

"I'm fine," she said in a quavery voice, then coughed.

"Oh, honey, no you're not. Look at you. You're shaking like a leaf. Are you going to have one of those panic attacks?"

"I'm fine, I said."

"Who the hell was that?"

"I don't know. I didn't get a good look."

"I'm going to have Luke turn this thing around right now. I'll ask the other guys who it was."

"No, Toby, don't. Please. Don't say anything. It was just a joke."

"If it was just a joke, why the hell did he run off like that?"

"You probably scared him to death. You looked like you were ready to take his head off. Now really, please, don't make a big deal of this."

The kids on the trailer were calming somewhat, and Corinne knew it was only a matter of minutes before the trailer started back for the community center.

"Come on, Sheriff, relax. It was all in fun."

"He looked like a pretty big guy. Did he feel solid to you? Or was that padding?"

"Toby, please. Let it go. Don't ruin everyone else's fun. It was no big deal. It's Halloween. You're supposed to get scared. See."

She held out a hand, hoping it would be steady enough to pass in the moonlight. "No more shaking. Everything's fine."

She started back toward the trailer, and felt his hesitation. But he followed and helped her back into the bed. This time when he sat beside her, she was the one who planted herself close to him and pressed herself into the crook of his shoulder.

She listened with half an ear to the rest of Luke's songs, trying to play along and have fun. Trying just to be grateful that she hadn't started wheezing and choking in front of her students. Trying not to think of the stocky body and iron-strong arms that pinned her.

Trying not to think of how much it didn't feel like a joke.

Chapter 11

By the time they got back to the community center, Corinne almost had herself convinced that it was just a joke. She helped clean up the center, and Toby folded down tables and swept the floor. He didn't ask if he could take her home, but when she picked up her coat and purse, he followed her and led her to his car.

When they got to her house, Corinne flipped on a lamp and tugged at her dress. "I'm sorry, but I've got to get out of this dress."

"Don't let me stop you."

His mouth twisted when she came back a few minutes later wearing baggy purple sweats.

"Something a little more comfortable, huh?"

She nodded and pulled the pins from her hair, shaking it out. "Much more comfortable. I'm going to have a cup of hot chocolate. Would you like some?"

He followed her into the kitchen and leaned against the counter while she heated the water.

"I think tonight was a success, don't you?" she asked as she measured powder into mugs.

"Mmm," he said quietly. He fiddled with a few things on the counter, his jaw tight. "Did you have fun?"

The memory of being hauled over the edge of the trailer flickered through her, giving her a momentary sense of panic. She gripped the spoon and pressed the feeling down. It was just a joke. Teachers were always targets for practical jokes. Nothing personal. Just a joke.

"Yes," she said brightly. "I did, actually. Did you?"

He didn't answer. He was probably still thinking about the prank. He was a little too sensitive where her safety was concerned, she thought. She wasn't afraid. She wasn't going to let herself be afraid.

In fact, the reason she didn't want to turn around and face him had everything to do with fear, but not from the hayride.

But he'd promised. No strings attached.

She turned and held the mug out to him, smiling too widely. "Here you are."

He took the mug without comment and set it on the counter behind him. He pulled the patch over his head, ruffling his hair so that one lock of it fell over his forehead, making him look even more rakish than before.

Corinne cleared her throat and sipped her hot chocolate. Toby's gaze was steady on her, unwavering.

"What?" she finally asked, slightly irritated at his silence.

"You had fun?" he asked again.

She nodded.

"It doesn't have to end now."

Her heart stopped. She didn't have to ask what he meant. The moment was here. She could hush the panicked voice in her head that urged her to get him out of the house, to be alone and safe again. She could close her eyes and walk into his arms and let the next step take care of itself. It had happened before.

And it had killed her to walk away. She wasn't ready for that. Not again.

"You promised no strings, Toby," she said.

"I know. And I'll stick by that. It's just one night."

She shook her head and set her own mug on the counter. "Who

do you think you're kidding? Yourself? Because I know better. If we're going to do this, let's at least be honest.''

He rubbed the back of his neck. ''Okay, let's be honest. If you can look me in the eye and honestly say you don't want me to stay, I'll go.''

He took a step toward her, his boots on the floor sounding like gunshots in the silent room. Corinne opened her mouth to stop him, but the words didn't come.

He took another step, his eyes blazing with an intensity that unnerved her, his face a mask of determination. Corinne took an involuntary step backward and found the counter at her back. The room shrank.

''Well,'' he said softly when his face was inches from her own. ''Be honest. I'm not asking what you *should* do. I'm asking what you want to do.''

He framed her face with one hand and his thumb caressed her cheek. He braced his other hand beside her, effectively blocking her in.

Her mouth grew dry and she felt as if she hadn't taken a breath since they walked in the house. Her blood hummed quickly through her veins, her heart beating a tattoo in her chest. His gray eyes remained on her, steady, not letting her look away, leaving her open and vulnerable.

''It's just one question, Corinne. Just one night. A one-word answer. Stay. Or go.''

His thumb dragged along her bottom lip, his eyes holding hers captive the whole time. She swallowed, cleared her throat. She opened her mouth to answer.

But instead of a word, only a soft sound came from her throat. She put her hand on Toby's wrist, closed her eyes, and brought his hand to her mouth. She kissed his palm, and opened her mouth to touch her tongue delicately to the sensitive skin there.

Toby's breath hissed in, and she felt his grip tighten on the counter beside her. ''I'm going to take that as 'stay,''' he said as he tilted her head and kissed her.

For Toby it was the moment he'd always known would come, the moment he'd put his faith in. He fisted his hands in her hair and tilted her head back, meeting her eyes.

Corinne's eyes were wide with mixed fear and longing. She closed them, and he kissed her eyelids softly, then her nose and finally her mouth. She sighed and drifted into him, melting a little in his arms. She opened her mouth and he took her offering greedily. His mouth moved over hers deeply, drawing her out, tasting.

He moved his hands down her neck, massaging and relaxing her in the way that he knew would have her purring like a content cat in a moment. His palms spread under the neck of her sweatshirt, and he felt her skin warming with his touch. He moved his kiss from her mouth to her neck.

He intended to take his time, savor every moment. He'd waited too long for this to rush it. But when Corinne moaned and dropped her head back to give him access, he could have swallowed her whole.

"Let's go to the bedroom," she said huskily.

"No." He nibbled on her earlobe. "I'm not done with the kitchen yet."

He closed his mouth onto the pulse at her throat and drew the skin in. She inhaled sharply. She probably didn't expect him to remember. But he did. He'd lost sleep night after night, remembering all the little things that drove her crazy. And he planned to ruthlessly use them all.

"Come on," she said again. "Let's go."

He shook his head against her neck, nuzzling.

"I've waited for this for over ten years. I'm not going to rush it now."

He wanted to sweep her off her feet in a moment of passion. He knew how to do it, too. He knew just the right places to touch, just the right things to say so that she'd forget all about the past and the future and focus on this moment alone. He wanted to make her safe, make her happy always.

At the same time, he wanted to take her now, roughly and quickly, on the kitchen floor.

He stroked her swollen lips with his thumb. She turned her head and took the tip of it into her mouth. Desire ripped through him, triplefold, sharp and hot. His breath shot from him, and he pulled her tightly against him.

''Corinne,'' he moaned. He wrapped his arms around Corinne's waist and brought her tightly against him, so tightly that he brought her feet off the floor. He kissed her deeply. Her arms went around his shoulders, and with a hitch of her breath, he felt the last bit of her hesitation fall away.

''Now,'' he growled. ''Now we can go to the bedroom.''

He cupped her bottom, and she wrapped her legs around his waist. He walked her back through the dining room, through the living room. Her body blocked his view of everything else. He bumped into tables and knocked over chairs, and kept going. He didn't care.

When his legs bumped the edge of her bed, he stopped and laid her carefully on it.

She reached for his shirt, her nimble fingers working quickly through the buttons.

Not quickly enough. Toby ripped at the material, rending the cloth off his body and casting it aside. He knelt over her.

Corinne spread her palms on his chest. Her skin felt cool on his burning flesh. She glided her hands up his shoulders, into his hair, and around to cup his face.

Toby took her hands in his. He breathed in the smell of her, and kissed her palms. She gasped as he took one of her long fingers into his mouth, sucking on it. Her free hand clutched at him. He was anxious to feel her against him. He lifted the hem of her sweatshirt and skimmed it over her head.

Her hair spread like a fan around her on the bed. Moonlight spilled through the window, bathing her smooth skin in a pale glow. Toby knelt above her. His breath caught in his throat at the sight. She looked up at him, her brown eyes damp, trusting.

He stretched full-length upon her, her skin like silk against his own. She was warm and soft, and he wrapped his arms around her, wanting to take her into himself.

Corinne clung to Toby, trying desperately to lose herself in physical sensation. She'd forgotten how it could be. She'd told herself that the incredible urgency she'd felt with Toby before was left in her youth. That it was due to the emotions and hormones that naturally raged out of control at that age.

But ten years later, the fire leapt in her, sharp and sweet, stronger even than it had before. Now nothing mattered except getting closer to Toby. Nothing mattered except the feel of him against her. Nothing mattered except losing herself, completely, to this moment.

And yet, her mind, her heart, churned along with her body. She felt as if she were made of spun glass, bright and shimmering, and if she stopped this moment she would be shattered forever.

Toby placed his palms flat on the bed on each side of her. He kissed a trail along her waist and across her flat belly. "I've dreamed of this," he murmured against her skin. "Every day since you left, I've dreamed of this."

His voice was husky with emotion, and Corinne closed her eyes, not wanting to think about the past, about the years that had separated them. She only wanted to think about this night. Everything else was too big to contemplate. She clung to his shoulders. "Toby, please," she moaned. "Take me."

"At night in my dreams, I remember looking at you, lying in the bed of my old pickup, underneath the peach trees." He breathed in deeply and threaded his fingers through her hair. "You were stretched out for me, your body trembling. I remember how wild you were, and hungry, and I remember how you cried after, because you said you didn't know you could feel like that, or that two people could get so close. Did you remember, Corinne? All that time you were away, did you remember us?"

Tears burned hot behind her eyelids. She'd been so confused back then—about everything but her feelings for Toby. But she'd needed desperately to leave Aloma, and she knew Toby would never leave. And in her heart of hearts she'd feared she didn't deserve a man like Toby. So she'd tried to forget. She'd made herself forget how it was with Toby. Because she couldn't remember and stay away.

But he wasn't going to let her do that now. She wanted him to take her in a frenzy of need, and he wasn't going to. He was going to make her face each moment, every emotion head-on. She could tease and tempt and seduce him, but in the end, she wasn't getting out of this with her heart intact.

He bunched the waist of her pants in his hands and dragged them down her legs. He sat on the edge of the bed and smoothed the pants down her legs and tossed them aside. He took one foot in his hand and massaged it, his eyes on hers. His hands moved up her knees, circling, touching every inch of her with his palms, moving up her legs.

He cupped her moist center in his hand, his gaze still locked with hers. She trembled beneath him, reaching for him. His touch seared her, a slow, excruciating inferno that built in her, completely out of her control and completely in his. His gaze stayed glued to hers as his thumb caressed her sensitive core, making her wince and jump and ache for more.

Her hips lifted involuntarily and moved against him, rotating against his hand. She couldn't catch her breath. Her heart pounded in her ears. "Toby, please," she begged, not sure if she wanted him to stop, or never stop.

He lowered his head and took her with his mouth. His tongue probed and shot straight to her center. She cried out and arched off the bed, her hands wrenched in his hair.

The climax slammed into her unexpectedly, rocking her and making her curl away from him.

"Toby!" She cried out his name in a whisper and he was there, beside her, holding her tightly. She clung to him.

He stretched out beside her, moving slowly, letting her savor the moment. He eased her knee back gingerly, moving between her legs. He moved gently, as if afraid to hurt her. She didn't want him to be gentle; she wanted him to be with her. She reached for him, even as the aftershocks of her climax made her body tremble. Her hand closed around him, rock hard and hot.

"Oh, Corinne," he groaned.

He thrust home in one stroke. She rocked her hips upward with the momentum and cried out, part in pain and part in pleasure. He covered her mouth with his, swallowing her cries. He thrust again, and again, and when she shuddered beneath him again, he tore his mouth away, and cried out with her.

* * *

Arms closed around her in the night, pinning her down, trapping her. Corinne tried to struggle, tried to fight, but she was paralyzed. She couldn't breathe. She whimpered, hating herself for doing it, helpless to stop.

Finally she wrenched her body free, flinging herself up and away. She flailed her arms and legs, finding her voice. Her own scream woke her.

She crouched at the foot of the bed. Light suddenly flooded around her, blinded her. She threw her arms up in self-defense.

"Corinne!" Toby reached for her. "Corinne, sweetheart, it's okay. It's okay."

Corinne batted his hand away. Her eyes cleared a little, and she reached for him.

"Toby." She breathed. "Toby." It was all she could say, the only thought her mind would form as relief washed over her.

He wrapped his arms around her and pulled her back down onto the bed.

"It's okay," he whispered, smoothing her hair and crooning in her ear. "It's okay, sweetheart. It was just a dream. It's okay."

The trembling stayed with her for a long time, but thankfully the hyperventilating didn't start. Toby's presence, warm and solid under her, distracted her, helped her bring her focus off her panic. She rested her head on his chest, listening to his heartbeat and his voice, feeling his breath soft against her hair, feeling the life course through him.

His hands roamed over her back, soothing her. Gradually, her breathing and heartbeat returned to normal.

She felt drained, her body hollow. She lay heavily on Toby, letting the warmth from his body slowly seep into hers.

He clasped his hands behind her back and hugged her tight, kissing the top of her head, her ear, her neck. "It's okay," he whispered. "I'm here now, and you don't have to be afraid ever again." After a few minutes, his breathing grew deep again, and she knew he was more than half asleep when he murmured into her ear, "I won't let anything happen to you. You're mine, Corinne, and I'll always take care of you."

His words echoed through her head, long after Toby had drifted back to sleep.

She lay awake for hours, wondering what she'd done.

She awoke with sunlight warm on her legs. She opened her eyes and lay staring at the empty pillow beside her. Toby was gone.

She could still smell him on the sheets. His words from last night rang again and again through her head. It was as though her body had slept but her mind was still stopped at that one thought. Never to be afraid again.

It was sweet. Sweet and a little sad, that he thought he could take on the whole world, could solve the most difficult problems with the strength of his own heart. He thought that, she knew, because that was what had always been expected of him, for as long as either of them could remember. John Haskell had controlled the entire county with a cigar in one hand and his badge permanently attached to his chest. How could Toby grow up to think any less of himself?

She smiled to herself, picturing Toby in a superhero costume, with his chest thrust out gallantly and the world resting in the palm of his hand.

She smiled, and wiped the tears from her eyes.

"Hey, what are you crying about?"

Corinne started at his voice. Toby leaned lazily against the door-jamb, his arms crossed over his chest. He wore only the tight black pants from the night before.

"Toby?" She sat up quickly and scrubbed her cheeks with her hands. "I thought you were gone. What are you doing?"

"Looking at you."

He crossed the room and sat on the bed. She shifted away as his weight tilted her toward him.

He put his hand on her knee to still her. "What's wrong?"

"Nothing."

"Liar. Did you have another dream?"

"No." She rose and walked restlessly around the room, one hand covering her breasts. "Where's my robe?" she asked, as if he would know.

He studied her for a moment, then walked to the closet, looked around, and pulled out her robe.

"Oh," she said. "Of course." She pulled it on and belted it tightly around her waist, avoiding his eyes.

"Corinne." Toby lifted her chin with his finger.

She took a deep breath and met his eyes.

"Are you sorry? For last night?"

She shook her head. She wasn't sorry, couldn't be sorry for what she knew was unavoidable. She turned away and stood before the window.

"Your Jeep is out front," she said.

"I know."

"But, Toby, everyone can see it. Mrs. Kirby will tell everyone you spent the night."

"So?" He stepped behind her and kissed her neck, wrapping his arms around her waist. "I don't think your mom will ground you."

"This could be bad, Toby. This could be very bad. I'm a teacher, even if I am just a substitute. I have to watch my reputation. I could lose my job."

"Now we have it. A convenient reason for us not to see each other again. I knew you'd think of something, Corinne."

His body stayed against hers, but tension suddenly separated them.

"This is a legitimate concern, Toby. A lot of the parents would be upset to learn you spent the night."

He laid his chin on her shoulder. "You're right. I should have thought of that before. Especially now, when half the town hates me."

"I doubt it would matter who you were. They won't want their children's lives in the hands of an immoral woman."

"Why don't you just get to what's really bothering you, sweetheart?" he asked after a moment.

"This is what's bothering me."

"You were upset before you saw my Jeep. Admit it, you're sorry about last night. You already regret it." He stepped away from her, his hands on his hips and his chin jutted out.

"I don't regret it. It's just that..."

"Just what?"

She sighed, raking a hand through her hair. His eyes steeled, and she knew he was waiting for her to say something that would hurt him. She couldn't do it. Wouldn't do it. "It's just—dammit, you said no strings!"

"And I meant it." He raised his hands, palms to the ceiling. "I didn't ask for anything from you, Corinne."

"It's not that simple and you know it." She blew out a gust of breath and walked slowly around the room, picking up objects and putting them down. Objects from her own past, mementos from growing up, little things that her mother had never put away, not because she treasured them, but because she'd simply never taken the time to notice them. She picked up a faded program from their senior prom. So long ago. Had it been that long since she'd felt as if she were in control of her life?

"Do you want me to leave?" Toby asked impatiently.

She shot him a look. "No, actually I don't."

"Then what do you want?"

"I don't know!" She tossed the program on the dresser and spun on him. "No, you know what? I do know. But since I stepped foot in this town, you have done your damnedest to see I don't get it. All I wanted was to be left alone. The students were just faceless creatures. It was my responsibility to teach them writing and Shakespeare and diagramming sentences. It was a job, and nothing more. You are the one who forced me to start seeing them differently, to get involved in their lives. You are the one who forced me to start caring about them, about you—" She clamped her mouth shut. She didn't dare say love.

Of course, Toby realized, she couldn't bring herself to say it. She couldn't talk about what passed between them last night. Because she didn't have control over it, over herself when she was with him. So again, she would use the students, the job, as a metaphor. She would tiptoe around the real issue and pretend it was the job that made her nervous.

Which was fine with him. It wasn't as if he were looking for undying declarations of love and devotion anyway.

"It will be okay, Corinne."

"You aren't the one who has to deal with it, Toby, if something goes wrong."

"Of course I will. That's what I was trying to tell you last night. I'm here now. I'll take care of you."

"It's not that simple. If there's one thing I learned through the whole ordeal with Sulley, and with getting shot, it's that no one is going to take care of me, except me. Period. It's not pretty, and a lot of people don't want to admit it. But that's just the way it is."

"It doesn't have to be that way. If you would just relax and let me—"

"I did relax!" Corinne snapped. She crossed her arms over her chest. "I did relax," she said again, looking at the wall.

"And now you wish you hadn't," he said flatly.

"No!" She plopped on the bed, all the energy draining from her. "God, Toby, can't we please just *slow down?* Please? I don't regret last night. But, you know, I made a pretty big concession. I let my guard down. Because you convinced me to. And now— now I feel like I'm not in control of anything. Does it have to be so...so—"

She groaned and flung herself back on the bed, her forearm over her eyes. "I *sang,* for crying out loud," she said, talking to the ceiling. "I sang in front of other people. I sang *Elvis* songs. And now we're—"

He stood over her, watching as she hid from him and, he suspected, from herself. From the moment he walked through the door last night, he'd expected her to ask him to leave. He was ready for it, he told himself. "And now we're what?"

"We're...we're together again."

"You're reading too much into a little sex, sweetheart." He rubbed the back of his neck. "Didn't I tell you no strings attached?"

"Yes, but—"

He knew what the "but" was going to be. He hadn't meant for her to see how he felt for her—hell, he didn't want to see it himself. But she must have seen it in his eyes, felt it in his touch. And that was what the "but" was.

He stuck his chin out, ready to deny that last night meant anything to him beyond a roll in the sheets, almost daring her to accuse him otherwise.

But she didn't. She sat up and looked at him silently, then her gaze slid away.

As for what he was going to do about those very feelings... Well, a bottle of Jack Daniel's and a decade got him over the last time she left him. It ought to do the trick again.

"But nothing," he said. "I meant what I said—no strings attached. So if you want to end it right here, sweetheart, that's fine. If you enjoyed last night as much as I did, that's fine, too." Because if he said more, he'd get himself into trouble, he clamped his jaw and waited for her to reply.

"So if I say the word, it ends now."

Toby shrugged and cocked his head, as if it were all the same to him.

"And if not, we keep things as they are."

"Would you like for me to spell out the terms of a contract, Corinne? Let's call it mutually exclusive dating, with sexual privileges thrown in when both parties are agreeable. And nothing more."

"Now you're trying to make me mad."

"No, now I'm trying to get you to chill out."

Corinne took a deep breath, stood, then smoothed her robe. "Okay, I'm chilled. Great. I know you were just joking, but those terms sound fine to me."

"Great. Want to kiss on the deal?"

He didn't give her a chance to answer. He cupped her jaw and kissed her with all the finesse he could muster. If nothing else, he would do his damnedest to make sure she was agreeable as much as possible.

Chapter 12

"Now, there's a guilty-looking grin if I ever saw one."

Corinne looked up from her desk to see Becca walking in. Corinne just shrugged and smiled smugly.

"I was picking up my mail and I brought yours in, too." Becca dropped a few envelopes on the desk. "What are you smiling about?"

Corinne flipped idly through the envelopes and bit her lip. She had been thinking about Toby, of course. The fact that she had actually been about to tell Becca the truth surprised her somewhat. When she decided to come back to Aloma, she'd pictured a quiet, solitary life, spent in her own company. And now, suddenly, she not only had a boyfriend, but a girlfriend as well.

But she wasn't sure if she wanted to share this with anyone, not even Becca. She was afraid to think of it too much herself, afraid to let her mind dwell on it.

"Mmm, it's Toby," Becca concluded, half sitting on the desk.

"I have an idea," Corinne said calmly. "Let's talk about something else."

Becca tilted her head. "Okay. How about Christmas week? How's the play coming along?"

Corinne groaned and raked a hand through her hair. "We've only had two practices, so it's probably too early to predict a complete disaster, but...are you sure we *have* to do a play?"

"The senior class does the play, Corinne. It's a thirty-year tradition. Don't worry, you'll have time."

"To have the sets made, the costumes chosen and made. Not to mention getting the students to learn their lines, which will probably be hardest of all."

"You should talk to Mr. Davis. He did the play for years. He could help."

"I'm planning on it. He's already helping me with some of my classes when he can. I'll ask him to come to the auditorium one day soon and watch a rehearsal. Come to think of it, I might ask him to drill the boys on their lines when they come over to sit with him."

"He'd love it. How's that working out?"

"Pretty well, actually. The students hate it, of course. He makes them work. They're learning as much from their visits as they do in my class. His mind is still sharp most of the time. One day last week he kept trying to give me his laundry to do, though. He thought I was the cleaning lady."

"What did you do?"

Corinne shrugged. "I did his laundry. I was there anyway, and he was helping me. He remembered *Hamlet,* if he didn't remember me all too well. No harm done."

Becca looked at the clock above Corinne's head. "I need to turn these lesson plans in. Let me know if there's anything I can help with on the play. What's wrong?" she asked as she looked back down at Corinne.

Corinne stared at an envelope in her hand, hidden among the rest of her mail.

It was a letter from a network affiliate in Atlanta, Georgia. Corinne had a friend there who had talked to her last year about moving to Atlanta and starting a local talk show. Before she was shot, the talk show was what she'd hoped for, fell asleep at night thinking about. It had been her dream. She'd believed that if she succeeded at that, she'd finally feel worthy. She'd finally earn her mother's notice...and love.

Together, she and her friend had envisioned a new kind of show, geared toward solutions, hope and fixing problems rather than just airing them. Instead of simply showing pregnant teenagers or feuding families, they would match them with organizations that could help them. They would focus on people who were making a difference—normal, everyday people who went out of their way to lend a hand when it was needed. They'd bring actual help, not just publicity, to different problems. Instead of just saying, "someone should do something," they would be doing it. And then her mother would see that her sacrifices had all been worth it.

Corinne stared at the logo on the envelope. She had been so excited when they were planning the show. Even Don had welcomed the thought of moving to Atlanta. There was talk of going network if things went well.

"What is it, Corinne?" Becca leaned forward over the desk. "You're as pale as a sheet."

Corinne shook her head and shuffled the envelope back into the stack. "It's nothing."

"It's not about...about that shooting, is it?"

"No." Corinne stood and smiled, somewhat halfheartedly. "It's okay, it's just a friend from a long time ago." She tapped the envelopes together and bit her bottom lip. She could trust Becca. "We were in the process of starting a new show when I got shot. I just...I haven't thought of all that in a while. That whole business."

"Are they going ahead with the show?"

Corinne gave a jittery laugh. "I don't know. I'm afraid to open the envelope."

"Don't worry, Corinne. When the time comes, you'll make the right decision."

Corinne gave a thoroughly unladylike snort. "I haven't made any of the right decisions so far."

"You made the decisions you were supposed to make."

"Don't tell me you're one of those people—" Corinne began, then broke off. So much for maintaining a polite distance.

Becca smiled. "One of those people who believe everything happens for a reason? Yes, I am."

"I believe everything happens for a reason, too. But sometimes that reason is because someone was sick or crazy or violent or just plain stupid."

Becca sat on the edge of Corinne's desk and swung her foot. "I believe that things happen to teach us something. Events take place so we can learn the lessons we need to learn."

"Yeah?" Corinne asked, her chin set stubbornly. "And what lesson was I supposed to learn from getting shot? Don't do my job? Don't get involved? All I did was care very much about what happened to one man."

"Sorry." Becca gave her a sympathetic smile. "You have to figure that one out for yourself."

"Big help you are," Corinne said as she leaned back in her chair.

"Just tell me this," Becca asked. "What would it have taken to get you back to Aloma?"

Corinne gave a short, sharp laugh. "Getting shot in the head."

"There, you see." Becca smiled, spreading her hands in demonstration.

"You sound like Toby." Corinne peered closely at the envelope. "Like it was my destiny to be here with him."

"I don't know if Toby has anything to do with your destiny or not. But you're here for some reason. God has a plan for everyone."

Corinne held the envelope up to the light and squinted at it. "I never really believed in fate and destiny and all that. I believe you make your own destiny."

"Sure you do," Becca agreed. "Everyone makes their own decisions. But life puts you into certain situations where you learn what you need to learn, before you go to the next step."

"Maybe this letter is destiny's way of saying I need to get out of Aloma," Corinne said. "Why else would it come now?"

Becca shrugged as Corinne held the envelope up to the light again. "You know, that's yours. You can open it."

"I know," Corinne said, looking at the envelope as if she expected it to do something besides lay silently on her desk. With a fortifying breath, she tore off the end and slid the letter out into her palm.

Becca was patient for a few seconds. But only a few.

"No fair. What does it say? Are they going ahead with the show?"

Corinne stared at the letter. She nodded.

"Do they want you to do it?"

"Yes," Corinne said remotely. "Yes, they do."

Corinne thrummed her fingers on the desk and tapped her foot. With a sigh, she opened her bottom desk drawer and took out the letter, staring at it without reading it.

Three days of staring at it hadn't given her a clue as to what to do.

I know you planned on getting out of the business, and I don't blame you. But you must consider taking this horrible event and making some good out of it. You've become a symbol to the country, Corinne, a symbol of the ravages of racism and violence. You can bring attention and help in one of the most racially torn cities in this country. I know this is low, but I'm not too proud to play on your sympathies. I need you. I need your vision. You're the perfect one for the job. Remember, this was our dream.

Words that filled her mind, occupied her thoughts. And just five days ago, other words whispered in darkness. *You're mine, Corinne. I'll always take care of you.*

They were all words with the power of a magnet, drawing her thoughts to them again and again. Except magnets sometimes attracted, and sometimes repelled. It all depended on what was held against it. It all depended on her.

In front of her, a throat cleared noisily.

Corinne jerked her head up to see Jeremy Huckaby standing in front of her desk, his hands stuffed in his pockets and his bangs in his eyes.

"Jeremy!" She dropped the letter on the desk, then picked it up and folded it closed, her fingers running again and again over the creases. "What can I do for you?"

He scowled and wrinkled his nose, then finally said, "They said I had to get an entry form from you for the contest."

"The essay contest? You don't have to enter, Jeremy—"

"I know I don't have to enter," he said slowly, as if to a dimwit. "They said I had to come to you, though, if I wanted to enter."

Oh. Corinne hid her pleased surprise and opened her desk drawer. She dropped the letter in it and took out an entry form. "You realize that the deadline is in two weeks?"

He mumbled something she took to be assent.

"I'll need you to fill this out here, and I'll assign you a number. Put the number on your story. Don't put your name anywhere on it, or you'll be disqualified."

"I bet I would," he muttered as he took the form.

"Do you understand that this is a Christmas story contest? It must have a Christmas theme."

"I get it."

"I won't be judging the contest."

"I said I get it. No gross stuff." He slumped into a desk and began filling out the form.

"Exactly. No gross stuff." Yesterday afternoon she'd read his latest story submitted for class—one in which a teacher was kidnapped from a Halloween hayride, held captive in the woods, and tortured by one of her students. Amazingly, and happily, she'd been more amused than upset. She didn't believe for a minute that Jeremy was the one who had hauled her over the side of that trailer, because whoever had done it weighed a good thirty pounds more than Jeremy did.

He'd tried to claim the rock through her window with the same method—by writing a detailed essay of the event and why he'd done it. Corinne hadn't believed that one, either, because of all

the people who were furious the night of the homecoming game—
and they were numerous—Jeremy had the least reason to be upset
with her. In fact, she got the feeling he was happy she'd endorsed
the football players' suspensions.

Jeremy chewed on the end of his pen now and studied the form
with great concentration. He finished filling in the blanks, and sat
staring at it, turning his pen around and around in his hand and
chewing his lower lip.

"Who's judging?"

"I can't tell you that."

"Why? You afraid I'll get mad at whoever it is and throw a
brick through her window or something?"

Corinne lifted her chin and met his defiant gaze with a stronger
one of her own. "Yes. Something like that."

He looked away and fidgeted some more. "So, you think they're
looking for some mushy, hokey, happily-ever-after kind of thing?"

Corinne stood and walked around the desk, then leaned back
on it. "They're looking for a good story, period. I'm sure a happy
ending would be nice, though it's not mandatory. But I'm telling
you, Jeremy, if you turn in something bloody and gruesome—say,
have Santa Claus break into my house and slash my throat, there
will be trouble."

He snorted a short laugh before he resumed his bored and un-
impressed expression again. "I don't care."

"The administration will see it, and I won't be able to protect
you."

He rose from the desk. "I never asked you to protect me. I
never asked you for anything."

"I know. Let's just say, I'm probably the only one around here
who can take a joke."

He snorted again in derision. "Yeah, you and your boyfriend.
You're both a real riot. The happy do-gooders."

He glowered at the form and finally dropped it on the desk
beside her. "Don't do me any favors."

He slunk out the door with his hands stuffed back in his pockets.

"They're very bad, aren't they?"

Corinne choked on her coffee and looked at Mr. Davis. He

watched their Christmas play rehearsal, and she was hoping he could help them to improve. If she'd been looking for some encouragement, however, evidently she'd come to the wrong person.

"Actually, this is a good day. Yesterday half the curtain refused to open, and Josh fell off the back of his throne. We have some time left to iron out the kinks. Do you think we have a prayer?"

Mr. Davis shook his head, his mouth grim. He stood and clapped his hands, signaling them to stop.

"No, no, this is horrible. You all act like a bunch of dimwits slogging through the motions. This is a disgrace."

Corinne pursed her lips to keep from smiling.

"We're all going to stay here until I'm satisfied each of you has grasped the right attitude for your character." Mr. Davis paced in front of the stage, his hand to his chin. "Now, if you want to be the one to cause your classmates to miss their dinner, be the one to continue to act like a slog. Now, elves, get in your places up front. And stand up! Elves are full of pep and energy, they don't droop. Now, where is young Mr. Steinbeck? We'll start with the opening speech of the town crier...."

Corinne frowned and rose to stand beside Mr. Davis. She'd noticed lately that his periods of confusion were becoming more frequent. She'd hoped, though, that they could get through an hour rehearsal without him forgetting things. But there was no Mr. Steinbeck in their class.

She placed a hand on Mr. Davis's arm and was about to ask him if he'd like to go home, when Jeremy stepped forward, his face red. "Right here," he mumbled.

Corinne looked at Jeremy in confusion.

"Very good. Now, do as I told you Monday. Your speech is short, but the entire play hinges on it. It sets the mood for the rest to follow. The rest of you, what are you doing standing around? If you're not in this scene, get back! Get off the stage."

The rest of the cast scrambled off the stage. Corinne looked at Jeremy, her head cocked. Steinbeck? Had Jeremy told Mr. Davis that was his name? Jeremy shrugged and took his mark.

"I know very well that the boy's name is not Steinbeck, Miss

Maxwell,'' Mr. Davis said, his eyes focused squarely on Jeremy. ''I call him that because that's who I think of when I see him. And I can't remember his real name.''

Corinne shook her head and tried to hide her amazement. ''Steinbeck?''

''Yes. The young man's writing has many of Steinbeck's qualities, the way he can capture the plight of the common man. Now hush, he's about to give his speech.''

Corinne hushed obediently. She turned to face Jeremy, who stood at the front right of the stage, his script curled tightly in his hand. ''Well, are the elves gonna sing or not?'' he asked.

Corinne cued the elves to sing. They warbled painfully off-key for three lines. Then Jeremy took a deep breath, looked at Mr. Davis, lifted his chin, and spoke his lines.

There were only five of them, but until this moment, he'd mumbled them with his hands stuffed in his pockets and his hair hanging in his eyes. Now he stood stiffly, his shoulders back, his eyes focused on the back of the auditorium. His voice was clear and firm, a quiet sense of dignity playing through his words. His lines came out clearly, in the perfect tone for the town crier. Corinne's jaw dropped in astonishment.

Mr. Davis perfunctorily nodded his approval, and Jeremy stepped back into the wings. Corinne could see the faint tinge of pink still showing at his ears.

''Now, crowd, mill about the stage and set the scene. Remember, it is two days before Christmas and everyone is in a rush, a happy holiday rush....''

Corinne watched in amazement as the play unfolded slowly. Whereas she'd felt as if she were banging her head against a brick wall with the students, they obviously felt nothing but respect for the old man. Maybe it was his age, or the fact that Mr. Davis was practically an institution in Aloma, but whatever it was, he got them to respond. They were by no means ready for Broadway, but at least they might be ready for Christmas week.

Toward the end of the hour, she noticed Mr. Davis had grown quiet, and was looking around the empty auditorium. ''Do you need something, Mr. Davis?''

He shook his head, frowning. "I left it here, I'm sure." He dropped his voice and mumbled to himself, then moved back a few rows and crouched down.

Corinne followed him back and whispered, "What are you looking for?"

"It was right here—my file. And my grade book. I need my grade book, I have to do semester averages tonight. I had it right here."

His brow furrowed and he made a fist in agitation. "I'll wager one of those little heathens took it. They try to change their grades, you know. But I remember each one of them. They can't fool me."

"I think it's up front, Mr. Davis. You wait here and I'll go get it."

Corinne hurried up the side steps of the stage and found Jeremy, slumped in a chair backstage, watching the play.

"Jeremy, Mr. Davis needs to go home. Can you take him?"

"I don't have a car. It's too cold for him to be out walking."

"You can take mine." Corinne pulled her keys out of her pocket. "Just come back here, and I'll drive you home after rehearsal."

Jeremy stared at the keys in her hand in mixed astonishment and wariness. "You're letting me drive your car?"

"Yes, and please hurry."

Jeremy shrugged, his pride keeping him from saying anything else about the car. He picked up his textbooks and they edged silently back to the auditorium.

"Did he take his medicine?" Jeremy asked quietly when they got to the seats.

"I don't know. But he's starting to forget where he is. I don't want the rest of the students to see him like that."

Jeremy nodded. "Mr. D., we're done here. Let's go home."

Mr. Davis was quiet now, his face grim and defeated. He followed Jeremy down the aisle. "I need my grade book," he mumbled.

"I've got it," Jeremy said easily, patting his stack of schoolbooks. He opened the door for the older man and stepped back to let him through. "We can work on it when we get home."

Toby was climbing into his Jeep when he saw Jeremy drive by in Corinne's car. Mr. Davis was in the passenger seat. With a scowl he headed after them.

He pulled up at Mr. Davis's house as they were going up the walk. Toby fell into step behind them.

"Good evening, Mr. D., Huckaby."

Jeremy turned and gave him a quick grimace. "Before you even get started, she told me to take the car. I'm going back to pick her up after play rehearsal."

Toby lifted an eyebrow but didn't comment. When they got inside, Jeremy went directly to the kitchen table and picked up a small pillbox. With a frown he took out a pill and drew a glass of water.

"Here, Mr. D. Time to take the pill."

"What's that?" Toby asked, taking the glass from Jeremy.

The boy went back to the table and picked up the box. "You should know, you're the one who got them filled when we were in Abilene." He shoved the bottle at Toby.

Toby studied the label. "He was supposed to take this at lunch."

"I know that. And he didn't, obviously. His pill for today was still in the box." He jerked a thumb at Mr. Davis, who sat limply in his chair and stared at the floor, mumbling incoherently to himself.

Toby handed Mr. Davis the glass and Jeremy gave him the pill. "He doesn't like to take them. Whoever was supposed to check on him at lunch probably gave up. Here, Mr. D. Drink up."

"Who was supposed to see him at lunch?" Toby asked as Mr. Davis meekly took the pill without incident. He swallowed the water.

"Don't ask me, ask your mom. She's got everybody on a schedule. You didn't swallow the pill, did you, Mr. D?" He gently squeezed the old man's jaw until his mouth opened slightly. "Uh-huh, I knew it. Trying to trick me, aren't you? Gotta take another drink now. Wash it down.''

Mr. Davis swung his head away and batted at Jeremy with his hands. Jeremy took firm hold of his arms, though, and eventually Mr. Davis swallowed the pill.

Toby stuck his hands in his pockets, feeling like an intruder. ''Does he always take his pills?''

Jeremy looked scornfully at him, as if he resented his presence there. ''I guess so. Sometimes he misses the lunch one. It depends on who comes and checks on him.''

Toby nodded. He didn't know quite what to say; Jeremy seemed to have everything in hand. ''Who separates the pills out for him?''

Jeremy stood upright suddenly and sighed. ''I do, okay? I do it when I come by in the morning. You wanna read all the labels?'' He stomped to the table and grabbed a handful of pill bottles. ''This one and this one are after breakfast. Then he takes another one of these after lunch. Then this one after dinner. The lunch one is supposed to keep him from getting depressed.''

''Is that why he's like this now, because he missed the pill?''

''Are you even listening to me? I said it's to keep him from getting depressed. He gets confused no matter what he takes. But if he takes the pill, he doesn't get so pissed off about it.''

''Watch your language,'' Toby said automatically.

Jeremy held the bottles out to Toby, his mouth tight. ''Everything meet with your approval, *Sheriff?*''

''Actually, I was just thinking what a good job you're doing with him. I hoped the kids would be able to take care of him, and you're proof that it's working. I'm really proud of you, Huckaby.''

Jeremy sneered and walked back to the kitchen. ''Spare me, please. Are you gonna stick around here all night? I've gotta get the lady's car back to her.''

''Actually, I have some work to do. Can you stay here with him for a while? I'll pick up Corinne, and we can come by and get her car and take you home later.''

Jeremy waved him away. ''Go. Get on with your do-gooder sheriff chores. Enjoy it while you can.''

Toby stopped. "What's that supposed to mean?"

"Everybody knows you're out of here. Old Man Buchanan says he's gonna run you out of town. No way you're getting reelected next year."

"Is that so?" Toby cocked his head.

"Yeah, it's so. He said he was gonna make sure you and your girlfriend both left town."

"Is that right?"

Jeremy shrugged and took Mr. Davis's cup back to the kitchen.

"What did he say about Corinne?"

Jeremy leaned against the doorjamb and crossed his arms over his chest. "Just that since he's the president of the school board, he'll make sure she doesn't stay past the end of the semester. It don't matter, though. She already got another job."

Toby went perfectly still. "What?" he asked softly.

"She already got another job. In Atlanta."

Toby crossed the room in two steps. "What are you talking about?"

Jeremy put up his hands. "Hey, it's the truth. Don't get pissed at me, I'm just telling you. She got this letter. They want her for this new talk show. They want her real bad, too."

"How do you know about this?"

Jeremy cocked his head and met Toby's eyes unapologetically. "I looked. The letter was in her desk drawer."

"You need to stay out of her desk," Toby said automatically. He sank to the couch and rubbed the back of his neck. A talk show? In Atlanta?

"She's leavin', man. Blowing off this Podunk, and you with it."

Toby rubbed his face and tried to think. Why hadn't she said something? "It was a letter?"

Jeremy nodded and plopped down on the couch beside Toby. "Yep, got it a few days ago."

A few days ago. He'd seen her just last night. Why hadn't she said anything?

Did it matter?

"Sounded like some old friend of hers," Jeremy said. "They've been talking about it a while, from what I understood. Got sponsors for the show and everything. Sounds real cushy, huh?''

"Yeah, cushy. A talk show? Are you sure it was Atlanta? Maybe it was Abilene.''

Jeremy rolled his eyes. "I know how to read. It was Atlanta." He clapped Toby on the knee. "Face it, man. You're looking at taillights.''

Toby rose with a groan. "Stay here with Mr. D. I've got to go.''

Chapter 13

Corinne was waiting outside when Toby pulled up in front of the school. "Where's Jeremy?" she asked as she climbed in the Jeep. She leaned across the seat to give Toby a quick kiss, but he turned his head and steered the car onto the road. Corinne quirked her brows, then silently turned to fasten her seat belt.

"He's at Mr. Davis's house. I'll take you by there right now to get your car."

"How is he? When Jeremy took him home, he was pretty disoriented."

Toby pursed his lips. "When I left, he was sitting on the couch staring into space. Whoever was supposed to check on him at lunch didn't give him his pill." Toby slammed his hand against the steering wheel. "The idiot!"

"What's wrong?" Corinne asked quietly.

"I just told you. These kids are old enough to do this, and this is their duty, part of their community service. They can't even give a pill to an old man."

"Which boy was it? Maybe I can have a talk with him."

"Just don't worry about it, okay, Corinne?" he snapped. "It's my problem, I'll handle it."

Corinne looked at him and opened her mouth. But it was obvious he was in a rare temper, so she let it slide.

"Okay," she said evenly. "Let me know if I can do anything."

When they got to Mr. Davis's, Corinne picked up her keys that Toby had dropped on the seat beside him. She retrieved them, then moved without a word to get out of the Jeep. Toby grabbed her arm. "Hang on," he said gruffly.

She turned back, and he kissed her roughly, demandingly. She was too surprised and confused to resist. And even though he was obviously angry about something, she wasn't afraid of him.

He pulled back, breathless, and wiped a hand across his lips, not looking at her.

"You want to talk about it?" Corinne asked quietly, leaning back against her seat.

Toby shook his head. "No. I'm just... I'm sorry. Go home. I'll talk to you later."

"Are you coming over tonight?"

He shook his head again. "No. I've got some things to take care of. I'll see you...later."

Corinne nodded and rolled her lips together. "Okay. I'll see you."

Later, Toby sat on Mr. Davis's couch, one ankle crossed over his knee, staring into space. Mr. D. was in that strange, silent limbo that gripped him more and more often. Toby more than half wished he could join the old man there.

Atlanta. She'd told him she wasn't going back into that business.

But if she wasn't at least thinking about Atlanta, the letter would be in the wastebasket, not her desk drawer.

And she'd never hinted that she might stay.

Toby dropped his foot to the floor with a thud, made a sound somewhere between a groan and a sigh, and scrubbed his face with his hands.

"It's not always easy running the entire show, is it, Mr. Haskell?"

Mr. Davis's thin voice startled Toby. He let his hands droop between his knees and looked at the old man.

"You have only yourself to thank, however," Mr. D. said archly. "You've set yourself up with this responsibility."

"Sometimes I wonder why," Toby muttered, more to himself than Mr. Davis. But he knew why. It was his heritage. His birthright. And, therefore, his responsibility.

"Because the whole town worships you, that's why. Ninety percent of these people believe you hung the moon. Of course," Mr. D. said with a thin laugh, "the other ten percent want to string you up. But you relish that as well. Adds an element of excitement."

Toby drew his head back. "I think your percentages are off a bit. A lot. And no, I don't like it. I don't like it at all." He rubbed the back of his neck. "But like you said, I wanted the responsibility."

Mr. D. rose on wobbly legs, then hobbled slowly toward the kitchen. "I'm going to heat a can of soup for my dinner. You are invited to join me."

Toby hung back and watched, not wanting to patronize Mr. Davis by jumping in and taking over.

Mr. D. poured two cans of tomato soup into a saucepan. He waited until the soup bubbled on the stove, then reached over and flicked the burner off. He poured the soup into two bowls and placed them on the kitchen table, where Toby sat down across from the old man.

Mr. Davis slurped his soup quietly for a moment, then he laid down his spoon and looked Toby in the eye.

"You're going to think this is none of my business, but so what. You wanted the responsibility because your father wanted you to have it. Any fool could see you would have done anything for that man. And I'm sorry, but I think he took advantage of your hero worship to manipulate you into a life you might not have chosen for yourself."

Toby rubbed the back of his neck. "That's not true," he protested. "I'm happy doing what I'm doing. I care about this town—about this county. I care about the people in it." Of that much, Toby was certain.

"Are you happy because you're doing what you want, or because you know it's what your father wanted?"

"What difference does it make? I've worked hard—my father worked hard—to make this town a good place to live, to raise a family. It's a good life here."

Toby looked at Mr. Davis, a little surprised at how strongly he wanted to defend his father. And to his surprise he found that he actually *felt* like his father. "My father taught me to face my responsibilities, not to walk away from them. I expect to work hard, to do as much as he did and more. It's a privilege."

"But is it a sacrifice for you?"

Toby opened his mouth to answer, then closed it again. Was he truly happy? Had his father been truly happy?

But of course he had, Toby thought. The man had been a hero. Of course he'd been happy.

"It's not a sacrifice," Toby said defiantly. "I'm here because this is where I belong. This is my home, and everything I could ever want or need is right here." If Toby had heard his father say that once, he'd heard it a million times.

"Well, that's very admirable. But I wonder if you really do have everything you need. Anyway, I meant what I said. You are a good sheriff."

Toby sat down, a little dazed. What the hell had just happened? "Yeah, well, thanks. I guess."

"You're quite welcome."

Mr. Davis went to bed not long after that. Toby didn't feel like going home. Luke was at the station and he didn't want to go there, either. He sat on Mr. D.'s couch in the dark, the bizarre conversation still running through his head.

Had his father been happy?

But that was ridiculous. Toby had heard him say many times that everything he ever needed or wanted was right here within Aloma county lines. He'd said it often.

Too often?

Had his father ever sat on an old man's couch in the dark, feeling as if it were all out of his control, wondering what to do next?

The very idea was absurd. John Haskell had never spent a second of his life feeling unsure about anything.

"I'm trying, Dad," Toby whispered into the dark. Though the words were new to him, he realized that the feeling was not. It was what he'd always done: tried to please his dad.

Toby sneaked into Corinne's house a few hours later. He didn't want to frighten her, so he kept as quiet as he could, tiptoeing into her bedroom. He slid into bed beside her and wrapped an arm around her.

She jumped, but she was accustomed enough to having him in bed with her that she wasn't petrified.

"It's okay," he whispered. He nuzzled her neck. "It's just me."

She moaned softly and rolled closer to him, fitting her nose into the V of his neck. She wrapped her arms around his waist. "Hello," she murmured sleepily.

He held her that way for a long time, until she roused herself enough to raise her head. "No fair. You've got clothes on."

He kissed her deeply, holding her tight, enjoying the feel of her, soft and warm and pliant with sleep, her bones seeming to have melted. A couple of months ago, she would have been terrified at waking to find him in her bed. He had made a difference to her. He had, he swore to himself, his teeth clenched.

"I thought you were mad at me," she said softly.

He shook his head. "No. I'm sorry. I was upset."

"About Mr. Davis? Is he okay? Who's with him now?"

"Mom came over to spend the night. He's doing better now. Jeremy gave him his pills. Everything's...everything's okay."

Corinne nodded and snuggled up to him again. "I'm glad you came."

"So am I," he whispered. "So am I."

Later, after Corinne had drifted back to sleep, he smoothed her hair down and kissed the top of her head. "I'm trying, Dad," he whispered into the dark. "I'm still trying."

* * *

When she was a kid, Corinne had read a book called *The Terrible, Horrible, No Good Very Bad Day.*

She was having that day.

And it was the very first day back from Thanksgiving break.

To start the morning, her lesson plans had had to be completely redone in the five minutes before each class, because the films she'd ordered didn't come in. She'd realized that she was a week behind in her grading. And she'd just learned that a school board member would be sitting in on her classes to observe her. When, they wouldn't tell her. So she had that cheerful thought hanging over her head.

It became a moot point when she looked up to see Mrs. Meddlar leading a young girl into the English room during the lunch break.

Corinne put down her yogurt container and smiled. "Hi. Are you a new student?"

The girl giggled. Mrs. Meddlar said, "No, this is Katherine Hart. She's the new English teacher."

Corinne swallowed her first reaction, which was a snort of disbelief. "Really?" she said with a stiff smile. The girl looked all of five minutes older than the students she would be teaching.

Katherine nodded enthusiastically. "I'm graduating in less than a month, and already I have a job." She grinned and clasped her hands to her chest. "This is it," she said, doing a slow twirl around the room. "My first classroom. I'm so jazzed."

Corinne kept the smile plastered on her face. What difference did it make how young the girl was, after all? Didn't her obvious enthusiasm make up for her lack of experience? Isn't that what Corinne had fought to get people to think about her in her early days of reporting?

But the bitter taste was still in her mouth at the end of the day during play rehearsal. She looked around at the stage full of students who were in a worse mood than she was, and wondered why it bothered her so much that her days of teaching were winding to a close. Rather than being refreshed by the recent Thanksgiving break, it seemed the students were already getting burned out with preparations for the Christmas events, not to mention the looming midterms. Corinne knew just how they felt.

So it really made no difference at all to her that she'd been replaced without a word. So what if she was being tossed out like yesterday's garbage? She was a substitute. That was the agreement, wasn't it? Just one semester.

One person she was definitely not going to miss was Carl Buchanan. He had grown progressively more surly and petulant as the days wore on. He was mad at the world since the fiasco with the football team, and specifically angry with Corinne. It seemed that being suspended for those few games had effectively ruined his life forever, and he wasn't about to let anyone else forget it.

There was forty-five minutes left of the play rehearsal before she could go home. The way she was feeling, if she ever got out of this place, she'd never come back.

A shout sounded backstage. The back curtain billowed in for a moment, then a chair crashed over. The students onstage whipped their heads around. They all rushed to the back of the stage.

Corinne hurried up the steps and slipped through the knot of students gathered at the back of the stage.

Carl kneeled on top of Jeremy, one meaty fist raised and aimed at Jeremy's face.

"Stop!" Corinne shouted. She shoved at Carl's back and toppled him over. "Get up." She grabbed onto the back of his shirt and hauled him up.

His face was mottled red, and his fist remained clenched. She thought for a moment that he would strike her. His breath hissed out through clenched teeth. A trickle of blood ran down his chin, and one eye was already swelling shut. He wrenched out of Corinne's grasp and swung away.

Jeremy stood; his lip was split, and blood dribbled down from his nose.

"What happened?" Corinne asked. "Carl? Jeremy?"

Silence. The two boys glared at each other, and the students around them shifted uncomfortably, but no one spoke.

Corinne gritted her teeth, wishing she could just walk away from the whole scene. The class looked to her expectantly.

Waves of animosity flowed from Carl and Jeremy. Dread filled Corinne. There was no way she was letting these two go to finish this fight somewhere else. "I'm going to call your parents and have them come get you," she said. "And you'll be in Mr. Sammons's office first thing in the morning."

Carl shook his head. "I have my pickup. I can take myself," he grumbled.

"I don't care. I'm calling your parents. They'll come get you." There was no way she was letting those two go, unsupervised. Jeremy would end up in a body cast if she did.

"Go ahead and call my *parent*," Jeremy said with a sneer, wiping blood from his lip.

"The rest of you go on home," Corinne said. "We're through for the day."

Corinne jogged down the dark, deserted streets of Aloma and tried to clear the day from her mind. It was cold out, and the chilly air burned her lungs as she drank in deep gulps. Her legs were growing heavy. She couldn't seem to get the adrenaline rush that usually accompanied her jogs.

And she couldn't seem to get Carl and Jeremy off her mind. What a terrible afternoon. Did teachers go through this kind of craziness often? She wouldn't have thought so, not in Aloma.

She almost wished she hadn't called the boys' parents after their fight. She didn't know what else she could have done, though. She couldn't have let them go.

But calling Dan Buchanan—that was almost as bad.

Corinne grimaced and pushed herself to run up the hill. She tried to block out the memory of Dan Buchanan's furious face. As her running shoes slapped the pavement, Corinne couldn't help glancing over her shoulder to make sure the man's enraged countenance wasn't still focused on her.

While JoAnn Huckaby had been apologetic and concerned about the situation, Dan Buchanan was livid that the school was once again persecuting his son. He'd stood in the school parking lot and ranted. This school had ruined his son's life, had robbed him of what future he had. Carl had no future now, thanks to Toby and Corinne. For good measure, he'd attacked Jeremy. The kid was a bad apple and got everyone into trouble with him, a damned derelict headed for the state pen just like his old man.

Corinne had watched in dismay as JoAnn's cheeks flamed, and she realized with deep regret that she'd thought close to the same thing about Jeremy once.

Dan had ranted on and on, until everyone left except Corinne. She'd tried to talk to him, tried to keep the situation from growing any more out of control than it was. But when it had become apparent that he just wanted to argue, she'd left, too. He was still yelling and waving a fist as she drove away.

She laughed to herself without humor. And she thought teaching was going to bring her peace.

She thought about jogging to the courthouse to see Toby. She was worried about Carl, though the trouble he was in was his own doing. But Dan had been in such a rage when she left them, she was uneasy with the idea of Carl being around him.

She turned at the corner to her street and headed home. She'd shower first, then head to the courthouse. Maybe she could talk Toby into driving out to the Buchanans to check on things.

But as she rounded the corner, she saw it wasn't necessary. Carl was driving toward her.

Corinne jogged over to the left shoulder of the road to get out of the way. Carl's pickup weaved down the road; he was driving too fast. He gunned it suddenly, and her heart leapt to her throat as she realized he must have recognized her. Instantly, the memories of the rock through her window, of arms that closed around her and pulled her off the Halloween hayride, along with the memory of a gun jamming into her cheek—all flashed through her mind at once.

The pickup roared closer. Corinne's heart stopped when she realized that he was intentionally heading straight for her. Her house was just ahead. She sprinted forward, and leapt over the low rock wall that surrounded her yard. She landed painfully, one knee striking the dirt, and rolled.

The pickup swept past with a cloud of exhaust and the rumble of a bad muffler. Inside, she could hear Carl laughing uproariously at the sight of her sprawled on her grass, terrified.

He sped past, careering into the middle of the street. He over-corrected. Carl slammed on the brakes and wrenched the wheel at the last moment. With the squeal of brakes and a crash, Carl drove through two mailboxes and into a low retaining wall across the street. The pickup bounced up a few feet, then came to rest.

Corinne rose from the ground and ran to check on Carl. He'd hit the wall pretty hard, and she seriously doubted he was wearing a seat belt.

She crossed the street and yanked open the passenger door. The stench of alcohol filled the cab of the pickup. An empty bottle lay on the floor.

''Carl! Are you okay?''

Carl slumped against the door, but he was conscious. A red gash slashed his forehead, apparently where he had struck the steering wheel.

''Carl! Answer me.''

Carl looked blearily at her and sneered. He muttered something unintelligible and looked out his windshield.

A light came on inside the house closest to them. Corinne waved and called to them. ''He's hurt. Call the hospital. And call the sheriff!'' She didn't know if anyone heard her or not.

She leaned back into the cab. Carl was reaching for the ignition. The pickup had conked out when it hit the wall, and Carl was trying to start it again.

''Oh no you don't,'' he said as he cranked the ignition. ''You're not getting me into trouble again. Screw that!''

The motor caught and rumbled to life.

''No, don't!'' Corinne cried. She leaned across the seat and tried to grab for the keys. They were out of reach. She slid onto the seat and tried again. ''You're drunk. You can't drive.''

He grinned wildly and showed her his middle finger. ''And screw you!''

Corinne lunged for the keys again.

''Get out!'' Carl slapped at her hand and put the pickup into reverse. They lurched away from the wall.

Corinne clutched the seat belt and hung on for dear life as the pickup began moving. Her feet skidded across the gravel. She braced herself on her elbows and lifted her feet into the air. "Carl, no! Stop."

Ignoring her, Carl weaved the pickup in a wide arc out of the yard, once again hitting the mailboxes. Corinne flung herself farther onto the seat and tried to roll over. Her door swung open wide as the pickup careened wildly.

"Carl!" she screamed.

"Get out!" he yelled, not looking at her. He slammed the pickup into Drive. She would have to jump out now, before he got going too fast.

Instead, as the pickup leapt forward, she grabbed for the handle and slammed the door shut.

Chapter 14

Toby's chair gave an agonized squeak as he leaned back and propped his boots on the scarred wooden desktop. He crossed his arms over his chest and studied Jeremy Huckaby who sat silently across from him. The boy stared at a spot on the floor. JoAnn Huckaby had brought him in ten minutes ago, eaten up with worry. "I don't know what I'm going to do with him, Toby. He just doesn't care anymore. I don't think I can handle losing them both." She meant, of course, having her husband and her son in jail. Which was where Jeremy seemed bent on going. She'd left her son with Toby, in the hopes that Toby could talk some sense into him.

Toby had talked to Corinne earlier, and she told him about the fight. She didn't know who had started it, just said that Carl had been acting like a jerk all day. Toby felt like belting both boys, just for making Corinne sound as drained as she had this afternoon.

"So," Toby said nonchalantly. "Did you get in any good licks before Miss Maxwell broke y'all up?"

Jeremy's eyes widened a little, but he didn't look up. "A couple," he mumbled.

"Good. I'm sure Buchanan deserved it."

Jeremy had no comment.

"Your mom looked run-down. I imagine this is hard on her, being alone now."

"She's not alone. She has me and my brother. We help out."

"Some help you are. Getting into trouble all the time, worrying her half to death. Have you thought at all about how all this makes her feel?"

"I know how it makes her feel," Jeremy said through gritted teeth, raising his head and meeting Toby's eyes for the first time. "I'm the one who can hear her crying in her room at night. So don't play family counselor with me, Sheriff. Are you going to call my probation officer or not?"

Toby shrugged. "I think we'll just stay in here and chat for a while."

Jeremy snorted and leaned back in his chair, looking as if he couldn't care less.

"So, what were you two fighting about?"

"Why don't you ask Buchanan?"

"I would, except you're here and he's not. Besides, I'm sure his dad is having this same discussion with him right now."

"Which is what started the whole thing in the first place," Jeremy mumbled.

"What's that supposed to mean?"

Jeremy set his mouth stubbornly and resumed his examination of the spot on the floor.

"I'm on duty until 6:00 a.m., Huckaby. You can sit here and keep me company all night if you want."

Jeremy lifted his brows and chewed the inside of his lip, but didn't say anything.

That was okay. Toby could figure it out for himself. Knowing what bullies both Dan and Carl Buchanan were, it wasn't difficult to see what was going on.

And obviously the threat of getting in trouble with the law wasn't going to get him anywhere with Jeremy. Maybe it was time to switch tactics.

Toby sighed, clicked his tongue, and shook his head sadly. "I tell you, Huckaby, I feel for you. I really do."

Jeremy looked at him and sneered.

"No, I'm serious. After all you've been through, no one could blame you for getting your feelings hurt."

"My feelings weren't hurt. He smarted off, and I popped him."

"Hey, don't take it personally. I've heard all the bull that Dan Buchanan has been spreading around town. He thinks Carl's not going to get into a good college now, since he has a record and all. Which means he won't be able to get into pro football. If you want to know my opinion, the kid isn't good enough to play pro ball in the first place, and I'm a good scapegoat for him, but that's just me."

Jeremy chewed his thumbnail and looked bored.

"As a matter of fact, if you want my opinion—"

"Which I don't."

"—I think they're just looking for something to complain about. None of the other kids arrested that night are even talking about it anymore. It's old news. But Dan Buchanan was always like that. Always looking for something to bellyache about. Always looking for someone to bully around. I guess Carl is a little too much like his dad."

"He wasn't bullying me around," Jeremy flared. "I told you. He said some things. I hit him. End of story."

Toby smiled sympathetically. "It's okay, man. I know how that's got to hurt—"

"Look, Sheriff," Jeremy said, his lips a thin angry line, "I don't need your pity. I handled things just fine, and if your old lady hadn't butted in, I would have handled it even better."

"Don't call her that," Toby said automatically.

"And he didn't hurt my feelings." Jeremy's eyes sparked, hot and angry. His breathing came harsh. "He said some things he shouldn't have said. I just got sick of hearing it, you know? He needs someone to shut him up. That's all."

"What did he say?"

Jeremy took a deep breath and looked away again.

"What did he say, Huckaby?"

Silence.

"Okay, let me guess. It was about your dad."

Jeremy snorted, shifted in his chair, and mumbled something unintelligible.

"It must have been, because that would be an easy target for Carl, and nothing else would have gotten you mad enough to hit someone twice your size."

Jeremy mumbled again.

"What was that?" Toby asked.

"He's not twice my size."

"Oh. Yeah, okay. Whatever you say."

Jeremy rose quickly from the chair.

"Look, man, am I under arrest or what? I don't have to stay here and let you play psychologist. I mean, I'm free to go anytime, right? If you're going to call my probation officer, do it and get it over with."

"That's what you want, isn't it?" Toby asked quietly.

Jeremy paced around the room, but instead of leaving, he walked to the window. His back was stiff, his hands shoved into his back pockets.

"Yeah," he said after a moment. "That's what I want."

"I don't blame you. It's got to be hard, staying around here where everybody knows you, knows what your dad did."

"You know what?" Jeremy asked, his back to Toby. "You ought to just stop talking about things you don't know anything about."

"I can imagine. Knowing that every time someone looks at you, they're thinking about Pete, and either thinking—"

"Shut up!" Jeremy yelled. He crossed his arms over his chest, still facing the window. "Just shut up. You don't know a damned thing. Your dad wasn't a sorry, no-good son of a—" He broke off with an angry growl.

"You're right." Toby stood and walked around to the front of the desk. He stayed there, maintaining a safe distance. If he touched the boy now, showed any sympathy at all, Jeremy would be out the door like a shot. So Toby would stay back, hopefully draw him out a little more.

"You're right. I don't know. Neither does anyone else in this town. Especially Carl Buchanan. So if he smarts off about your dad, you can't take it all that personally. He's just—"

"He didn't say anything about my dad. He was..." Jeremy shook his head and sighed deeply, scratching his arm agitatedly. "He was talking about this story I wrote. This Christmas story. Talking about how hokey it was and all."

Toby rubbed the back of his neck and chewed on that for a moment. This was a curve he wasn't expecting.

"You wrote a Christmas story?"

"Yeah," Jeremy said, irritation in his voice. "I like to write sometimes. Big deal. There's this contest, and they're going to publish the winner in the *Aloma Sentinel*. I entered. It was supposed to be confidential."

"How did he get ahold of it?"

"How the hell should I know? Maybe his mom was a judge or something. Anyway, it was about this family being reunited at Christmas, and he guessed it was mine. He said it was sappy and I should send it to *True Confessions* magazine."

"It sounds really nice—"

"It was a sappy load of bull and Carl was right."

"I think it's a good idea for you to write about your family. It's good therapy—"

"Did I say it was about my family?" Jeremy rounded on him. "Did I say that? No, I did not. Because it's not about my family. Quit reading into things."

Toby took a deep breath and chewed his bottom lip. "Okay, it wasn't about your family. My mistake."

"Why does everything have to be about him, anyway? No matter what I do, that's what it's all going to come down to from now on—" His voice broke suddenly, and tears sprang into his eyes. He clenched his jaw, breathing hard through his teeth, his hands fisted at his sides. The veins in his arms stood out. Toby wasn't sure if the boy needed a shot to the jaw or a hug.

He moved away from the desk. Jeremy took a step back, murder in his eyes.

"It doesn't have to be about him."

"Of course it does. You don't know anything, Sheriff. You don't know what it feels like to have everyone think you're trash. Hearing the things they say when they think you can't hear, or when they intentionally say it loud enough for you to overhear."

"You're right. I don't know." Toby stuck his hands in his pockets to keep from reaching out.

Jeremy shook his head. "I don't get it, man." He wandered idly around the office, the tension whirring off him like a live wire. "Why would he do something like that?" His voice was soft now, as if he were thinking out loud. "Why?"

Toby leaned a hip on the desk and folded his arms across his chest. "It's a mistake a lot of people make, Jeremy. I guess it's all about the money."

"Of course it's about the money. It's always about money, isn't it?"

It was Toby's turn to shrug.

"I mean, why would he do it, though? Any idiot could see how it was going to turn out. Was a bigger house, a bigger car, or a big-screen TV worth everything he's putting our family through? And we probably won't even get to stay in our house. The bank's going to foreclose any day now. And how's that going to make Mom feel? Or Bradley? He's just a little kid."

Toby chose his words carefully. "You have to know, Jeremy, that no one in this town blames Bradley, or thinks any less of him because of what your father did."

"Yeah, right."

"It's true."

"Which explains Carl Buchanan and his dad. You should have hard him yellin' this afternoon. 'A no-account hoodlum, headed for the state pen just like his old man.' That's what the old fart said about me. Because I had the nerve to stand up to his stupid kid."

"Don't blame Dan for that. You are doing your best to land yourself in jail."

"And why not? Everyone thinks the worst of me anyway. That would really make him proud, wouldn't it? A chip off the old block. Maybe we could get a cell together."

At last Toby understood what this was all about. To hurt his father, to get even with him, Jeremy would throw away his life, would purposely get himself into trouble. He would hurt his father in the same way his father had hurt him.

And it would work, too. Toby had been the one to arrest Pete Huckaby. And the thing Pete had been most worried about was his family. He hadn't wanted his wife and kids to see him in handcuffs. As stupid as he'd been to put himself in the situation in the first place, Toby couldn't help but feel sorry for the guy.

Toby wondered what he was going to say next. Was it moments like these, crucial seconds in a person's life, that determined the next direction, the choice between one road or another? He wished suddenly, fervently, that Corinne were here. She would know what to say.

Thinking of Corinne gave him an idea.

"You can throw your whole life away just to get even if you want to, but the only person you're going to be hurting is yourself. You have a bright future ahead of you, no matter what Dan Buchanan says. Mr. D. told me you have keen insight." Toby pulled a face and shrugged. "Of course, we have to take into account his questionable state of mind."

Jeremy smiled feebly at his joke, surreptitiously wiping a tear from the corner of his eye and sniffing.

"And Miss Maxwell says you're the best writer in the school."

"I'll just bet she did," he said, sniffing again. He cleared his throat. "I'm sure she told you all about my essays."

Toby raised his brow. "Not really. Just that you had a good imagination and a flair for vivid descriptions."

"Yeah, right. She never told you how I was trying to scare her, I'm sure." Jeremy's voice was full of derision.

Toby's blood chilled. "What are you talking about?"

Jeremy looked at him warily. "She really didn't tell you?"

"No, but you'd better. Now."

Jeremy stuck his hands in his back pockets and studied the floor. His obvious regret didn't stop Toby's rising anger.

"The first day of school, we were supposed to write an essay. I was really—well, I didn't want to be there, and so..."

"And so what?" Toby went perfectly still, his fists clenched at his sides.

"I was going to scare her. So I wrote this story about this reporter who, um, who got shot in the face."

Toby's blood went from hot to cold and back again. It didn't matter that the person standing before him was a kid, a kid who obviously regretted what he'd done. It didn't matter that a moment ago, he had recognized that the boy was lashing out from his own pain and sense of betrayal. He'd lashed out at Corinne. And that changed everything.

"You sorry son of a—" Toby took two steps forward, then hung there on the balls of his feet, trembling with impotent rage.

"I know, I know," Jeremy said. He took a few cautious steps backward. "I shouldn't have done it. I wish I hadn't, now."

"Then why the hell did you?" Toby roared.

"I don't know. She thought she was so smart. I was just—I was really mad. I thought she'd tell Sammons and my probation officer. I thought I'd get sent somewhere. I didn't want to go to school where everyone knew me. But no matter what I did, nobody would really do anything to me except tell me to straighten up and then they'd look at me and I knew they were feeling sorry for me, and I just—"

He broke off and grimaced with frustration. "I mean, what does a guy have to do to get sent away around here? I tried everything I could think of."

He shook his head miserably. "I was just really mad. And she was so cool and sure of herself. And I don't know why, but that made me even madder. I just took it out on her, I guess."

Toby nodded, his jaw clenched tight, anger humming through his veins. "Yeah, I guess you did. Just like Dan takes it out on Carl, and Carl takes it out on you. Everybody's angry, and everybody's passing it around." His mouth flattened into a grim line. "Just get out of here. Get the hell out."

Now that he was free to go, Jeremy hung there, hesitant.

"Go on," Toby said, walking back behind the desk.

Jeremy took a step backward, but didn't leave.

Toby worked his jaw and picked up a handful of papers, having

10 idea what he was looking at. He could happily have throttled the kid, right then and there.

"Was that the only time?" His voice grated between his lips. "That first day?"

Jeremy scratched his forehead and cleared his throat. "Not exactly."

"Tell me, exactly," Toby said icily.

"Later, when she told us to write a short story, I wrote about this English teacher that gets...umm...gets harassed by her students."

"Harassed?"

"Yeah, you know, students giving her a hard time." He bit his lip and shuffled his feet.

Toby put down the papers and leaned his fists on the desk, glaring at Jeremy. "And in your story, what did these students do to her?"

"They, um—well, actually it was just one kid, and he threw a rock through her window one time, and another time he kidnapped her from the Halloween carnival and held her hostage out in this little shack in the middle of this pasture."

In a flash, Toby was around the desk and had Jeremy by the collar.

"Hey, it wasn't me, man. It wasn't me."

"You're about to get your wish, Huckaby. I'll have you locked up so fast, it'll make your head swim."

"It wasn't me, either time. I just heard about it, and I wanted to give her a hard time. I didn't do it, I swear."

Toby's face curled into a snarl. "Why should I believe a word you say?"

"I promise, man, it wasn't me. I just heard the others guys talking about it. And I wanted her to think it was me."

"Then who was it? If it wasn't you, who was it?" Toby jerked Jeremy by the collar and glared into his eyes, inches from his own.

Jeremy hesitated for a moment, his eyes darting around the room.

"It was Buchanan," he finally said. "It was Carl, both times. He said that if it wasn't for her, you would probably back down and drop the charges. And he would still get to play football. He blamed her for the whole thing. He said she should keep her mouth shut and stick to what she was good at—keeping you happy.''

Toby let go of Jeremy and walked around the room, his mind numb with rage. He would kill him. When he got ahold of him, he would tear him apart. "He's a—" He rattled off a few choice words inappropriate for the company of a teenager. "He was going to kidnap her?"

"He said he wasn't going to hurt her. He was just going to drag her off into this old shack out there. Scare her. Said he wanted to see her cry. Then he would say it was all a part of the act, the whole haunted hayride thing. She couldn't do anything to him. He'd get away with it, scot-free. But then you chased him.''

"Why would he do that to her? I'm the one who arrested him.''

"What, do you think he's going to do something to you? He's a putz. He only messes with people weaker than him.''

Toby dragged a hand through his hair and shook his head in disbelief. "Why would he do that? Why would anyone want to hurt her?''

Jeremy chewed on his lip. "I guess he just wanted to get to her because she was tight with you. He couldn't get to you, so he did the next best thing.''

Toby walked around the office, scrubbing his face with his hands. "Just get out, Huckaby. I don't care anymore what you do.''

Jeremy stood there and cleared his throat awkwardly. "I thought she would tell you about the essays. I thought she would tell you I was dangerous and should be sent away. I did everything I could think of. I tried to convince that stupid shrink in Abilene that I was unstable. And what does he do? Sends me home and tells me to get more involved in after school activities. That's why I wrote the one about the hayride. Because I thought she would tell you it was me, and you would..." He trailed off as he realized Toby wasn't listening anymore. "I thought she would tell you," he mumbled.

"Yeah, you would think she would tell me," Toby said grimly. He leaned a hip on the desk and rubbed the back of his neck.

"I wish—I wish I hadn't done it. It was a stupid thing to do. She's pretty cool. She's a good teacher."

Toby remained silent. Corinne had called him idealistic. He must have been blind. His town. His people. Where had all this hate come from?

"Maybe you should try to talk her out of going to Atlanta," Jeremy offered tentatively.

Toby snorted.

"You could ask her to stay. She likes you. She would, maybe, if you asked."

"Why would she want to stay here? So you idiots can threaten her and harass her and make her life hell?"

"You could tell her that...that I'm sorry. That I didn't mean anything. I was just—"

Toby shook his head and moved back behind the desk, feeling wiped out. "You have something to say to her, say it yourself. I'm not going to clean up after you."

Jeremy nodded unhappily. Toby didn't care how remorseful he looked. He thought of Corinne, and he was ashamed. Ashamed of Carl, of Dan, of Jeremy. Of himself. Here he'd been trying to convince her this place was some kind of Utopia, and it was really just a hateful little hole-in-the-wall town. He'd gone wrong somehow. To think she'd come back for some peace—

The phone rang.

"Sheriff's office," he mumbled into the receiver. He groaned and rubbed the back of his neck. "What is it this time, Mrs. Kirby? Someone break in and change the channels on your television?"

He listened for a minute and sank into his chair. "Yes, yes, I know," he said tiredly. "You're only trying to do your part as a good citizen. Yes, I appreciate it. No, I do. Really. Now, what is it?"

A second later he jumped from his seat. "What? What the— why didn't you say so? Okay, okay, I'm sorry—when? How fast was he going? She was in there with him? Are you sure?" He listened for a second longer, his body taut as a pulled bow. "Which way did they go? Think!" He picked up the Rolodex from the desk and hurled it at the wall. "Think! Are you sure? Okay."

He slammed down the phone and headed for the door, grabbing his hat off the rack as he shouted to Jeremy, "Call Luke and tell him to get down here. Carl Buchanan just ran down a row of mailboxes and took off, hell-bent for leather. Corinne's with him."

Corinne's hands trembled as she dug between the seat cushions to find the clip to the seat belt. The knowledge that she'd made a huge mistake screamed in her mind. She tried not to think about how fast Carl was driving.

"Carl, pull over and let me drive. We can go down to the Dairy Queen and get a hamburger."

"Go to hell. Nobody asked you to come along."

Corinne took a deep breath. She'd covered a few hostage situations in her life. Hell, she thought wildly, she'd actually *been* a hostage. Surely she had learned something.

"Carl," she said evenly, though her heart rocketed along almost as fast as the pickup. "I understand that you are upset. That was a bad scene today at the school, and I know that it's bothering you. But believe me, we can work it out. We can talk to Mr. Sammons, and I'm sure—"

He slammed down on the accelerator and the pickup fishtailed. "Shut up!" he yelled. "You just shut up. You don't know what you're talking about."

"Then tell me," Corinne said. "Pull over and let's talk about it." She reached a hand out to him.

He jerked, and the pickup hit the shoulder of the road. Gravel spun up and knocked loudly against the undercarriage.

He pulled hard back onto the road, sending them into the oncoming lane. Corinne gasped.

"Carl! Watch the road!"

Carl laughed. "Scared ya, huh?" He twisted the wheel back and forth, swerving over the road, laughing. Corinne shrieked and put her hand on the dash to brace herself.

"Stop it! Pull over now." She forced some authority into her voice. "Pull over, and I'll drive."

Carl grinned idiotically at her. "Okay." He slammed on the brake. Tires squealed, and Corinne flung forward until her seat belt caught her.

"Psych!" Carl yelled, and accelerated again.

Corinne closed her eyes and leaned back in the seat, bracing her feet against the dash.

Carl saw her and laughed again. "Where's your snotty attitude now, you interfering bitch? Knocked you down a peg or two, didn't I? Should have done it that night. Shoulda gone through with it."

Corinne started to ask what he meant, then decided she didn't want to know.

But evidently the thought had reminded Carl of something. "Yeah, that's what we'll do. We'll take a little trip out there and show you what happens to people who screw up my life."

He mumbled to himself and looked out at the black night around them. For a moment he seemed to forget she was there.

But then he turned on her again, grinning maliciously. "Gonna take a little trip to the middle of nowhere. Where there ain't no lover-boy sheriff to save you."

He nodded to himself. "Yeah, see how you like it. You should have kept your mouth shut and got it over with at Halloween. I was just gonna scare you then. Who knows what I'm liable to do now?" He smiled again and reached across to pinch her cheek, hard.

She jerked away. "What are you talking about? I don't even know—"

"Shut up!" Lightning fast, his mood grew dark again. "I'm talking about Halloween. I had it all planned out. You were gonna come out to the pasture and stay a while with me. Then I'd let you go, and it would all be like a big joke. Part of the Haunted Hayride experience," he said mockingly. "But then you and lover-boy got back together, so I changed my mind. He can't take a joke."

He scowled and swerved off the road. Corinne choked on her own breath, her heart lurching as the pickup bounced hard off the pavement and barreled down a dirt road.

"That was...that was you?" she asked, one arm braced on the seat beside her, the other against the door. "The one who pulled me off the hayride?"

The scene Jeremy described in his story came back to her. Except it had been Carl, not Jeremy, who had planned to stand over her with a gun, laughing hysterically as she pleaded for her life. Carl behind the mask. "But you would never have gotten away with it. Someone would have found me—"

"Of course they would have found you, eventually. I wasn't going to do anything to you, just scare you. Bring you down a notch or two—" The pickup swerved and went into the ditch. The pickup leaned hard to her side, and for a second Corinne could see weeds slap against her window. Carl wrenched the wheel hard, and they lurched back up to the dirt track.

"Carl, please, pull over." The pleading was strong in her voice. Just like before, she was begging for her life. Just as he'd planned.

He ignored her. "Gonna take a little trip out to the country," he sang off-key. "Gonna have a little fun with the teacher."

"Why did you do that?" Corinne asked, as much to keep his attention as to know. "Why did you want to scare me?"

"Because, you interfering bitch, you ruined my future. If you hadn't opened your fat mouth, Haskell woulda dropped the charges and I still would have gotten to play. But no." He threw her a hateful glare. "You holier-than-thou, self-righteous, interfering..." He trailed off. Corinne was glad. If he called her a bitch one more time, she was going to slap him and damn the consequences.

"And now I have nothing!" His furious voice filled the cab. He turned angry eyes to her, ignoring the road. Corinne stared straight ahead, watching in terror as they hurtled over a hill. She caught flashes of wooden fence posts, and tumbleweeds built up against them. They bounced hard over the road, and in the impact her teeth cracked together and she tasted blood.

Another hill, another hard bounce. Carl's face drew tight, and he growled low in his throat. He stomped hard on the gas, and the pickup fishtailed in the dirt. This made him angrier. He wrenched on the wheel.

Corinne saw fence posts looming ahead, and screamed. They

hit the dirt embankment with a loud thud, and sailed over the ditch. For a moment, they were airborne. She heard a metallic scrape and a loud knock. Barbed wire and a crooked wooden fence post hung from the passenger mirror. They touched down with a mighty crash. The bed of the truck bounced up. For a heart-stopping moment, Corinne thought they were going to flip end over end.

She heard a loud inrush of air, and looked over at Carl. His door was open. He was gone.

It was then that she looked up and saw the tree, straight ahead. It was the last thing she saw.

The first thing Corinne saw when she came to was a thin, crooked branch of mesquite, half an inch from her face. She blinked, licked her lips, and stared at it for a moment, before pushing it away. It broke off and fell to the seat beside her.

She looked across the cab. The driver's door hung crookedly open, letting in the frigid air. Carl was gone.

''Carl?'' she tried to call. Her voice was weak and rusty. Silence weighed heavily around her. She wondered how long she'd been unconscious. The moonlight was barely bright enough to make out the shapes around her—an empty cotton field, slim stalks plucked bare in the recent weeks, and a small stand of mesquite trees, directly in front and to the left of them. The branch that cracked through the windshield extended to a tree, imbedded in the front bumper of the truck.

She tried to get out of her seat so she could find Carl, but a heavy weight held her fast. She opened the door with an agonized metallic screech, and tried to slide out. Her mind fogged and her muscles felt weak as pudding. She struggled for a moment, then collapsed back against the seat with a tired sigh.

Maybe she had died in the accident. The inane thought flitted through her head that it was probably her just due to end up in a cotton field. A bit ironic. Then she thought of Toby. He would be upset that she'd left him again. She was always leaving him. He would never know that she'd fallen in love with him again. That she'd never fallen out of love with him.

Then she realized her seat belt was still fastened. She pushed the red button and stumbled onto the cold field.

She moved around the front of the pickup, tripping on tall grass and stumbling over low branches. She moved around the tree, pushing aside branches that scratched at her face and arms. Carl lay on the ground, under the back wheel.

Corinne froze when she saw him. He was very still—a dead stillness that went beyond mere absence of movement. He was dead, she knew. And she didn't want to know any more.

She waited for the panic to come, to overwhelm her. Almost welcomed it, because it would come and take her away from this, give her somewhere to go besides here. She waited, and stared at Carl.

But instead of the roar of her breath and the thud of her heart, she heard only the voice of Toby.

I'm here now. I'll take care of you.

She felt him beside her, encouraging her. He would be the one to encourage her, she thought. He and her aunt were the only ones who'd ever believed in her.

Of its own volition, her body moved forward, until she knelt beside Carl. As if it were someone else doing it, she reached out and touched cold fingers to the side of his neck.

She wasn't sure if it was his pulse she was feeling, or the rapid beat of her own heart, throbbing in her fingertips. But he moaned and shifted, and she let out the breath she didn't know she'd been holding.

"Carl," she said softly, tapping him on the face. "Carl, wake up." She looked around them again, disoriented. She couldn't even remember which direction they'd taken from town. A blessed, numbing fog clouded her brain. "Carl."

He remained silent, breathing shallowly. Corinne started to lift him, but stopped, not knowing how badly he was hurt, not wanting to make it worse. Gingerly she ran her fingers over his head, checking for wounds. Her fingers came away sticky with warm blood, but not a lot. Detached, she continued her exploration down both arms and his torso, checking for anything.

His legs stretched out under the bed of the pickup, and she

squatted, feeling with fingers gone numb either from shock or cold. Her head reeled, and she braced herself with one hand on his stomach to keep herself from falling over.

Her hand stretched down, across the cold denim covering his thigh—and struck metal.

Confused, she bent and searched the shadows under the bed of the pickup. The back tire was flat, punctured somewhere along their violent ride through the field. The cold metal of the wheel bit through the material of Carl's jeans, through muscle, and straight to bone.

"No!" Corinne suddenly jolted into action. The numbness that had protected her since she woke fled in an instant. She scrambled down and felt again the warm sticky blood that flowed out of the wound. She lay her hand there for a moment, until she felt the blood pump out, again and again, in a hot flood over her hand.

She reeled back, horrified, the smell of blood thick in her nose. He couldn't live long, not bleeding like that. "Carl!" she cried. "Wake up!"

She felt it now, the terror, building out of control. *I'll take care of you.* Her heart thundered, and her breath pounded out of her. *I'm here now, I'll take care of you.*

"Oh, Toby, what do I do, what do I do?"

She spoke the words to herself, and tried in her panic to push the wheel back, to draw Carl's leg out. He woke, and screamed.

Corinne jumped up and dove into the cab of the pickup, wrenching the key in the ignition. The truck wouldn't start.

Carl screamed in agony, again and again. Corinne ran back to him, the panic building in her chest, choking her. She didn't know what to do. She whipped her head around again, searching fruitlessly for help from some quarter. But she was alone. Alone, again, with impending death.

You're mine, and I'll take care of you.

She dropped down beside Carl and tried to think. She had to stop the bleeding. She grabbed at his belt, fumbling with the buckle, and finally yanked it from his belt loops with a mighty tug. She looped the belt around his thigh, above the wound, trying to ignore his tortured screams. She wound it around his leg twice, tugging it tight, and tucked the ends in.

Suddenly, Carl stopped screaming. Corinne put her ear to his mouth; he was still breathing, just thankfully passed out, either from the pain or the blood loss.

She pulled her baggy sweatshirt off then over Carl's head, tugging him upright to do it. He rested limply against her, and she prayed that he wouldn't wake up again. She was left in only her thin tank top, and her skin pebbled instantly with the cold. Her body felt the icy air, and the hot tears that coursed down her cheeks, but her mind didn't register it.

She scrambled to get his arms into the sleeves, thinking only to keep him as warm as possible. She lay his head gently back on the ground.

"I'm going to get help," she said to the still form. She knew he couldn't hear her; she said it to reassure herself that there was something she could do.

She remained for a moment, not wanting to leave him alone. But there was nothing she could do. With a silent prayer that he not wake until she returned with help, she started running back toward the road.

Toby burst through the elevator doors as soon as they opened. "Corinne Maxwell?" he said to the nurse at the desk. "She just came in on the helicopter."

The nurse shrugged. "A boy came in on the helicopter. He's in trauma."

"There was a lady with him." He knew she was there, he'd listened to the transmission on the radio on the way over.

The nurse gave him a blank look. "I didn't see a lady. If you want to talk to the doctor..."

Toby groaned and walked away, wandering frantically around the emergency room. He batted back the curtains to cubicles and opened doors, searching. He moved to the back of the room. A door swung open across the hall, and he caught a quick blur of green scrubs and frenzied activity. He lunged and pushed his way through the door.

The mayhem inside the room was concentrated around a gurney. His legs suddenly leaden, Toby crossed the white room. A dozen people swarmed around the patient on the bed.

Toby stepped close, his hat in his hand and his heart in his throat. A nurse moved aside. Carl lay on the bed. His face was as white as the sheet he lay on. An IV dripped blood into his arm. An oxygen mask cupped his face. A team of doctors and nurses covered his body like a giant team of worker ants.

Something in Toby's stomach unclenched at the knowledge that it wasn't Corinne.

"Who is that? Somebody get that guy out of here!" a doctor yelled. "What's the blood alcohol level?"

Toby stepped back, but he was still in the midst of the mayhem. He asked a nurse hurrying by, "Is he going to make it?"

"They're doing everything they can." Her face was an impersonal mask. "Please step into the hallway."

Toby swallowed and turned away. He saw Corinne then. She was on the other side of a window, sitting on a gurney along the hallway outside. He rushed through the door to her. Her thin white tank top was covered with blood, and she held a towel in her hand. An ugly gash slashed across her forehead, over her eye. She stared through the window at the bustle of activity going on around Carl.

"Thank God!" Toby crossed the hall and reached to hug her. He stopped, his hands in midair, not sure if he should touch her. "Are you okay?"

"Yes," she said tiredly. "Carl's hurt. He lost a lot of blood."

Her voice was robotic, her eyes dead. Toby cupped her shoulders and looked hard at her. "Have you seen a doctor about your head? Your skin is like ice."

She wrinkled her brow and craned her neck to look behind him, saying lazily, "They gave me a blanket...."

"You need to see a doctor, sweetheart." The blank look in her eyes terrified him. Her hands were blue, and she seemed to be in a daze. Was this shock?

Dan Buchanan burst through the swinging doors. "Where's my son? Carl?"

His wife, Belinda, hurried behind him, her face pinched with fear. They both ran toward the table.

A nurse headed them off. "I'm sorry, but you'll have to wait outside. The doctors are doing everything they can. Please give them room to work."

Dan refused to be budged. "I want to see my son! Someone tell me what's going on."

Toby walked up and took Dan by the elbow. "Dan, you need to wait outside so—"

"What the hell are you doing here? What happened to Carl?"

"He was in an accident. He drove off the road and into a tree in the Huckaby's pasture. The doctors are doing everything they can, so please step back—"

"You step back. I'm going to see my son."

Toby collared Dan and pushed him outside the swinging doors. Corinne dropped her blanket and followed them.

"You?" Dan said when he saw Corinne. "What the hell are you doing here? Trying to get my son into more trouble, I'm sure."

"Do not talk to her like that," Toby said sternly. "She was in the pickup with Carl when he wrecked it." He put an arm around Corinne. "You should go back and sit down, sweetheart. You're too pale."

"What were you doing in my son's pickup, lady?" Dan's voice was a grating roar. Toby motioned to silence him, but Corinne stepped past him and turned to Dan.

"Mr. Buchanan, I believe your son has a drinking problem. He was drinking when he drove past my house tonight. He was very upset, talking about how he had no future—"

"My son doesn't have a problem except for nosy jackasses like you—"

"Don't talk to her that way," Toby ordered again. He placed a hand on Dan's massive arm. Dan tossed it off, drawing his own fist back.

Toby glared at him. "Do it," he said softly. "Hit me. I'm just waiting for an excuse."

Dan swung just as Belinda screamed. "Dan, no!"

Toby ducked the punch easily, and delivered one quick shot to Dan's jaw. He pulled back his fist for another shot, when movement to his side caught his eye.

Corinne collapsed in a faint, and Toby caught her just before she hit the floor.

Chapter 15

Toby pulled a chair to the side of Corinne's bed and took her hand. The space around the edge of the hospital curtain was growing lighter; the sun was up. A new dawn. He closed his eyes and prayed his thanks that the woman in front of him would see it and many more. He thought she was asleep, but she opened her eyes and gave him a weak smile.

"Don't look like that, Sheriff," she said groggily. "It's just a bump on the head. I'll be home tomorrow."

Toby swallowed and kissed her forehead softly, beside the bandage. "It could have been worse."

"It wasn't. How's Carl?"

Toby shook his head solemnly. "I still haven't heard anything. He's out of surgery, but that's all I know."

Corinne nodded and closed her eyes.

Toby rubbed the back of his neck and looked at her. He'd looked at her all night, afraid that if he closed his eyes she would be swept away from him again by some malevolent force bent on having her. There were bruises everywhere. One side of her face was discolored, her eye swollen, her lip stitched where she'd bitten through it.

"Corinne?" he whispered.

She opened her eyes.

"What were you doing in that truck? Why did you go with him?"

Corinne pursed her lips and tried to sit up.

"No, lie down. I'm sorry. If you don't want to talk about it, we can wait till later. I was just wondering why you didn't call me. I could have taken care of it."

"There wasn't time, Toby. He was taking off and I didn't know how to stop him. I just climbed in the cab, hoping I could talk some sense into him. It was a stupid thing to do, but I couldn't think of anything else. I tried to stop him, but he was stronger than me." Her voice rasped with exhaustion.

Toby cleared his throat and looked at the floor. "He hurt you," he said finally, quietly.

"No, I'm okay."

Toby reached out and touched the bandage over her eye lightly. She flinched.

"You should have called me the moment he showed up. He was drunk. You should have called me. I should have been there to help you."

"Toby, I told you, there wasn't time. You can't be everywhere at once—"

"Dammit, Corinne!" He sprang from his chair, knocking it backward. "Don't lay there all bruised and battered and tell me there's nothing I could have done." He paced the room, tight with rage. "Look at you! Beat up and bleeding. You could have died! You could have died, Corinne. Again. And again, there was nothing I could do to stop it. You shut me out, you keep me at a distance when all I want to do is keep you safe."

Corinne watched him pace the floor, his fists clenched and his jaw tight. She held out a hand. "Toby," she whispered.

He swallowed and took her hand.

"I'm sorry," she whispered. The eyes that met hers were red-rimmed, bloodshot.

He shook his head. "I'm not mad at you."

"I know."

"It's not the easiest thing, you know, watching you get knocked around all the time."

She smiled weakly at him. "I'll try not to let it happen again."

He edged down onto the bed beside her and pulled her gingerly into his lap. "Promise me."

"I promise."

"Can you really go home tomorrow?"

She nodded against his chest. "The doctor looked at the X rays and said I could probably check out in the morning."

The door squeaked open. Dan Buchanan poked his head around the corner.

Corinne gestured for him to come in. Dan entered the room slowly, followed by his wife, Belinda.

Dan cleared his throat. "I wanted you to know, they had to—" He cleared his throat again. "They had to cut off Carl's leg. Just above the knee."

"I'm so sorry," Corinne said.

Dan nodded. "Yeah, well..." There didn't seem to be a lot to say to that.

Belinda stepped up. "They said he would have died, if you hadn't put that tourniquet on his leg. He lost a lot of blood. They didn't think he was going to make it at first. You saved his life."

Dan nodded. "That's right. We owe you a debt of gratitude."

"You don't have to thank me," Corinne said.

"Yes, we do," Belinda insisted.

Dan nodded again. He looked a bit shell-shocked. Like Toby, they had probably spent the night in sleepless worry. "She's right. We do." Dan stood there awkwardly for a second. "I—I guess I should apologize, too."

Belinda made a noise and turned away discreetly.

"I shouldn't have—" He shook his head. "It's amazing, you know, how your priorities can change in the blink of an eye. That doctor told us they were taking him into surgery, but they didn't seem very hopeful that they'd be bringing him out. Those were the longest hours of my life, I tell you. All of a sudden, it didn't matter about football or college or anything else. All that mattered was that I got to talk to my boy again.''

"Is he awake yet?'' Toby asked.

Dan shook his head. "We saw him in recovery, but he didn't really know we were there. Anyway, Toby, Miss Maxwell, I know I was probably unfair to you—well, no probably about it, I was out of line. That whole mess with the football team and the drinking and everything. I never thought it would come to this.''

Toby and Corinne exchanged a look, and Belinda faced Dan with her brows raised. "Well, yeah, I guess I should have known. You tried to tell me. I just had it in my head that boys will be boys and as long as there was no harm done... But now there is harm done. A lot of it.''

Corinne braced herself on the pillows and raised up. "Mr. Buchanan, I believe Carl has the idea that if he can't play football, he doesn't have a future. He thinks that's all he's good at.''

Dan studied the floor. "Yeah, I guess he probably got that idea from me. I get a little carried away when it comes to football.''

Corinne gave him a sympathetic smile. Despite all the trouble he'd caused her, she felt sorry for the man. "He's going to need your encouragement and support now more than ever to help him find his way.''

Dan rubbed his jaw. "I'm just grateful I'm being given a second chance. If I can just take him home, I won't ever be—'' His voice broke and he looked away. He swallowed thickly and rubbed the bridge of his nose fiercely.

Belinda put a hand on his arm and started to lead him away. "We just wanted you to know, Miss Maxwell. And to thank you.''

Dan stopped and turned back to them. "Listen, all that nonsense about you not getting reelected next year, Haskell, that was just...''

Toby stood and put his hand out to shake Dan's. "That's water under the bridge, Dan.''

"No, this needs to be said. I was wrong and I apologize. Believe me, I've been making deals with God all night, promising everything I could think of if he'd just let me keep my boy. And I intend to follow through with every one of them. And don't worry about the election. You have my support. As much noise as I made against you, I'll double that in your favor. And you, too, Miss Maxwell. I know you don't want to stay in Aloma, but if there's anything I can ever do for you, you just let me know.''

"There are a few things you can do. First, get Carl some help for his drinking.''

Dan nodded again and Belinda said emphatically, "We will.''

"And second, let him know what you just told us. That he matters to you more than football does.''

"Don't worry,'' Dan said as they were walking out the door. "I intend to, every hour of every day. Until he gets sick of hearing it.''

Corinne forced Toby to go home and get some rest a few hours later. He was so tired, he couldn't think straight. He was drifting off to sleep when he remembered Mr. Davis.

Between the episode with Jeremy last night, and then the accident with Corinne, Mr. Davis hadn't crossed his mind. But Toby found that once he remembered, he couldn't go to sleep. His mother and one of her friends who was also a nurse took turns spending the night at Mr. D.'s, but still Toby usually made sure the older man was squared away before going to Corinne's at night, and then checking again first thing in the morning.

He looked at the alarm clock by his head. Two-thirty in the afternoon. It had been almost twenty-four hours since he'd last visited Mr. D. He groaned and closed his eyes. His body felt as if it had been clenched tight with fear for hours on end.

Probably someone else had been by hours ago to check on Mr. D. Probably.

Toby rolled over and buried his face in the pillow. He was so worn-out, he couldn't sleep. His body refused to relax, after being strung taut for so many hours.

It was no use. He hauled himself out of bed and cupped his chin in his palms, his elbows on his knees. He might as well drive by the man's house right quick, just to check. Then he could go to the office and catch up on paperwork. That always put him to sleep. He could catch a quick nap on the cot in the cell—it wouldn't be the first time.

He pulled on a flannel shirt and pinned the star to his pocket. To hell with the uniform.

Jeremy was sitting on Mr. Davis's recliner when Toby walked through the door. The boy had a box of dry cereal in his lap, and he was watching television.

"Why aren't you in school?" Toby asked.

"I'm taking a personal day," Jeremy said, tossing a handful of cereal into his mouth.

Toby decided not to pursue that at the moment. "Where's Mr. D.?"

Jeremy indicated the bedroom with a toss of his shaggy head. "Snoozing."

"Everything okay?"

Jeremy shrugged his bony shoulders. "Sure. Except for taking Mr. D. to the emergency room last night, things have been pretty quiet. How 'bout you?" Jeremy smiled in exaggerated politeness.

"The emergency room? Why?"

"I found him down at the football grounds, conked out. Big bump on his head."

Toby hurried to the bedroom and looked in on the old man. He was sleeping peacefully, a wide white bandage over his forehead.

He returned to the living room. "What the hell happened? What was he doing at the football grounds? Was this after we talked last night?"

Jeremy shook his head. "Nah, it was before. I just forgot to tell you. Of course, it was after. Get ahold of yourself, man. It's not that big a deal. Look at you, your face is all white."

Toby fought the urge to strangle him. He was still a minor, for a few months at any rate.

"Jeremy," he said with deadly calm. "Tell me what happened."

"I don't know what happened. After Luke came to the station last night, I was going to hike it home. I thought I saw Mr. D. tottering to the school. It was dark, and by the time I found him, he was out cold. He fell—you know, there behind the concession stand where the retaining wall is crumbling a little? He must have slipped.''

Toby nodded and rubbed his head so hard it started to burn. It was all slipping out of his hands. He wasn't handling anything. "How did you get to the hospital?"

"I flew."

"You smart off one more time and I'll shoot you, I swear."

"Jeez, okay. You really need to look into getting a sense of humor, you know. I told you it was okay. I woke the old guy up, and he was kind of woozy, you know, calling me other people's names and stuff. He could walk, though. I was walking him back home, and your mom found us. She was out looking for him."

"She took him to the hospital?"

"Yep."

"What did the doctor say?"

"That he needs to watch his step. Hey—" Jeremy lifted his hands helplessly and pressed back against the chair. "That's what he said, I swear. He stitched Mr. D. up and said he needed to watch his step."

"Does he know about the Alzheimer's?"

"Yeah, he asked what medicines he was taking. I told him the ones I remembered. Your old lady—sorry, your mother—filled him in on the rest. He didn't act like it was a big deal. He said this happens to people with Alzheimer's all the time. Mr. D. came around while we were there, thinking straight and everything. It's cool, man. He pulled it off. How's your squeeze?"

"Don't call her that," Toby said automatically. He felt suddenly as if the world had started turning a different way or something, and he couldn't keep up. Corinne in the hospital. She was going to be okay, thank God, but it could have been a lot worse. Carl losing his leg. And Mr. D. The temperature had been in the high thirties last night. A man his age, out in the cold all night, could have died from exposure, gotten pneumonia, all kinds of things. If Jeremy hadn't been walking by just then...

Toby stared at the braid rug on the floor, stared until the pattern blurred and lifted toward him. He rubbed his jaw, his hands scraping stubble. He thought inanely that maybe he should have shaved; maybe then he'd feel more in control of everything.

"Were you planning on staying here for a while?" he asked.

Jeremy nodded and rose hesitantly. An uneasy concern replaced his sarcasm. "I told your mom I could stay while she went home and took a nap—she sat up with Mr. D. all night. My mom said it was okay. She already brought me some clothes. She told me about the accident. How are they? Your—Miss Maxwell and Buchanan?"

Toby sighed. "Corinne's okay. Just a bump on the head." Much like the one Mr. Davis had. "Carl is—they had to amputate his leg."

"Man," was all Jeremy could say. He looked a little dazed. "They cut it off? Like, for good?"

In spite of everything, Toby smiled wanly. As if they were going to cut it off and then put it back on. "Yeah, for good."

"Man," Jeremy said again.

"Listen, if you don't mind staying, I need to go out for a while. I need to take care of some...business."

"This one is from the junior class," Becca said as she read the card attached to the huge bouquet of flowers just delivered to Corinne's room.

"That's nice," Corinne said absently.

"I'll just put them with the rest of the jungle." Becca slid aside a potted ivy and a bouquet of mums to make room for the new addition.

"Why don't I make a list of everyone who sent something and what they sent so you can send thank you notes?"

"That's a good idea." Corinne shifted on the bed and looked at the door.

"The doctor should be here any minute to discharge you," Becca said hopefully. Corinne didn't answer.

"Do you want a magazine?"

"No, thank you."

"How about a drink of water?"

"No, thank you."

"A soda?"

"No."

"Then what do you want?" Becca asked, exasperated.

Corinne met Becca's eyes. "I want to know why I'm here."

"Put your hand up to your forehead and you'll remember."

"Not here in the hospital. Here, in this position. At this point in my life. You said everything happens for a reason. What am I doing back in Aloma?"

Becca sat down beside the bed. "Deep philosophical questions are a pretty tall order for someone on painkillers. Are you sure you don't want to leave this for later?"

"I'm sure. There's a kid down the hall who had his leg cut off. There was a definite sequence of events that led up to it, too. You can see it plain as day, if you want to look. First, he's arrested for drinking. Then he's restricted from football. A decision I played a hand in—"

"Hold it," Becca said, putting out her hand. "Don't even go there. Carl is the one who chose to drink. Carl is the one who chose to drive. I feel sorry for him, too. But the fact is, it's his own fault."

"I'm not saying it wasn't. I'm just saying, I put myself into the equation. And I can't help but wonder how things would have happened, if I hadn't come back. If I hadn't spoken up, would Toby have backed down? Maybe Carl would have gotten to play football. Maybe he would have done great and gotten a scholarship and gone on to play professional football or something. Is this what was supposed to happen, Becca? Was Carl supposed to lose his leg? He's only eighteen."

"I don't know," Becca said. "Some blessings are disguised as tragedies, until you look a little closer."

"I just can't help thinking there's something else. I keep thinking about what you said. I mean, if I had anything at all to do with him losing his leg, then surely my responsibility extends beyond that as well. If I had a part in something bad happening to him, then I have to also play a part in something good. Don't I?" She looked beseechingly at Becca.

Becca squeezed Corinne's shoulder. "I can't answer that."

Corinne scrunched up her face and sat up. "You drive me crazy, you know that? If you weren't such a good friend, I'd never speak to you."

Becca smiled and stood, unperturbed. "I know."

"This is not what I had in mind at all, when I came back."

"What did you have in mind?"

Corinne shook her head and leaned back. She still tired very easily. "I just wanted some peace. I wanted to be anonymous. That's how I felt before, growing up in Aloma. Like nothing I did would ever affect anyone. Like nothing I did mattered. That's why I left. And it's why I came back. I wanted to be completely unimportant. I didn't want anything I said or did to affect anyone." *So I couldn't screw up again,* she thought.

"Everyone affects someone, Corinne. Haven't you ever seen *It's a Wonderful Life*?"

"Yes, a couple dozen times just like—"

The door creaked open. Jeremy Huckaby stood in the doorway, a sheaf of papers curled in one hand. He gave a halfhearted wave. "Hi."

"Hi," Corinne said with a smile. He hung there in the doorway, hesitant, until she gestured for him to come in.

She raised herself higher on the pillows. "This is a nice surprise."

"Yeah," he said uncomfortably. The room was silent for a moment, until Becca asked, "Did your mother drive you over?"

"Nah, she's staying with Mr. D. I brought the car." His pride at coming to the city by himself showed through even his awkwardness.

"Have you been to see Carl?" Becca asked.

Jeremy shook his head. "No. I'm going to. I guess. I don't know what I'm going to say."

Corinne nodded. "It will be awkward. But I think you should talk to him, even if it is. That way it won't be so hard when he comes back to school."

"Yeah, I guess you're right."

"What's that in your hand, Jeremy?" Becca asked.

Jeremy looked at the papers curled in his hand as if he expected them to do something.

"It's just—it's this thing I wrote. I thought you might get bored and want to do a little reading. If you don't have time, though, or don't want to, it's okay."

Corinne reached out and took the papers from him. "I'd love to read it."

"Don't worry. It's a real story. Not a true story—I don't mean that. But it's not gross or violent or anything like that."

Corinne smiled and nodded. "I understand."

Jeremy cleared his throat and scratched the back of his head. "Listen, the reason I came is because me and the sheriff—the sheriff and I, I mean—we had a long talk the other night. And I came to tell you that I shouldn't have written those things in school. I was trying to...well, I guess I was trying to get into trouble. I don't know if you heard about my father?"

"I heard."

"Of course you did," Jeremy muttered, shaking his head. "It's Aloma. Anyway, I really just wanted to get out of here, and I heard that you were tight with the sheriff. I thought I could scare you and make you think I had done all that stuff, and you would tell him I should be sent to some home or something like that. My probation officer kept telling me that if I got into any more trouble, I'd get sent to the county correction center."

Corinne leveled her gaze at him. She decided to forgo the lecture about how tough those places were. "I thought that was what you were after. I just didn't understand why."

"Because I couldn't go anywhere or do anything without knowing that everyone was staring at me, and talking about me. I wanted my mom to transfer me to another school, but she said she couldn't afford to drive me twenty miles each way every day. And I think..." His voice trailed off and his face became grim. "I was really mad. At him. For screwing up like that, for making my mom so unhappy and everything. And I thought that was the worst thing I could do to him. If I got locked up somewhere, he would know it was his fault. He would know how he had made everyone else feel."

He looked at the floor and frowned. "Pretty dumb, huh?"

Corinne gave him a sympathetic smile. "Yeah, pretty dumb. But understandable. People do dumb things when they're hurting."

"I wasn't hurting. I was just mad."

"But you've changed your mind now? You're going to stay out of trouble?"

"I guess so. It wasn't doing me any good, anyway. I might as well stick around here and tough it out till the end of the year. Hopefully I can get a student loan or something and go to college. Do they have some kind of special rate for children of cons?" He gave a feeble attempt at a laugh.

"I know it's difficult, Jeremy. But I'm glad you've forgiven your father," Corinne said.

Jeremy scowled. "I didn't forgive him. I just decided I'm not going to screw up my life just because he screwed his up."

Corinne and Becca looked at each other. Corinne shrugged. "It's a start, anyway."

She turned to more pleasant topics. "What is this story about?" she asked, holding up the pages.

He shrugged awkwardly. "It's just this Christmas thing I wrote. It was for the contest. I know it's supposed to be confidential and all that, so I'll probably get kicked out of the contest for showing you. But I don't care."

Corinne shook her head. "The judging is already done, so it's okay."

"I thought maybe—" He cleared his throat again. "I thought maybe you could critique it for me. Not like a grade or anything, but tell me what you really think, so maybe I can send it to a magazine or something...." He drifted off awkwardly. "If you have time. And feel like it. And all that."

Corinne bit down on a smile. "I'd be happy to see what I can come up with. There's a book in the library with a list of magazine publishers. We'll check it out when I get back—"

Corinne faltered when she realized that by the time she got back to school, the semester would be almost over. And so would her time as Jeremy's teacher. "Or, I suppose Miss Danvers can help you, or the new English teacher."

Jeremy nodded grimly. "Yeah, I guess you'll be headed for Atlanta as soon as semester finals are over."

Corinne remained lost in thought for a moment, until she realized what Jeremy had said. "How did you know about Atlanta?"

Jeremy blinked. "Oh— I...well...I was—"

"Snooping?"

"Yeah. Snooping. Another thing I guess I need to apologize for. But it's true, isn't it? That woman wants you to come to Atlanta so you can have your own talk show."

"Yes, it's true." Corinne idly rubbed the bandage over her eye.

"I'm sorry I was snooping. And I'm sorry you'll be leaving town. I wish you weren't going. But really, Miss Maxwell, it sounds like a great chance. You could get really rich and famous."

"Mmm," was all Corinne would say.

"It's true, Corinne," Becca said. "It could be a great opportunity."

"I know. It would be everything I wanted and worked for, everything I dreamed about for almost ten years."

"A dream come true."

Corinne nodded. "Yes, my dream come true. Recognition. Respect. The knowledge that I affected a lot of people. Made a difference in the world."

"It sounds like a person would be crazy to pass it up."

"Yes," Corinne said slowly. "Crazy. What was that?"

"What?" Becca asked.

"I thought I heard something. Is someone in the hall?"

"I didn't hear anything," Becca said. "But I'll go look."

"When you get rich and famous, will you get me an introduction to Alicia Silverstone?" Jeremy asked.

"When you're a rich and famous author, she'll be calling you herself. What was it, Becca?"

"It's Toby," Becca said over her shoulder. She stuck her head back out the door. "Hey, Toby, you can come in. She's awake."

Corinne sat up straighter in bed and smoothed her hair back. She wasn't crazy about Toby seeing her like this; she hadn't show ered or brushed her teeth. But the moment Becca said he was there, she realized she wanted to see him.

After a few seconds, she leaned forward. ''Becca? Tell him to come in.''

Becca walked back into the room, a puzzled frown on her face. ''I tried. He just kept walking away.''

Chapter 16

Toby held his hat in his hand and slipped into the dim, deserted hospital chapel. The cold ball of fear had slipped from his throat and settled with a solid sourness into the pit of his stomach, and promised to stay here.

My dream come true.

Three short pews faced a backlit cross. Toby moved to the front bench and sat.

He'd intended to pray, but now that he was here he found that between sleep deprivation and worry, his mind couldn't hold on to a solid thread of thought. Jumbled images tumbled around inside his head, whirling like a tornado around and around. Corinne, falling in a limp heap in his arms. Corinne, prone on a city sidewalk, a dark maroon puddle spreading too rapidly under her head.

Corinne's dreams coming true. Corinne leaving again. And the dark gulf that awaited him when she did.

He heard movement in the doorway behind him, then felt the cushion shift as someone sat beside him. He stared straight ahead at the glowing cross, not interested enough to turn his head and see who sat beside him. He smelled vanilla, though, and knew without looking that it was his mother.

"I stopped by the home you chose and picked up some paperwork. Mr. Davis will have to go in, of course, for an interview. The decision is still up to him, though, Toby."

"I know," Toby said gruffly without looking at her. "But if it's what's best, I can convince him."

"It is what's best, Toby." She wrapped her fingers around Toby's arm and leaned on him. "You're not turning your back on him, Toby. He'll only be forty miles away."

Toby nodded and swallowed. Jeremy had already promised that he'd check on Mr. Davis at least once a week. He'd joked that it gave him a good excuse to borrow his mother's car, but Toby knew the joke was meant to cover up the boy's very real affection for the old man. Uncool as it was, Jeremy cared about Mr. Davis.

His mother squeezed Toby's arm. "When are you going to tell him?"

Toby shrugged. "No point putting it off. This afternoon, maybe tomorrow."

"Do you want me to do it?"

Toby shook his head. "No." He didn't walk away from his responsibilities, and he didn't pawn them off on someone else. He'd told Corinne that, just a few months ago. But then, he'd felt at least a shred of confidence that he knew the right thing to do.

The thought of Corinne brought back the black feeling, and he closed his eyes for a second.

"Have you been to see Corinne yet?" his mother asked.

Toby made a noise that could have meant anything. The answer to that question was a bit ambiguous. He'd been to her room. He'd heard her. He hadn't needed to see her after that.

"She'll be okay, you know."

Toby nodded, still facing front, then he put his hand over hers and squeezed back. Corinne would be okay, and for that he was eternally grateful, even if he couldn't find the words to express it now. She would be okay.

She would live to leave again.

After a long moment of silence, Toby shifted and cleared his throat. "Do you suppose Dad pulls any weight up there?" He gestured to the cross with a slight nod.

From the corner of his eye, he saw his mother give a wistful smile. "If I know your father, he's charmed his way up to second in command by now. And looking to improve his position."

Toby lifted the corners of his mouth, but the movement didn't feel like a smile. "Yep, that sounds like Dad. He always did the right thing, knew the right things to say. And he didn't let the right woman slip away."

His mother gave him another sympathetic squeeze, as tears filled her eyes. "Toby, it's time for both of us to let your father be who he really was—a man. Not a legend, or a god. But a man. And it's time for you to go for your own dream."

Toby put his hands on his knees and looked at the cross. "I love what I do, Mom. I started this to make Dad proud, but I love what I do."

"Is it enough?"

"I thought it was."

"Until Corinne came back to town."

Toby nodded. "Yep. Until that very second."

"Then get up there and tell her that."

Toby sat with his chin in his hands. "I honestly don't know if I can give her what she wants."

"You'll never know if you let fear hold you back. There are a lot of good reasons not to do something, Toby. Fear isn't one of them."

Toby stood. "I asked her once before, you know. And it didn't do any good."

"She's not the same person she was then. Are you?"

Toby swallowed the lump in his throat. "No, I suppose not."

"Then get out of here. You'll make your father and me both proud."

Corinne sat up and smiled at Toby when he walked in her room. "I was wondering when you'd get here. The doctor should be by in a few minutes to discharge me."

Toby didn't answer. Silently, he pulled the chair up to the side of the bed and sat down across from her.

He rubbed the back of his neck, licked his lips, then took her hands in his. He cleared his throat.

"Corinne, I..." He looked at her hands, then back into her eyes. "Marry me."

Corinne's mouth dropped open, and she blinked a few times. "Marry you?"

"I love you, Corinne." His tone was solemn, his eyes dark with intensity. "I want to marry you."

She took a deep breath and chewed her lower lip. "But, Toby, I don't know—"

He reached up and gently but firmly put one hand over her mouth. "You know everything you need to know."

"This is a little sudden."

Toby's jaw steeled and he looked off.

Corinne squeezed his hand. "Give me some time to think about it."

"No," he said flatly.

She drew back and wrinkled her brow. "I just need some time to think about—"

"No." His face was haggard, his eyes red-rimmed from lack of sleep, deep lines bracketed his mouth. But for all that, he was calm. "No," he said again, shaking his head. "No more time, Corinne. I can't do it anymore."

"Toby, you told me you would give me room to breathe."

"That was before you decided to go out and get yourself almost killed! Again!" He stood suddenly, knocking his chair back. "Dammit, Corinne, I can't do it anymore. If it's about Atlanta, that's fine. I can go to Atlanta." He held his arms out and paced the room. "Hell, I can be a cop anywhere, I suppose. Or I could do something else. It doesn't matter. All that really matters is us, Corinne. You and me. So, what's it going to be?"

"Toby, I don't know. This is a little out of the blue. How did you know about Atlanta—?"

"This is not out of the blue!" He made a slashing motion with his hand. "I have been in love with you from day one, and you damned well know it, Corinne. You've always known it. But this is it. You make up your mind right now. It's either yes or no. You're either with me forever, or you're leaving now. Because I don't want to...I can't—''

His voice broke, and he sat down as abruptly as he'd stood. He leaned forward, elbows on his knees, his face in his hands. She thought for a second that he was crying, and she reached out to him. He raised his head. His eyes were dry. They were cold, flat and dry.

"I can't do it anymore, Corinne." His voice was deadly calm. "You were right. I was trying to play God. No, I was trying to be my dad. With you, with Mr. Davis, with the whole town. I thought I could make everything okay for everybody, if I tried hard enough. But look where it got me. You're shutting me out, trying to get yourself killed every time you turn around. Carl's leg." He shook his head, muttering to himself. "And Mr. D., going into a nursing home."

"I wasn't shutting you out, Toby," Corinne said, starting to grow angry. When did he become so impatient? "I told you, there wasn't time—wait. You're putting Mr. Davis in a nursing home?"

"What choice do I have?" he asked hotly. "He's going to get himself killed, too. I can't watch everybody at the same time, no matter how much I want to. Go ahead and say I told you so. Go ahead."

There was no way she could say that. "I'm sorry, Toby. I know you didn't want to do that."

He shook his head. "Yeah, well, things don't always work out the way you want them to, do they? Sooner or later you have to face that fact. And you have to let it go."

Corinne chewed her lip. He wasn't talking about Mr. Davis anymore. "Toby," she said, swallowing. "Just give me a little more time. I don't even know what I'm doing—"

"No," he said again flatly. "I can't make things happy-ever-after for everybody. I know that. And for the most part, I'm okay with that. I know I can't do anything about Mr. Davis. Or for Carl, or Jeremy, or anybody else, except help out where I can and hope for the best. And for everybody else, the best I can do is okay.

For them, I can do what I can, give it my best shot, and still sleep at night.''

He faced her, his expression a stony mask. "But not for you. I can't go on waiting and hoping, and then standing by watching while you shut me out and get yourself hurt—"

"I didn't shut you out!" she cried. "I told you. Dammit, Toby, I told you already. There wasn't time."

"I'm not talking about Carl. I'm talking about Jeremy. You never told me what he was doing. You never told me about how he was trying to scare you. You knew I would have done—"

"Exactly! I knew you would have stepped in and done something, tried to protect me from him. I didn't think I needed protection from him, Toby. But you would have barged in and done exactly what he wanted. You would have shipped him off to some reform school, and that's not what he needs. Just because it was me, and not someone else, you would have been a lot tougher on him.''

"You could have given me a chance." His drawn face loomed inches from her own. "You could have given us a chance."

She sighed and sat back on the bed, rubbing lightly at the bandage over her forehead. "The point is, Toby—"

He raised his brows when she stopped. "What is the point, Corinne? Or do you even know?"

Corinne twisted the sheet in her lap and clenched her jaw. "I'm not ready, Toby."

Toby stared at her for a long moment. "I'm willing to give up everything, Corinne. I'll follow you, anywhere you want to go. I'm willing to do just about anything, except wait. Except listen to any more of your excuses. I'm offering you everything I have."

He lifted her chin with his thumb and forced her to meet his gaze. "But I won't take one bit less from you."

Corinne's eyes shimmered with tears. She swallowed. "I'm sorry, Toby," she whispered.

His face hardened, and he put his hat on his head. "Yeah, me too." He turned on his heel.

"Toby, wait."

He ignored her, pushing his way out the door. As he did, Aunt

Muriel walked in, looking at Toby in surprise. Toby brushed past her silently.

Muriel looked at Corinne. "Did I come at a bad time?"

Corinne closed her eyes, then opened them again. "No, it's just...he wants—" Corinne broke off, looking helplessly at her aunt.

Muriel sat on the edge of the bed gingerly. She took Corinne's hand in hers and peered closely at her. "That's a nice little bump there. You sure you're okay?"

Corinne nodded, not trusting herself to speak.

"Good. Linda said she wanted to come see you herself, but she's having some kind of problem with her car. She told me to give you this." She leaned down and gave Corinne a hug.

Corinne could see what Muriel tried to hide in her smile and embrace—no doubt Muriel had tried unsuccessfully to talk Linda into coming to the hospital. Corinne told herself once again that it didn't matter, as she returned the hug she knew her mother had never mentioned.

"It's okay, I talked to her yesterday." Corinne had a hard time talking around the lump in her throat. "She told me to be more careful."

"We don't want anything to happen to our best girl."

Corinne couldn't face the sympathy in her aunt's eyes. She swallowed and nodded, looking hard at the flowers beside her bed, wanting desperately to call Toby back.

"Want to tell me what that was all about?" Muriel asked softly as she cocked her head in the direction of the door and squeezed Corinne's hand.

Corinne opened her mouth to tell her. Instead, she did something completely uncharacteristic. She burst into tears. "Oh, Aunt Muriel, I've made such a mess of things!"

Twenty minutes later, after Corinne was drained of tears and energy, Muriel sat on the bed and cradled Corinne's head in her lap and stroked her hair. "So he had the unmitigated gall to be in love with you and agree to follow you anywhere?"

"I told you he was crazy."

"Certifiable. How could anyone love you?"

Corinne laughed and sniffed. "It's not that I don't believe he really thinks he loves me—"

"It's just...?"

"It's just, he doesn't really know me. Not really."

"Corinne, he's known you since you were five. He knows you."

"But..." It didn't make that much sense, trying to explain it to someone else. "Not the real me."

"And who is that, sweetheart?"

"I don't even know anymore. But I know I'm not the wonderful person he thinks I am." Corinne smiled sadly. "He calls me sweetheart, too. It's silly and hokey."

"And wonderful," Muriel said as she stroked Corinne's hair. "Now tell me—besides almost getting yourself killed again, how have you been?"

Corinne sighed. "Wonderful. Horrible."

"Sounds like love to me."

It did sound like love, Corinne thought. It felt like love, too.

"And what about the nightmares, Corinne? And the anxiety attacks?"

Corinne thought of the other night with Carl, and the strength she'd derived from Toby's words. *I'll take care of you.*

"I haven't had either in several weeks. I guess I just needed to get out of the house, focus on something."

"You've found what you need, all right. Let's hope you're smart enough to see that."

Corinne knew what her aunt was talking about. "I can't," she whispered, as much to herself as to Muriel.

"Why not?"

Corinne didn't answer.

Muriel gently took Corinne's chin in hand and forced her to meet her gaze. "Go ahead, honey. Say it. Why can't you?"

Instead of answering, though, Corinne sat up, took a cleansing breath, and smoothed her hair back. Enough of self-pity. "Because...because I don't deserve him. I need to do more."

"More than what?"

"Just more. The fact that I love him doesn't mean it's enough."

Muriel was silent for a moment. "We're not just talking about Toby here, are we? Say it, sweetie. Not enough for whom?"

"For Mom." Corinne's voice came out thin, almost whispered. "It's never been enough for her."

"Can I tell you a secret?"

Corinne closed her eyes and nodded slightly.

"Sweetie, it's never going to be enough. Not until she learns to love herself. Nothing you do or I do or she does or anyone else does is going to make her happy, until she learns to be happy with herself. You could single-handedly end poverty and cure cancer, and it would not be enough for her. Because she despises herself, and always has."

"But why?" Corinne sat up and brushed her hair back from her face. "Why is she like that?"

Muriel shrugged. "Probably because our mother was a lot like she is, bitter and resentful, always finding fault no matter what happened. And because she never had it from her mother, *your* mother looked for love and acceptance wherever she could get it."

"Which got her pregnant at seventeen. And ruined her life."

"Right on the first part. Dead wrong on the second. She did try to find approval by being available to anyone she could find. And that did get her pregnant at seventeen. Oh, Corinne." Muriel stroked Corinne's cheek, brushed away a tear. "I wish I could tell you that your parents loved each other, and you were conceived in love. But thanks to your mother, we both know it's a lie. The truth is, your mother wanted to find a place of her own, and so she created it. Your poor father was blindsided. Not," Muriel said with a finger pointed at Corinne, "that he shouldn't have taken responsibility for his own actions. He tried, Corinne, he really did, at first. But she just became more and more unhappy, and harder to be around. Since he didn't love her to begin with, her bitterness made her even more difficult to live with."

Corinne nodded. "I know. So she was a divorced single mother by the time she was twenty. Her life would have been a lot easier if—"

"Her life has been hard because she's made it hard!" Muriel

framed Corinne's face with her hands. "Corinne, I know you've always blamed yourself for your mother's unhappiness, because she's always blamed you. She's also blamed me, her mother, her ex-husband—anyone who was handy. But none of it's true. A person's happiness is their own responsibility. That includes yours and mine. And if you don't watch out, you're going to lose your chance at it.

"You just turned away a wonderful man who wants to spend the rest of his life with you. He's crazy about you! And you're going to lose him. Do you want to end up unhappy and bitter like your mother?"

"Of course not. But—"

"But what? You're not good enough for him? That's bull. And don't tell me you don't love him. I can see it all over your face."

"It's not that, it's just..."

"Just what, for crying out loud?"

"How can I be happy, when she isn't?"

Muriel just stared at her, and Corinne realized for the first time how nonsensical it sounded.

"So as your penance for being born, you plan to spend your life being unhappy?"

"I just wanted to make her proud. I wanted to show her that everything she gave up wasn't for nothing. That it meant something. That I really wasn't a mistake."

Muriel reached out, taking Corinne's hand in hers. "Sweetie, you were never a mistake. God sent you here for a reason."

"Toby thinks it's to be with him."

"What do you think?"

"I don't know. I just..."

"What do you want?"

Tears swam in Corinne's eyes, and she had to swallow twice before she could speak. "I want to find Toby."

"Good. Now quit trying to please someone who can't be pleased, Corinne. When she learns to love herself, your mother will open her eyes and see what a wonderful child she has. And if she doesn't..." Tears shone in Muriel's eyes, too.

Corinne leaned forward and hugged her tight. "If she doesn't, could you be my mother?"

Muriel squeezed her back. "I'd be honored. But I have one condition. No, two."

"What's the first?"

"Quit trying to get yourself killed."

"Done. What's the second?"

"Go after that cowboy. I want some grandkids."

Corinne snuffled a laugh through her tears. "I will, if he'll still have me."

Chapter 17

Corinne knew she had one more thing to do before she faced Toby. She tiptoed into the hospital room, edging the door open, not sure if she wanted to find Carl awake or not. If he was asleep, she could sneak out easily.

He was awake. The door squeaked, and he turned his head to look at her.

She smiled weakly. "Hi," she whispered.

He croaked in response. "Hi."

She moved to the bed and looked down at him. His head was bandaged. She avoided looking at the lower half of his body.

"How are you?" she asked inanely, wishing the words back as soon as they came out.

"They cut off my leg," he said dully.

"I know," she said, her voice a whisper. "I'm sorry."

"Yeah, well. No point being sorry. Got what I deserved, I guess."

"You didn't deserve this," she said firmly.

He frowned and looked at the wall. "What do you want?"

"I want..." Now that she was here, she wasn't sure what exactly she was going to say. She could feel it; a bond had been forged between them. An unlikely bond, to be sure. And not one that she would have asked for. But life had put her here, in this place, and she was finally wise enough not to fight it.

"I want you to know that it doesn't matter. It's only your leg."

He kept his face averted, and she saw his jaw muscles clench.

"I know that it sounds stupid, Carl. And I'm not going to pretend this is a minor thing that you should immediately get over. It's a terrible thing that's happened, and it's going to take you a long time to adjust. But you can adjust. I want you to know that what you have lost is a leg. Not your life. Not your identity. It's your leg. You are the one who can make it more than that. Only you."

"You don't know what the hell you're talking about!" He turned to her, his face flushed hotly, his breath harsh.

She smiled down at him, feeling for the first time a kind of tenderness toward him. "I know a little—more than you think I do. Because I've lost everything I based my life on. Everything I'd worked toward and dreamed about."

He glared at her, derision in his eyes. For some reason, it made her smile. "You know, this could be the best thing that ever happened to you."

"You have a serious head injury, don't you?" He tried to roll over, but couldn't because of his leg.

She had to admit, she felt a little dreamy, but not because of a head injury. No, for the first time in her life, she'd given herself permission to follow her heart.

"Yes, I took a bump on the head, and for the most part, that's your fault. I'm partly to blame, of course. Getting into that pickup with you wasn't my brightest hour. But mostly, it's your fault. It's your fault you were drunk."

"I wasn't drunk, I was just blowing off steam. If Huckaby hadn't made such a big deal out of a little joke—"

"Uh-uh," Corinne said, shaking her head. "Don't blame this on Jeremy, or on the fight you two had. This wasn't the first time you got drunk. Don't try to pawn the blame for this off on someone else. It's your fault we ran off the road and hit that tree. And as hard as it's going to be to face, it's your fault you lost your leg.''

Carl turned his head and ignored her.

"You've blamed me and Sheriff Haskell and everyone else you could think of for everything that's gone wrong in your life. And right now is a good time for it to stop.''

"Thanks for the sympathy," Carl said sarcastically. "You can leave now. Be sure and sign the guest register on your way out.''

"Believe it or not, I do feel sympathy for you. You've got a hard battle ahead of you. I feel enough sympathy, in fact, to come in here and say what I really believe needs to be said, though I know you'll hate me for it.''

"You've got that right.''

"You have a choice to make, Carl, right now. You can let this be the end for you. You can turn bitter, and hate yourself and everyone around you. You can feel sorry for yourself from now on. You can let this little drinking problem of yours turn into a big one. Or—'' She turned her palms up. "Or you can decide to turn this tragedy into something good. Let it open your eyes. Start taking responsibility for yourself. For your own happiness.''

She reached out and cupped Carl's shoulder. Amazingly, he let her hand stay there. "Do you want to be happy, Carl?''

Carl looked at her and rolled his eyes. "What kind of idiot question is that?''

"Not as idiotic as it sounds. Happiness is a choice, Carl.''

"And I'm supposed to choose to be happy about this?'' He gestured angrily to the lower part of his body.

"Of course not. But you can choose to let it ruin your life. Or you can choose to find what else is inside Carl Buchanan besides football.''

Instead of growing angrier as she'd expected, Carl faced the wall again. She saw the muscles of his throat convulse. "Yeah, well, there's nothing," he said huskily. "Nothing else. So you can save the pep talk.''

"That's not true.''

"Don't tell me to look on the bright side!'' he said hotly, trying futilely to pull himself up. "Don't you get it? I screwed up! I

screwed it all up. I was supposed to play football. I was supposed
to be a star! And I screwed it up. Now...I don't have anything.
Now I'm nothing." He collapsed against his pillow.

"That's not true. You have your whole life ahead of you."

Carl whipped his head around. "That's what Mom and Dad
tried to tell me. But we all know my life is over."

Corinne leaned forward and made him look at her. "Listen to
me. That isn't true, Carl. You're more than that—more than football."

Corinne pulled back, frustrated, searching for some way to make
him understand. "Look, I could tell you the sky was green every
day for twenty years, and the sky would still be blue. Just like you
being told all your life that a football player is all you are—all
you're good for—doesn't make it true. It's still a lie, no matter
how many times you've heard it."

Carl pulled away, breathing hard. He swiped at his cheek, and
Corinne realized he was crying. "What the hell am I supposed to
do now?" he asked her. "What do I do now?"

Corinne smiled and wiped away her own tears. "Now, you decide what *you* want. What you want from yourself. Not what your
family wants, or what you want from everyone else."

She looked at Carl, and hoped what she said made some kind
of impression on him. But in her mind, she also talked to Toby,
and her mother. And as she talked, Corinne felt at last a sense of
the reality of her relationship with her mother. Not just her own
perspective of that relationship, not just the way she'd always per-
ceived the problems between them, but the whole picture.

It's not my fault, Mom, she thought. *It's not my fault now, and
it wasn't my fault then.*

She spoke to Carl, but in her mind, she spoke to her mother.
And she spoke to herself.

"Now you take a good, honest look at yourself, and decide what
you have to give. And you focus on that, instead of every wrong
you think has been done to you. Instead of dwelling on everything
that could have been, or should have been. You focus on what is,
and make the most of *that.* There's a lot in there, Carl. I know
there is. You just have to be willing to look for it, and accept it."

Corinne felt something small but significant inside her loosening, accepting the message she tried to convey to Carl. She felt a sense of letting go, and that letting go felt a little intimidating. But it also felt right.

I'm sorry, Mom. But I'm going to live my life now.

Carl cleared his throat and wiped under his eye again. "No matter what I do, it won't be enough. He told me last night it would all be okay—that we'd deal with the future. But... He's never going to forgive me for this."

Corinne didn't have to ask; she knew Carl was referring to his father. She squeezed his shoulder again. "I have a feeling that won't be as big a problem as you might think."

"You don't know my dad."

"Sure I do. And I happen to think people can change, if they really want to." She leaned forward and met his gaze again. "If they want to, Carl. That means you, too. I meant what I said. You have to start taking responsibility for yourself. You can't go through your life blaming everyone else for your mistakes."

"You're right. I've got nobody to blame for this but me," he said. He looked down at his lower body and shook his head.

Corinne surprised them both by leaning down and giving him a hug. "Give your dad a chance to accept this, Carl. And give yourself a chance."

A nurse came in just then, and Corinne told Carl she needed to leave. "I'll be back. Think about what I said, okay?"

She walked out the door, and saw Toby. He leaned against the wall outside Carl's room, his hat in his hand.

He looked at her solemnly. "Do you think he'll listen?" he asked quietly.

Corinne shrugged. "I hope so. Time will tell. I just hope it doesn't take him ten years." She bit her bottom lip, suddenly nervous.

He looked horrible—beaten and tired and heartsick. She'd done that to him. She closed her eyes for a second. "Listen, Toby. There are some things I really need to talk to you about—"

"No." He pulled away from the wall.

"But I need to tell you—"

"I said no. I came to talk to Carl."

The nurse emerged from Carl's room and looked at Toby. "He's very tired. He asked if you could come back later. He told me to tell you he wasn't going anywhere."

Toby nodded and pulled his hat on. "Yeah, I'll be back." With that, he turned and walked away.

"Toby, wait." Corinne hurried to keep up with him. He ignored her, his long strides carrying him down the hall and out a side door.

With a muttered oath, Corinne followed him. The cold winter air cut through the sweats Becca had brought for her to wear home, and Corinne gasped with the shock.

"Would you—oh!—would you wait just a minute? I need to talk to you."

"I told you, I've heard plenty of your excuses." He moved quickly down the sidewalk and into the parking lot. Corinne hugged her arms against the cold and followed him. "I don't need to hear another one of your reasons for putting me off." He reached his Jeep and unlocked the door.

"I'm not going to give you an excuse, and—" she grabbed the door before he could shut it in her face "—and you're going to listen!"

Toby glared at her, then shook his head. "You're going to freeze to death." He pulled off his jacket, and despite his anger, there was a tenderness in his touch as he took her hand and started pulling his jacket on her. "You need to get inside."

"Not until you hear me out."

"Hear you say what, Corinne? That I spent ten years of my life trying to please my dad? That I should have followed you back then? That I should have gone after what I wanted and if I had, we would be together now?"

She wrinkled her brow and shook her head. "No, that's not what I was going to say—"

"I heard it, Corinne, loud and clear, when you were talking to Carl. I got the message."

"I wasn't trying to say—"

"Aw, hell. Are you going to stand out here and freeze? Get in." He reached over and unlocked the passenger door.

Feeling as though she'd missed an important step somewhere along the way, Corinne walked around the Jeep and opened the door. She turned to see Toby had followed her. He gingerly guided her in and shut the door behind her.

"You think I was talking about you in there?" Corinne asked when he got in on the driver's side.

"It fits, doesn't it? And you're right, in a way. The only reason I got into law enforcement was to make my dad happy. It was what he wanted, and I wanted to please him. But you know what?" He lifted his chin defensively. "I *like* what I do. In fact, I love it. It suits me, right down to the ground. Maybe I can't solve every problem in the county single-handedly. Maybe I couldn't do anything to stop Mr. Davis from getting sicker. And it will probably always bother me that I can't. But, Corinne, I like trying."

"I know," she said quietly. She leaned her head back against the seat. "And you were ready to give it up for me."

"Yeah, well..." He made a tossing-off gesture with his hand. "Some people never learn."

Corinne bit her lip and looked down at her hands. "And some people finally do."

When she raised her gaze, she saw Toby looking at her with that same dead look that had come into his eyes when she told him she wasn't ready to marry him. She wanted to move across the seat and into his arms. She wanted to tell him, finally, a decade late, how she loved him.

But she hesitated, because at the very least he deserved an explanation. And because she was no longer sure of how she would be received.

She twisted her hands together and squeezed. *Just say it,* she told herself. "I was an accident," she blurted.

Toby's brow furrowed. "What?"

"My...my birth, my conception—whatever—was unplanned, to put it kindly. In fact, if everything I learned in my eavesdropping was correct, I was conceived on the first or second date, between two people who had no real affection for each other, and grew to hate each other. I'm sorry I never told you that.''

"Corinne, do you honestly think that matters to me?''

"It matters to *me*. It's always mattered to me, because I've always felt that if I hadn't been born, my mother's life would have been drastically different. Better. I thought that because she made it plain that was what she believed. 'Single mothers don't have the money for this and that.' I heard that one too many times to count. Or, 'I had to grow up too fast...I missed my youth. When I should have been out partying and having fun, I was home changing diapers and heating formula.' I heard that one a lot, too. And the topper—'None of the good men want a ready-made family.' Which told me pretty effectively that it wasn't only her past I'd ruined, but her future, too.''

Corinne clenched her jaw. She didn't want Toby to think she was feeling sorry for herself; she just wanted him to understand. "And so I tried to make it up to her. If I could just do something, anything, to make it up to her, to show her that it was all worth it—everything she'd sacrificed and missed out on—she would forgive me. She'd see, in the long run, that I wasn't a mistake after all. If I could make enough money, have enough prestige, do enough good in the world...'' She shrugged. "But I couldn't make her happy. Nothing I ever did was enough. And I allowed those feelings to spill over into my relationship with you.''

Toby looked at the dashboard and rubbed the back of his neck. "Would having your own talk show make her happy?''

Corinne shrugged. "I don't know.''

He just stared at the dashboard in silence. Was she too late? Had she killed his love for her, once and for all? She choked back her panic at his carefully blank look.

"When I left Aloma ten years ago, I didn't say goodbye, and I didn't look back, because I couldn't, Toby. I hope you can understand now why.''

Toby nodded slightly. "Yeah, I suppose I can.''

"Toby, I wasn't thinking about you when I was talking to Carl. I was thinking about Mom. And about me. And about finally letting go of my need to please her. About learning how to please myself.

"I still need to prove that I wasn't a mistake, Toby. I still need to know that I can make a difference in the world. Not for her. For me."

"Sweetheart, you can't think you were—"

"Please, Toby, let me finish. This has been a long time coming. The other night, when I was alone with Carl out there in the middle of nowhere..." The words poured out, and she wasn't even sure what she was trying to say, just that she needed for him to know. "I was so afraid, Toby. I was so afraid. And I was about to panic. But I heard your voice, telling me you'd take care of me. Telling me you were there for me. And it helped me, Toby. It really did, knowing that, even though I was alone, I had someone out there who really cared about me, who believed in me—"

She choked off abruptly, and attempted to swallow the lump that had built quickly in her throat. She had to get this out. "What you do, Toby—being sheriff—it's a part of who you are. A big part. I finally realized, just today, that what I've been looking for, you already have. Here, in tiny little Aloma, you've made a difference. Don't look at me like that," she said with a small laugh and a sniff. "You have. And I really think I have, too. I think we might have helped Jeremy with a very difficult time. And maybe, just maybe, what I told Carl will make him think. The point is, Toby, from this little corner of the world, you're affecting people. This is where you belong, Toby. I wouldn't take that from you, not for anything. Just as I don't want to leave it."

Toby was silent, but she saw his throat working as he swallowed hard.

"I turned the Atlanta job down."

He remained perfectly still. "You said it was your dream come true."

"It was. But the person who wanted that is gone. My dream has changed."

"And what is your dream now, Corinne?" Toby looked at her intensely.

"Ask me again, Toby," she whispered. "Please."

His gaze still glued to hers, he shook his head and spoke just as quietly as she. "Not this time. This time, you go first."

She didn't expect to cry, didn't know she was going to until the tears ran and her throat closed. She barely managed to get the words out. "I love you, Toby. I always have."

Still, he just stared at her, frozen.

"Say something, please."

Toby shook his head slightly, as if to clear it. "I'm sorry. It's just...I've waited so long to hear that. I wanted to make sure I wasn't dreaming."

Corinne gave a short laugh and sniffed back her tears. "You're not dreaming, but..." She took a shaking breath. "Would you propose again?"

Toby rested his arm on the back of the seat and looked at her solemnly. He wasn't going to do it, she thought. She'd blown her last chance.

He swallowed, his gaze locked on hers. Finally, he said softly, "Will you marry me?"

Just as softly, she said, "Yes. Yes, I'll marry you. And I want to stay in Aloma. You need to stay. It's where you belong." She felt as if she were babbling, but he remained frozen and it made her nervous. Maybe he didn't understand. Or maybe he no longer wanted her.

"I want to be your wife. I want to live in Aloma. I want to be a teacher, Toby. I can't believe it, but I really *liked* teaching. So I want to go back to school and get my teaching certificate—"

The rest was cut off as he reached across the seat and hugged her tight. "I'm sorry," he said. "I haven't heard one word past 'yes.' Do you mean it, Corinne? Are you sure?"

She laughed through her happy tears. "I'm sure. For the first time in my life, I'm sure."

He held her close and kissed her. "I love you, sweetheart. God, I love you."

She winced, and he pulled back. "I'm sorry, did I hurt you?" He tenderly fingered the bandage over her eye.

"No, the emergency brake is cutting into my hip. But I don't care. Kiss me like that again."

He complied, then pulled away quickly. He dug his keys out of s pocket and started the ignition.

"Toby," Corinne asked with a laugh, her heart racing. She iped tears away with the back of her hand. "What are you do- g?"

"Driving to the courthouse to get married. Buckle your seat :lt."

"Right now?"

"Yes, now. I have to make up for lost time. I'm not giving you chance to change your mind."

"But—but Aunt Muriel is in the coffee shop, waiting for me."

"We'll call her from the courthouse—she can be one of the itnesses."

He drove to the edge of the parking lot and stopped, then he rned to look at her intensely. "You're sure? You really want is?"

She smiled, then nodded. "More than anything. You're right, heriff. We have a lot of time to make up for."

* * * * *

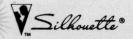

If you enjoyed what you just read,
then we've got an offer you can't resist!

Take 2 bestselling
love stories FREE!

Plus get a FREE surprise gift!

Clip this page and mail it to Silhouette Reader Service™

IN U.S.A.	IN CANADA
3010 Walden Ave.	P.O. Box 609
P.O. Box 1867	Fort Erie, Ontario
Buffalo, N.Y. 14240-1867	L2A 5X3

YES! Please send me 2 free Silhouette Intimate Moments® novels and my free surprise gift. Then send me 6 brand-new novels every month, which I will receive months before they're available in stores. In the U.S.A., bill me at the bargain price of $3.57 plus 25¢ delivery per book and applicable sales tax, if any*. In Canada, bill me at the bargain price of $3.96 plus 25¢ delivery per book and applicable taxes**. That's the complete price and a savings of over 10% off the cover prices—what a great deal! I understand that accepting the 2 free books and gift places me under no obligation ever to buy any books. I can always return a shipment and cancel at any time. Even if I never buy another book from Silhouette, the 2 free books and gift are mine to keep forever. So why not take us up on our invitation. You'll be glad you did!

245 SEN CNFF
345 SEN CNFG

Name	(PLEASE PRINT)	
Address	Apt.#	
City	State/Prov.	Zip/Postal Code

 * Terms and prices subject to change without notice. Sales tax applicable in N.Y.
** Canadian residents will be charged applicable provincial taxes and GST.
   All orders subject to approval. Offer limited to one per household.
   ® are registered trademarks of Harlequin Enterprises Limited.

INMOM99   ©1998 Harlequin Enterprises Limited

This March Silhouette is proud to present

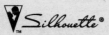 *Silhouette* ®

SENSATIONAL

MAGGIE SHAYNE
BARBARA BOSWELL
SUSAN MALLERY
MARIE FERRARELLA

This is a special collection of four complete novels for one low price, featuring a novel from each line: Silhouette Intimate Moments, Silhouette Desire, Silhouette Special Edition and Silhouette Romance.

Available at your favorite retail outlet.

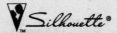 *Silhouette* ®

INTIMATE MOMENTS ® *Silhouette* ®

invites you to go West to

Cameron, Utah

Margaret Watson's exhilarating new miniseries.

FOR THE CHILDREN…IM #886, October 1998: Embittered agent Damien Kane was responsible for protecting beautiful Abby Markham and her twin nieces. But it was Abby who saved him as she showed him the redeeming power of home and family.

COWBOY WITH A BADGE…IM #904, January 1999: Journalist Carly Fitzpatrick had come to Cameron determined to clear her dead brother's name. But it's the local sheriff—the son of the very man she believed was responsible—who ends up safeguarding her from the real murderer and giving her the family she's always wanted.

Available at your favorite retail outlet.

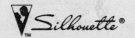
Silhouette ®

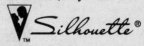

COMING NEXT MONTH